Desirada

ALSO BY MARYSE CONDÉ

Desirada

Maryse Condé

Translated from the French by
Richard Philcox

SOHO

Published by Soho Press, Inc.
853 Broadway
New York, NY 10003

Library of Congress Catalog-in-Publication Data

Condé, Maryse.
[Desirada. English]
Desirada : a novel/Maryse Condé ; [translation, Richard Philcox].
p.cm.
ISBN 1-56947-263-7 (alk. paper)
I. Philcox, Richard II. Title.

PQ3949.2.C65 D4813 2000
843'.914—dc21
00-030121

Designed by Kathleen Lake, Neuwirth and Associates, Inc.

10 9 8 7 6 5 4 3 2 1

For Sylvie, Aïcha, and Leïla

Happiness is all there is.

—Song from Martinique

This translation has been supported by a grant from
the National Endowment for the Arts

NATIONAL
ENDOWMENT
FOR THE ARTS

Part One

Chapter 1

anélise had described her birth to her so many times that she believed she had actually played a part—not that of a terrorized and submissive baby whom Madame Fleurette, the midwife, wrenched out from between her mother's bloodied thighs—but that of a clear-sighted witness, a major role, her very mother, the mother in labor, Reynalda herself, whom she imagined sitting rigid, lips pursed, arms crossed, and a look of inexpressible suffering on her face. Years later, standing in front of Frida Kahlo's painting of her own birth, it had seemed to her that this woman, this stranger, must have been thinking of her.

It was three o'clock in the afternoon. The atmosphere shimmered and tingled with excitement. It was Mardi Gras, a day of jubilation when all the companies of masked dancers charged through the streets of La Pointe. The previous Sunday they had secretly plotted to converge on the Place de la Victoire from the outlying districts. The throbbing of the *gwo-ka* drums could already be heard. Some of the masked dancers were wrapped in dried banana leaves. Others had tarred their bodies and ran through the streets cracking whips that coiled like snakes. Another group had devised buffalos' and bulls' heads for costumes and pinned to their

3

apparel all shapes of mirrors, pieces of glass, and mica that attracted the light and glittered in the sun. These were the formidable
mas'a kon dancers, said to have come straight from the Casamance.
In the meantime respectable families and their children crowded
the verandas between the bougainvillea in flower and the latanias
in pots. They had saved up their silver coins with holes in the middle to throw down to the crowd below. At their feet the rabble
shuffled along shouting at the top of their voices.

The Vatable Canal district was deserted since everyone had
gathered at the center of town. A few *moko zombis* who had strayed
that way soon realized their mistake and proceeded down the rue
Frébault kicking violently with their stilts at the closed wooden
doors as a reminder of their presence. In Ranélise's four-room
house, behind the shutters, you could hear neither the din of the
gwo-ka drums, nor the piercing shrill of the whistles, nor the clack-
ing of the *rara* rattles accompanying the masked dancers. You
couldn't hear the screams of pleasure from the crowd either. The
silence was broken only by the muffled moans of Reynalda, whose
too-narrow, fifteen-year-old pelvis refused to make any conces-
sions, and by the maternal yet exasperated berating in Creole from
Mme. Fleurette: "Push, push, I'm telling you, for God's sake!" and
finally, out came the frail, persistent wail of a newborn infant.

Mme. Fleurette was a handsome mulatto woman, an experienced midwife, without a diploma to her name, who was goodness
itself. Rainy season come dry season she cycled through the poor
neighborhoods on her "Flying Pigeon" to deliver the babies of the
poor wretches who were turned away by the General Hospital and
whom the sisters of the Saint-Jules Hospice could not accommo-
date. When Reynalda went into labor, Ranélise, who had rescued
her a few months earlier after her failed attempt at drowning, recognized the bicycle parked in front of a shack, even on this day of
festivities, and together with her younger sister, Claire-Alta, inter-

cepted Mme. Fleurette. After the laborious delivery was over they were thanking Mme. Fleurette and leading her out toward the pool of clear water in the yard when Reynalda, looking like death, uttered such a mournful groan that the three women turned around in alarm. In an instant the threadbare sheet covering her had turned red and was already dripping blood. Fortunately the Saint-Jules Hospice was close by. There they bundled Reynalda into a bed still burning from the puerperal fever of a poor woman who had just passed from this life to the next, and the good sisters went to work.

When Ranélise left the Saint-Jules Hospice around midnight, the fireworks that had been set off over by the harbor were zigzagging across the sky in a multitude of colors and vanishing over Dominica way. The streets were swarming with children, women, and men yelling. Drunks were dancing their entrechats. Amid a hellish din the masked revelers were having their final fling.

Back home she found the newborn infant fast asleep, set down where they had forgotten her. Her tiny face streaked with excrement and dried blood, she smelled of rotting fish. In spite of this, rays of love beamed from Ranélise's heart and shed a glow over the tiny body. She had always wanted a child. Instead the Good Lord had sent her miscarriage after miscarriage, stillborn after stillborn, infants baptized at the very last minute, one after another. She clasped the baby to her heart, convinced that the Good Lord had finally repented for having mistreated her so. Showering her with kisses, she chose the name Marie-Noëlle, though she was born at the height of Carnival. For Marie is the name of the Holy Virgin, mother of all virtues, and Noëlle a reminder of that miraculous night when Jesus became a child to wash away our sins. She prepared a bath of lukewarm water, mixed in some essence of roses, and plopped in soursop leaves as well as a pinch of sweet violets and sweet-smelling husks to soak. Then she dried the baby with a soft towel and laid her on her belly to protect her from the fear of the dark, the wind, and nightmares.

Ranélise was a tall black woman, a cook at Tribord Bâbord, a restaurant with a shabby appearance but a reputation for good food, situated at the Bas de la Source. Her speciality: conch. Nobody could match the way she extracted the mollusk from its shell, left it to soak in a homemade mixture of brine and bay-rum leaves, pounded it with a pestle she had made from a piece of lignum vitae, and served it up juicy and succulent as lamb in a thick reddish sauce. Her customers came from far and wide. Sometimes from as far away as Le Moule or La Boucan, and Gérardo Polius, the Communist mayor of La Pointe, took four meals a week at Tribord Bâbord, sitting down with his entire municipal council. A few months earlier, as she was walking down to the Carenage to meet the fisherman she usually dealt with, she saw a bundle of clothes floating on the water like a buoy. Intrigued, she went over and made out an arm, a leg, then a sliver of buttock. Her shouts had attracted passersby, and, using a pole, they had fished out a bedraggled girl whose heart was still beating unsteadily.

A young girl, almost a child. Fourteen years old. Certainly not more than fifteen. Her breasts the size of guava buds. Ranélise, who wore her heart on her sleeve, had taken her home with her. She had rubbed her with camphor oil and given her an infusion of watergrass mixed with a little rum to warm her up. Then she wrapped her in one of the flannel nightdresses she wore during the bad weather season. The first day they got little more out of her than a few reluctant words. She said her name was Reynalda Titane. Her maman, Antonine, whom everyone nicknamed Nina, hired herself out to the family of Gian Carlo Coppini. Gian Carlo Coppini was an Italian jeweler in the rue de Nozières whose shop, Il Lago di Como, was always full of customers come to buy but mainly to browse in admiration. Gian Carlo Coppini looked a little like Jesus Christ: curly, silky hair and a beard to go with it. He reigned over a host of women: first of all his own wife, always pregnant or in labor; his two sisters, always dressed in black, their heads covered with lace mantillas; and his daughters. It was thanks to him that Nina had been able to send Reynalda to the Dubouchage elementary school. Reynalda loved school. French, history, natural science. She worked hard and passed the exam for her elementary school certificate.

People advised Ranélise to send Reynalda back where she came from. Who knew whether she wasn't a thief or a good-for-nothing wanted by the gendarmes? But when Ranélise mentioned taking her back to Il Lago di Como, Reynalda had knelt down at her feet and like Mary Magdalene soaked them with her tears. That was when she revealed she was pregnant and why she had thrown herself into the sea. Ranélise had stood speechless, facing her. How could she think of killing herself because someone had given her a belly? Didn't she know that a child is a blessing from the Good Lord? A sign that His elixir has enriched your heart as well as your body? A woman who sees her belly swell and grow round should throw herself on her knees, strike her breast, and cry: "Thank you, Lord!"

Reynalda did not breathe a word to anyone. Except sometimes to Claire-Alta, who was about her age. Ranélise ended up keeping her and found her a job at the restaurant Tribord Bâbord—in the kitchen, because in the dining room, customers complained she prevented them from enjoying their rum.

The second thing Marie-Noëlle imagined was her christening. It had been held right in the middle of Lent on a Saturday, the day reserved for illegitimate children, those who don't know their papa's name. The Church of Saint-Jules, adjoining the hospice of the same name, was a wooden building with a nave in the shape of a ship's hull. It had withstood the fires and earthquakes that devastated La Pointe since it was founded. At that time a good many of its louvered shutters were missing; its stained-glass windows were broken in places, while its bell tower sat askew like the madras headtie of an old woman who has seen far too much of life. Ranélise, her godmother, was carrying her in her arms like the Holy Sacrament. Ranélise was a sight to behold that day. She was radiant, dressed in her polka-dot blue satin two-piece suit with white lapels and a wide hat with a sagging brim. One of her countless good friends, dressed in a double-breasted wool suit and tie, stood in as godfather and joined her in singing: "We give thanks unto Thee, O God;/We give thanks for Thy name is near."

The font stood in front of one of the remaining unbroken stained-glass windows depicting the Annunciation. With her thumb pressed against her palate and her cheek resting against Ranélise's bosom, Marie-Noëlle was interested in neither the priest's homily nor her godfather's and godmother's well-intentioned resolutions. She could not take her eyes off the celestial image of the archangel Gabriel, with his blue cape and great outspread wings, holding a bunch of lilies. All around her the other babies wailed or sucked on the salt of good behavior. Absorbed in her vision, she felt infinitely superior. Hadn't Ranélise proclaimed her to be the most wonderful child on earth? The day of the christening they had listened to music. Not just the usual mazurkas, *wa-bap* beguines, and others. Monsieur and Madame Léomidas, who worked in Senegal for the Ministry of Overseas Development, had played records on the gramophone and everyone had sat in silence listening to their explanation of the *griots* in Africa.

Curiously enough, although Ranélise must have recounted the incident fairly frequently, Marie-Noëlle had no memory of her mother leaving. All she could gather was that she had left in September. A September laden with the threat of hurricanes and storms as if the sky were flushed with anger. One or two weeks after the christening Reynalda announced that she was leaving to work in metropolitan France. In France? Yes, France! The BUMIDOM agency had found her a job, as they did for so many fellow islanders at that time—with Jean-René Duparc, who lived on the boulevard Malesherbes in the XVIIth Arrondissement in Paris. This Jean-René had a family of three small children who needed a nurse. The mayor, Gérardo Polius, did not mince his words. Nor did the neighbors, whereas Ranélise was beside herself with joy, and to show it gave Reynalda three hundred-franc notes. Before she left Reynalda had come straight to the point and told Claire-Alta that she had no intention of ending up a maid.

She intended to go to college and become somebody.

ᵭ

Marie-Noëlle's childhood was an enchantment. Hand in hand with Ranélise she walked in a woodland carpeted with tree ferns, milky white trumpet flowers, and heavy-petaled heliconias rimmed with yellow. Here and there blossomed the purple flower of the wild plantain. A cool wind tickled her nostrils, mingling with the scent of flowers, earth, wind, and rain, and her childhood was a perfumed garden. To some people Marie-Noëlle's possessions would not have amounted to much. A chain bracelet engraved with her name. A necklace with three medallions, one of which was of the Infant Jesus, her patron saint. Some clothes at the bottom of a wicker basket. She never had a tricycle or a toy car with pedals or a Barbie doll. Merely a homemade scooter with which she whisked along the Vatable canal and the streets on the Morne Udol. But a child's joy cannot be measured in gold or expensive toys. It is measured by motions of the heart, and Marie-Noëlle was the only reason Ranélise's heart throbbed. Ranélise's hand was gentle, so gentle, even when she untangled Marie-Noëlle's thick mass of long hair. Never a slap, never a blow, never the mark of a belt on her buttocks. Never a punishment standing up or kneeling down, arms outspread under the merciless sun in the yard. Not even a word spoken louder than the next. Rather cascades of affection, with pet names and showers of kisses on the nape of her neck.

On Easter Monday they would load up a hamper with pots of conch in hot Colombo sauce and rice and set off with friends in a minibus to the beach at Grande-Anse, Deshaies. Marie-Noëlle chuckled and paddled in her Petit-Bateau panties while Rastamen with long fauve-colored dreadlocks played ball in the sand or beat the *gwo-ka*.

Marie-Noëlle's presence in the house turned Ranélise's life upside down. Until then she had been a woman who took in men. A lot of men. Inquisitive neighbors spied on those who went in at dusk to emerge only at dawn when the stars were fading. Starting with Gérardo Polius, the Communist mayor who had been a regular visitor for twenty years; and Alexis Alexius, his deputy, who slipped inside as soon as the mayor had turned his back. People did not gossip too much because Ranélise was a good soul. Always ready to help a neighbor, slip a banknote into the hands of the destitute, find a job for the unemployed or a place in the nursery school for an infant. From one day to the next, her reckless behavior changed. Except for Gérardo Polius, no man ever came to spend the night with her again. Although she abstained from taking the Holy Sacrament, she had nevertheless always been on good terms with the priests of Saint-Jules and organized carol singing in her yard at Advent. Now, without going so far as to take confession and communion, she never missed a mass, vespers, or rosary. She could be seen walking in the processions of the

Holy Virgin, head lowered in prayer and striking her chest as if she never stopped thanking the Good Lord for all the happiness in her life.

Very early on, as soon as Marie-Noëlle started school, it was obvious that He who deals the gift of intelligence had not forgotten her. First in everything. When the prizes were handed out, she never stopped walking up to the podium. It was first prize after first prize, leather-bound books after gilt-edge books, and Ranélise paraded around, already the proud mother of a future schoolteacher. Even a midwife. For she had completely forgotten that Marie-Noëlle had not come out of her belly. Not that Reynalda did anything at all to remind her child she existed. Time passed. Days lapsed into months, months into years, and they received practically no news of her. A card at New Year's without an address. Clodomire Ludovic, a retired postman from the XIIIth Arrondissement in Paris, swore that one day he met her in the very middle of the Place d'Italie. She had looked him straight in the eye and pretended not to recognize him. In spite of the passing years, people often mentioned the name of Reynalda Titane. It's not every day you fish out a drowning girl from the waters of the Carenage. And why did she try to drown herself, come to that? If every girl who paraded around an unwanted bun in the oven did the same the earth would soon be emptied. Gradually all that was left in people's minds was the memory of an eccentric, sullen girl who had not been content with her daily lot.

Every time they talked of her maman Marie-Noëlle sensed a feeling of danger. It was as if an icy wind blew stealthily over her shoulders and she might catch pleurisy. She quickly tried to change the subject, showing off her latest composition or asking to recite a lesson. Sometimes in the middle of the night the thought of her mother gripped her and woke her up like a nightmare. She would start to cry inconsolably, and only the dawn light would dry her cheeks.

On her way to school she could not help making a detour via the rue de Nozières to look at Il Lago di Como, situated on the ground floor of a two-story wooden house that needed a fresh coat of paint. She sensed that this shop, which did not look like much, nothing more than a dark, narrow passageway, where the electric light was left on day and night, held the secret of her birth. What events so terrible had occurred a few years earlier to make her barely fifteen-year-old maman throw herself into the sea and seek death?

One day—she must have been almost ten—Marie-Noëlle plucked up enough courage, pushed open the door, and mingled with the flow of customers admiring the cameo brooches and pendants and all the Florentine engraving. The wife of the owner, pallid and fatigued, sat enthroned at the cash register. The two sisters wearing mantillas were talking to customers. In a corner three or four little girls were playing with rag dolls. Gian Carlo Coppini, a jeweler's loupe inserted into his right eye, his beard and handsome silky hair, now pepper and salt, reaching almost to his shoulders, was examining a green-colored gem. A thin black skullcap sat tightly on his head, which probably meant he was Jewish. After a while he laid the stone down on the counter and cast a look around him. He caught sight of Marie-Noëlle standing in a corner of the shop and gave her a suave, magnanimous smile, revealing a carnassial set of teeth, as if he were Our Lord Jesus Christ surrounded by his apostles. At that moment a young servant girl came out from the back of the shop carrying a small tray set with a white embroidered cloth, a gilt-edged cup, a sugar bowl, and a coffeepot. The girl poured the coffee into the cup, cautiously— like somebody fearing a reprimand—added two spoonfuls of sugar, and the penetrating aroma filled the shop.

Gian Carlo Coppini thanked her with a motion of the hand that dismissed her at the same time. Then, with the unctuousness of a priest drinking the Communion wine and yet with the theatricality of an actor, he lowered his eyes and brought the coffee cup level with his lips, which were like rosebuds set among his mass of hair. When Marie-Noëlle found herself back on the street under the sun, she leaned against a wall and almost fainted with emotion.

Yes, there was no doubt about it, this stranger had played a major role in her life.

On July 5, 1970, when Marie-Noëlle had celebrated her tenth birthday and was now old enough to enter the Lycée Michelet, the postman slipped notification of a registered letter addressed to Mademoiselle Ranélise Tertullien between the shutters.

It caused a sensation.

First of all Ranélise never received any letters, apart from Reynalda's cards, the mail-order catalog from the Trois Suisses and the *billets-doux* from the tax man. Second, she didn't know how to retrieve the registered letter. Where had she placed her identity card, which she never used? Inside the drawers of her bedside table? In her bureau? In her wicker basket with the silverware? After having searched for hours she was about to strike up a prayer to Saint-Expédit, patron of lost causes, when she found it under a pile of good sheets in her chest of drawers. Then she set off for the post office that had recently opened in the Bergevin district, not far from the new bus station.

Since she could not read very well she gave the letter to Marie-Noëlle who, even before opening it and reading its contents, knew that what she had dreaded most in the world had finally arrived.

The strong brown paper envelope contained a money order, a plane ticket, some Air France forms, and a short note.

The writing on the cream-colored paper was in a firm, even elegant hand:

Savigny-sur-Orge, June 27

Dear Ranélise,

Contrary to what you may think I have not forgotten my daughter. The time has come when I can fulfill my duties toward her, for I am now in a position to provide her with the decent life any child deserves.

I would be grateful if you could send me by return mail her school report and health records. You will find enclosed some money to buy her clothes and a plane ticket for mid-October. You only have to sign the forms: she travels as an unaccompanied minor.

I don't know how to thank you for the goodness of your heart.

Reynalda Titane

P.S. I am now a welfare worker at the city hall in Savigny-sur-Orge.

Ranélise collapsed into a fainting fit. The neighbors who had rushed over had to rub her forehead and palms with camphorated alcohol. Then she regained consciousness and started to weep hot tears, moaning out loud and cursing fate. Had she raised and cherished a child for ten years only to bundle her off to a deranged individual who had done nothing less than abandon her defenseless infant on this earth? Who was the child's real maman? The one who had cared for her measles, her smallpox, and her ear infections or the one giving herself airs in France? Aren't there laws to protect people and right the wrongs in this world? No! She would never give up Marie-Noëlle. The chorus of neighbors nodded their approval. Then she stood up and armed herself with a parasol to go out. She was not in the habit of disturbing Gérardo Polius at work or making a show of their relations. But on that day she felt she needed his expert advice. After all, Gérardo had studied law. He was a lawyer, even though he no longer practiced. When she arrived at Town Hall, beside herself with rage and her eyes swollen with tears, he was locked in his office with two of his councilmen and the director of garbage disposal. So she told her story to any sympathizing employee while she waited two full hours for him to finish. He carefully considered the letter she had received, listened to her patiently, then knowing how fond she was of Marie-Noëlle he said sadly: "I told you over and over again to legalize the situation by adopting her. As things stand you can't do anything. The biological mother has every right."

However much she hammered his chest with her fists and accused him of being heartless, he merely repeated what he said and she finally collapsed cursing the Good Lord. When she had calmed down somewhat, he had her driven home in his Citroën DS 19.

That evening Marie-Noëlle was gripped by a high fever. At nine o'clock her temperature was running well over a hundred, and her eyes, as red as the embers of a bonfire, seemed about to leap out of her head. Around ten she began to moan and whine like a tiny infant and utter unintelligible sounds. At times she appeared to regain consciousness and shouted in a heart-rending voice: "I want to stay with my maman!"

Then she was seized with such violent convulsions that she almost fell off her bed, and they had to tie her to the bedposts with the sheets.

Mme. Fleurette, the only person who consented to leave her bed in the middle of the night, diagnosed a pernicious fever and called for her to be admitted to the emergency room at the General Hospital. There the young doctor on duty ascertained the symptoms to be nothing but a common attack of dengue fever, which he treated with sulfonamide. At four in the morning Marie-Noëlle drained herself like a sick person suffering from typhoid fever, vomiting up a thick, foul-smelling custard, after which, as stiff as a corpse, she fell into a coma. The doctors declared her a hopeless case, and people were already predicting a double funeral, for everyone knew that Ranélise would not survive her. Marie-Noëlle, however, recovered. After a week in a deep coma, her bed hidden behind a screen so as not to frighten the other patients, she opened her eyes and asked for her maman. Ranélise, who had not left her bedside for one instant, went down on both knees weeping and crying Hosannah in the Highest. It should be said that the Marie-Noëlle who left the General Hospital one morning in July in the arms of Ranélise was not the same Marie-Noëlle who had gone in almost a month earlier. The chubby, mischievous little girl, temperamental and tender, who had been the delight of Ranélise's heart, was gone. In her place a great gawk of a girl, nothing but skin and bone, with a glazed look, staring at people in a way that made them feel ill at ease, for she seemed to be looking through them to pursue some personal obsession. Once so imaginative, a real chatterbox filling Ranélise's head with fantastic stories, she now said virtually not a word. She sat for hours on end without moving, staring straight in front of her; then she would rest her cheek on Ranélise's shoulder while tears streamed down her face.

Ranélise, who in her entire life had never thought about taking a vacation and had worked like a beast of burden every day the Good Lord made, borrowed some money from Gérardo and with it rented a house in Port Louis, steps from the beach at Souffleur, to give the child a change of air.

Before it was devastated by hurricanes and the demise of sugar-cane, Port Louis was undoubtedly the prettiest town on Grande-Terre. Its clear blue sky knew nothing of rain; its air, nothing of miasmas. A row of tall elegant wooden houses with flower-filled balconies and deep attic windows lined the seafront. They belonged to the representatives of the financiers in metropolitan France who had taken over from the white Creoles, the former masters of the sugar plantations. On Sundays they filled the church with their arrogance, perfume, and starched linen and placed in the collection basket the equivalent of one month's pay of one of their workers.

Port Louis was also a bustling little town. And Beauport was the focus of activity. During the cane harvest, lines of steel wagons drawn by tractors rumbled toward the factory, for the oxcart had become obsolete and was now scarcely used except by some small-holders. Furthermore it was the hub of forty kilometers of railroad track traveled daily by five locomotives and two hundred wagons.

The house Ranélise had rented was at the very end of the seafront. From the somewhat unkempt plot of garden, where a few tall canna lilies managed to grow, you could see the graves in the cemetery splashed by the red blossom of the flamboyants and the yellow clumps of allamanda. Ranélise had her own thoughts on how to cure a sick person: She knew that the sea had a healing effect on everything. Just before dawn, when the fishermen's boats were the first to sully the blue of the sea, she would wake Marie-Noëlle and take her down to the beach. Wrapped in her loose, faded dress, she cautiously stepped into the water, crossed herself twice, scooped up three mouthfuls of water in the palm of her hand, swallowed them, then went back and sat on the sand. Marie-Noëlle, however, who had taken swimming lessons at school, swam with great strokes out toward the open sea as if she wanted to reach for the horizon. When the houses grew tiny in a golden arc, she stopped swimming, caught her breath, and let herself float. The slow motion of the waves comforted her, rocking her to and fro like a baby in a cradle. Her hair untangled itself. She felt herself become a seaweed towed by the whims of the current or a sea animal, a spider crab or a seahorse. The peppery scent of the water penetrated her nostrils while its gentleness washed over her, coating her like a balm. To the south was the open sea—an infinite blue. But if she looked north, the jagged blue ridge of the mountains scarred the horizon. If she looked down below the water, the great white seabed attracted her, and she felt tempted to kick her way down to eternal peace. Then she thought of Ranélise waiting for her, and she swam back to the shore.

These daily swims, together with a careful diet and walks, hastened Marie-Noëlle's convalescence. Sometimes they walked as far as Massioux, Gros-Cap, and Pombiray. And the hordes of kids from the Indian families, who under the Second Empire had replaced the blacks deserting the canefields, came out on their doorsteps to take a look at this mismatched couple: a handsome, well-built black woman, walking under her parasol looking neither left nor right, followed by a puny girl with bobbing braids reddened by the seawater, who, on the contrary, gaped in wonder at everything. This was the first time Marie-Noëlle had left La Pointe and the Vatable Canal district, so everything enchanted her. She paused out of curiosity in front of the red-and-yellow-striped temples dedicated to Mariamman under the sheltering green of the trees. What went on behind those high tricolored walls? What comings and goings from the ghats of the Ganges to these limestone paths? Or else she ran until she was out of breath along the driveways lined with dwarf coconut trees and palms, remains of the sugar plantation houses that in times past had dotted the canefields. She breathed in the smell of the crushed cane juice from the Beauport factory and dreamed of clinging like the little black ragamuffins to the back of the sugarcane trains as they smoked their way across the scrubland. And so she regained a little strength, cheered, almost in spite of herself, by the hustle and bustle of her island.

⅁

She never returned to the child she once was. That time was well and truly over. Due to her sickness and long convalescence she wasn't able to leave for France until October 31 and was late for school.

Years later Marie-Noëlle still retained the sensations and images that flickered through her head while she was in a coma at the General Hospital.

At times she was cold, a cold that cut her to the bone. Other times she felt herself next to a blazing furnace. It seemed her skin was about to scorch, burn to a cinder, and leave her naked, an unwholesome heap of entrails. Daylight had been snuffed out. She remained in darkness. Behind her eyelids, shapes raveled and unraveled, taking flight or floating, like the flying ends of melancholy scarves made of silk or plastic. Then suddenly blurs of color in blue and violet hues or monochrome, here and there a red or yellow flash, emerged and grew into dazzling shapes. When she blinked, the spots burst and grew smaller. Small and menacing. They drew a constellation of tiny dots, glittering like car headlights in the distance or the eyes of a pack of animals prowling in the forest. Suddenly everything melted, clouding over again with a thick velvet folded in four, and she remained in this jet black darkness, panting and terrified.

At other times her head filled with noise. She thought she would explode and the wax of her brain ooze soft and lukewarm onto the rough pillowcase with G.H. stitched in large blue letters. It was as if a hurricane were looming up from the other side of the earth, greeted by the rustle of the cane and the screaming of the great wind. The breadfruit, mango, and coconut trees fell one on top of another, preceded by an ominous cracking. The doors of the huts banged and were torn off, their hinges twisted like mere pieces of scrap iron. The louvered shutters were smashed to pieces. The roofs sliced the air with their sheets of rusted zinc. While the terrified kids crouching under the kitchen sinks never stopped squealing, she listened to the din. Until it all stopped and silence enveloped her. A silence more terrible than the noise. It was then that she traversed immense open spaces.

Some days, however, things improved. It was as if daylight broke through. She managed to distinguish the blue-and-white square of the window, the narrow bell tower of the Saint-Pierre-and-Saint-Paul Cathedral and the clock, which always showed one-fifteen all year round. She could make out the doctors, always in a hurry. She could see the nuns' winged coifs fluttering around the drip feed or their hands holding their syringes level with their eyes. She could see Ranélise sitting at her bedside or leaning over her or pacing up and down in her room, openly crying. Sometimes she could even hear the familiar music of Ranélise's voice, lamenting, taking stock of all the sacrifices she had made, all the tribulations she had endured during these ten years of maternity. Oh, no! The Good Lord could not take away her child! Was she talking about sickness and death or else the reunion with Reynalda? Whatever the case, for her it was nothing but grief. Marie-Noëlle would have liked to answer her. She would have liked to comfort her, assure her that wherever she was she would continue to love her more than anyone else. But she couldn't. The words got stuck in her throat and became clogged. She remained nailed to her bed, unable to respond, a prisoner of her solitude. Her eyes then filled with tears. Her suffering swelled around her and she huddled down under the threadbare sheet that was too small.

Marie-Noëlle still carried these images and sensations deep inside her. Without warning they would surge up and take possession of her. Time would stop. Right in the middle of a sentence or a gesture she appeared to fall into a trance, go numb, and her eyes glazed over.

People did not fail to notice these absences of mind. At first they remarked on them. Then they got used to them and thought her a bit cracked. Like her mother before her. Quite simply cracked.

Chapter 3

But nobody had ever described to Marie-Noëlle the day she arrived in Paris. Her memory had taken good care of that for her.

Once she had accepted the inevitable hand of fate, Ranélise acted as best she could. She dried the tears from her eyes and began to fill a suitcase full of woolen clothes. Then she asked Father Simonin to celebrate four masses for Marie-Noëlle. Four Saturdays in a row she took her to confession. For four Sundays, hands piously joined under her chin, she marched with her to the altar to receive Holy Communion. Finally, one evening after work, she opened the album she kept locked in her chest of drawers and showed her a photo of her mother taken the day when they and some close friends had celebrated the first election of Gérard Polius as mayor of La Pointe. Reynalda was almost nine months pregnant. Her protruding belly strained the checkered fabric of her shapeless dress in an unseemly way. Surrounding her, Ranélise, Claire-Alta, Gérardo Polius, and Alexis Alexius, his deputy, who was still a regular visitor to the house and Ranélise's bed, looked completely inebriated. They were raising their glasses level with the camera and grinning. Everyone looked tipsy. Except for her.

Her triangular face with its somewhat sickly features did not express grief or revolt, but rather an extreme weariness. As if she had only one idea in mind: put an end to it all. Marie-Noëlle had not let herself be moved, neither by this expression nor by the sight of this mountain of flesh behind which she, the fetus, was hiding from the world. When Ranélise babbled on in a torrent of words that Reynalda should be forgiven for her ten years of neglect as Jesus had forgiven Peter his three denials, Marie-Noëlle had forcefully interrupted her and asked who her papa was, for there isn't a child on this earth without a papa. You had to have a papa to make a child. It was not the first time this burning question had weighed heavily on her tongue. At the very last minute, she always managed to swallow it back. To be truthful she was afraid of the answer she might hear. Because of the color of her skin that stood out against those around her, who were decidedly black, because of her mop of hair that was the color of straw, and her eyes that were striped green or yellow by the light, depending on the hour of day. Her papa must have been a man of light skin. A mulatto? An islander from Les Saintes? A malevolent high-yellow *chaben* as red as a land crab? Perhaps even a white man? A white Creole or a French Frenchman, gendarme or officer in the riot squad? How could she bear such a paternity?

Ranélise became flustered. What does it matter? Does a papa count? The only thing that counts is your maman's womb, a fortress whose door you once painfully pried open. Long, long time ago, the masters decided that the child follows its maman's womb. If she was black, the child was black. . . . Marie-Noëlle was no longer listening to this useless chatter. She swore to herself she would take as long as it needed, but one day she would decipher the undecipherable.

From the photos she got the impression her mother must be ugly. Tall, whereas in fact she was quite short. Plump, whereas she must have weighed the weight of a teenager. Middle-aged, like Ranélise or her classmates' mothers at the Dubouchage school, whereas she was still a young woman. She could have been an older sister. Or a young aunt like Claire-Alta. Marie-Noëlle could not help devouring her with her eyes and, hiding her grief at having lost Ranélise, she felt like hugging her and whispering into her neck: "You are the treasure I did not know I had."

Reynalda was waiting in a corner of the airport reserved for the parents of the unaccompanied minors, leaning against a pillar like a plant against a prop. Her face betrayed nothing, as if she were wearing a mask, a wolf hiding its real emotions. She was cramped into a navy-blue, military-style coat that was buttoned up to the neck and did not suit her. But a red, green, and yellow cap provided an unexpected touch of color. She looked at Marie-Noëlle furtively, almost fearfully, forced a smile, then quickly turned her eyes away without leaning over to kiss her. While signing the forms she asked the hostess in a voice that contrasted with the loud, drawling accents of Ranélise and Claire-Alta: "Did everything go all right?"

Then she grabbed Marie-Noëlle's case and preceded her to the exit.

Outside the sky shimmered gray and overcast, skimming the rooftops. It was snowing.

Was it snowing? It seldom snows in Paris. And not on November 1. In any case in Marie-Noëlle's memory big snowflakes were falling and fluttering like insects around the flame of an oil lamp. The buildings, the paving stones, the buses, and the parked cars were coated with a white powder. Here and there trees brandished their stumps bandaged in white. Marie-Noëlle was shaking and did not know why. She had trouble following Reynalda as she quickly twisted and turned through the airport. Finally she stopped in front of a black car and Marie-Noëlle was amazed. Not because she was going to climb into a car. Wasn't it Gérardo Polius's DS 19, still bravely holding the road despite its aging bodywork, that had driven her to the airport? It was simply the first time she had seen a woman sit behind a wheel. At La Pointe it was always the men who occupied this seat, and Joby, Gérardo's chauffeur, swaggered officiously as he manipulated the gears, as if he were handling the controls of a Caravelle. From what she gathered from Ranélise, she was convinced her maman was poor. Was Reynalda deceiving everyone and was she, in fact, rich? The car set off along the deserted streets (it was the morning of a public holiday), so dismal after the streets of La Pointe, brightened merely by the red and green lights blinking at the intersections. Since Reynalda did not utter a single word, neither to ask for news about her, Ranélise, or Claire-Alta nor to enquire about the changes to La Pointe, the journey seemed endless, and Marie-Noëlle sank numbly into despair.

At that time the Jean Mermoz housing projects at Savigny-sur-Orge were like any other suburban apartment houses. Unattractive but calm and residential. From time to time a quarrel flared up between neighbors. A husband beat his wife. A dance ended in a brawl. The police showed up, but it was never anything serious. The housing projects consisted of a dozen buildings an architect who was a poet at heart had painted the colors of clouds. White, pale blue, dark blue, light gray, and darker gray. On the concrete squares, now padded with snow, hordes of brown-skinned children played, for the buildings housed a high percentage of Africans, West Indians, and Réunion islanders. The West Indians and Réunion islanders got along well together. They spoke Creole among themselves. They paraded together through the streets at Carnival time. They celebrated their weddings and christenings in the communal hall, whose walls were painted with frescoes by a

Martinican who passed as an artist. By common accord they did not mix with the Africans. Not one. Neither from north or south of the Sahara. They were people of another race who did not mix well together.

Since the elevators were out of order Reynalda and Marie-Noëlle took the stairs, still one behind the other, in building A (pale gray). Reynalda lived in a third-floor apartment, empty in comparison to Ranélise's four-room house cluttered with low tables, pedestal tables, poufs, sofas, chests of drawers, wardrobes, cupboards, beds, with and without posts, and mirrors. Except for some reproductions on the walls, there was nothing but a few mismatched pieces of furniture scattered haphazardly over the floor strewn here and there with mats. But it wasn't the bareness that struck Marie-Noëlle. In a playpen filled with toys, a well-built little boy about one year old, standing sturdily on his bare feet, was methodically wailing for wailing's sake. At times he halfheartedly scratched his cheeks, varnished by his tears. On seeing Reynalda he stopped crying and began to stomp on the playpen mat, waving his arms. Marie-Noëlle turned to Reynalda who, barely motioning her head, said: "That's your little brother, Garvey."

Marie-Noëlle had always wanted another child in the house. She knew full well she shouldn't count on Ranélise, who had laid two or three stillborn babies in the Briscaille cemetery. Even less on Claire-Alta, who was scared to death of getting an unwanted infant. So she consoled herself with other people's children. Along the Vatable Canal she was known for this love of children. On Wednesdays, when there was no school, the women who had to run to market had no trouble entrusting her with their newborn infants. When she returned from the Tribord Bâbord it was not unusual for Ranélise to find her learning her lessons or finishing her homework with a wailing child lying in her lap. A little brother? The gift was enough to lift the veil of mourning of this first day.

With a pounding heart she leaned over Garvey, who let himself be embraced. At that moment a man appeared. Very tall, all skin and bones, a tangle of unkempt reddish hair around his face. He was holding a plate full of baby cereal and a goblet. He smiled at Marie-Noëlle as if he had met up with an old acquaintance and softly said: "There you are!"

Then he drew her close and warmly kissed her. That was the second silver lining of the day.

Ludovic always hesitated a moment when asked where he was from. His father had left Haiti for Ciego de Avila in Cuba, where the caneworkers' pay was much better. There he had had three boys with a woman who also broke her back working in the cane-fields. He had lived for some time in Santo Domingo, where he fathered other children. Then he went back to Haiti, for he was homesick for the acrid smell of its burnt earth. As soon as he turned eighteen Ludovic began to wander in his father's footsteps. He put far behind him the bottomless despair of Haiti, tried his luck in the United States of America, Canada, Germany, and Africa before ending up in Belgium and striding across the border to Paris. He had been a docker in the Port of New York, an elementary school teacher at Koulikoro in Mali, a journalist at Maputo in Mozambique, and a musician on the Place de l'Horloge in Brussels. All these twists and turns had left their mark on his face, drawn crow's feet at the corners of his eyes, dug two trenches around his mouth and traced wrinkles across his forehead. A hint of melancholy permanently glimmered at the back of his eyes, as if they could not forget all the misery they had laid sight on. After elementary school he had received no other education except from life itself. But because he spoke five languages, he now worked at a municipal center for young delinquents. Ever since she was quite small Marie-Noëlle had heard the neighbors' wives cry on Ranélise's shoulder and relate to her the bitter taste of their daily lot: abuse from their husbands, all sorts of ill treatment, and at the end of it all, abandonment. She herself had grown up without the presence or the affection of a papa, and she could clearly see she was not alone. So she had finally been convinced that men were apart and belonged to a different, somewhat malevolent species who were only concerned with their own well-being.

As soon as she arrived at Savigny-sur-Orge, this conviction began to crumble. Ludovic was the mainstay of the home. He was the one who did the shopping, the cooking, the housework—less often, it's true the laundry in the basement, hung it out to dry in front of the windows, and drove Garvey to and from nursery school after having washed and dressed him. Likewise he took full charge of Reynalda. He spoke to her only in Spanish, the language of his childhood, as if he wanted to go back to a time before enduring the stormy tribulations of his life. He put up with her constant lassitude, interpreted her silences, and, without being servile, anticipated her slightest desire, like an understanding older brother. One day while she was passing in front of their bedroom door, Marie-Noëlle saw him sitting beside Reynalda and watching over her as she slept, with the expression of a maman tending to a sick baby.

What was Reynalda suffering from?

Marie-Noëlle never stopped wondering, though she never came up with the answer. As a woman Reynalda did not concern herself with things that are a woman's lot around the house. Some days she bustled about in a frenzy, but in a selfish way. In a cubbyhole she used as an office she would type for hours on her typewriter. On those days Ludovic gaily explained to Garvey that his maman was working on her thesis and that in no way should he make any noise. Other days, back from City Hall, she drew her bedroom door over her like a tombstone. When she yielded to Ludovic's insistent calls, it was to sit at the dinner table without touching her plate and stare in sulky silence at the thousand colors of the television screen, absorbed by an obsession she shared with nobody. She had no conversation. She listened in silence to Ludovic, who provided his own call and response. In a word she did not seem to be interested in anything. Neither culture, nor politics, nor the ups and downs of Africa that fascinated Ludovic. Sometimes a book passed between her hands. Whenever this happened, Marie-Noëlle had the feeling that only her eyes registered the printed characters on the page, while her mind remained the prisoner of images she could not forget. Even Garvey and his little games could not capture her attention. She would hug him for a moment, then quickly set him down, wearied and once again gripped by her indifference. Marie-Noëlle understood immediately that her presence inconvenienced her more than anything else. So she asked herself the same question over and over again: Why had she broken Ranélise's heart and sent for her in Guadeloupe where she was so happy? Reynalda was not like one of those monsters whose revolting crimes you read about in the tabloids. She was worse, Marie-Noëlle decided. Neither brutal nor quick tempered, she was generous with pocket money and did not skimp on clothes and school supplies. It was simply as if her heart had no feelings for anyone.

Ludovic, on the other hand, put a lot of warmth into their lives. He was the one who taught Marie-Noëlle how to smooth her hair back with a wet brush, how to iron her jeans, and how to polish and clean her boots. He made her do her homework and work on her English, the only subject she hated at school. For her first Christmas at Savigny-sur-Orge he gave her a bicycle to ride around the squares like the other children from the projects. He let her choose the records, which she herself carefully positioned on the record player. Ludovic was a music fanatic. When he was home, the apartment vibrated with noise and commotion.

Waltzes, rumbas, boleros, operas, gospels, requiems, reggae, concertos, and symphonies merged one into the other. The LPs and singles were stored, labeled, and numbered in different-colored boxes. In La Pointe, Marie-Noëlle had only been exposed to the melodies of the beguines they played on birthdays or the rhythms of the carnival processions she followed from the Assainissement district with Claire-Alta. So she made him angry when she confused Sarah Vaughan with Bessie Smith and *The Marriage of Figaro* with *The Barber of Seville*. To begin with she mistook his kindness for that of her lost father. Then she realized that, even in his eyes, there wasn't really any room for her in the triangle of affection he formed with Reynalda and Garvey. He pitied her, that was all. She held that against him. Reynalda and Ludovic did not have any friends. They did not go out in the evenings. Their car remained in the garage collecting dust while they spent their vacations locked in the prison of the housing project. Never a friend or a colleague from work climbed the stairs to their landing. The telephone never rang except when Ludovic's cousins called from Belgium, and the postman slipped only bills or mail-order catalogs under the door. But Marie-Noëlle soon learned through her classmates' chatter that both of them were in a way extremely active. Ludovic was the founder of a political-cum-religious association called Muntu. The miracles he worked with the delinquents, mainly Arabs and blacks, could be attributed to the association. Guided by its principles the gangsters no longer ganged together, the robbers gave to charity, and the most rebellious became as gentle as lambs. Marie-Noëlle could not believe her ears when she learned that Reynalda too belonged to the association. That's how people explained her success at City Hall, where, together with

another social worker, she was in charge of difficult cases. Her speciality was rape. But she was ruthlessly efficient at taking charge of
every wretched woman who had fallen under the merciless grip of
life. African women from north and south of the Sahara, West
Indians from Guadeloupe and Martinique, Réunion islanders,
abandoned by lovers seeking ever younger flesh, humiliated, ill
treated, battered, and sexually abused. Nobody could match the
way she induced the defenseless to defend themselves and the lifeless to stand up to life, the way she transformed the docile into
furies and urged them to demand their rights as well as those of
their children. More than one man, obliged to pay alimony and
other tribulations of this sort on the basis of her family investigations and testimony before the court, swore he would teach her a
lesson she would not soon forget. Marie-Noëlle thought she could
see in these revelations the key to a number of small mysteries that
had so intrigued her. Why the walls of every room were decorated
with curious drawings. Why they never ate meat or shellfish. Why
Ludovic, eyes lowered, made a silent invocation before every meal.
Why neither he nor Reynalda nor Garvey went to the hairdresser,
hiding their mop of hair under tam-o'shanters with three identical
colors. Why they regularly disappeared every Saturday afternoon.
She was not surprised at being kept away from Muntu. She knew
full well she was not part of the family. What disconcerted her was
imagining Reynalda as a vigilante, an activist in an association. It
was beyond understanding. Reynalda sought out her victims so far
away and ignored the girl who was being driven to despair under
her very eyes. Why heal the wounds of strangers?

Owing to her troubles Marie-Noëlle ended her childhood on a
taciturn and morose note. The summers were spent at holiday
camps along melancholic seashores. No friends. No boyfriends or
love letters at school. She attracted nobody, not even the dirty old
men who haunt the stairwells. The only things that warmed her

heart were the unending letters from Ranélise, who recounted all
the gossip from the Vatable Canal neighborhood in every detail,
and her parcels of pickled peppers, grapefruit jam, peanut nougat,
and pink-topped coconut candies packed in shreds of paper that
brought with them all the smells of the lost island. As for
Reynalda, she never enquired about Ranélise. She never bothered
to send her regards when Marie-Noëlle was writing to her. Not a
card at New Year's. Nor Christmas. Nor her birthday on April 24.

You could have sworn that her benefactor of years gone by had
never existed.

ven so, she did have one friend.

"Madame Esmondas, Clairvoyant." It was printed on her visiting cards left at the baker's. Mme. Esmondas lived on the top floor of building A and since the elevator was broken, by the time you arrived on her landing you were out of breath. This did not prevent people from climbing up to pour out all their misfortunes. Men. Women. Young people. Not-so-young people. The unemployed in search of a job, the ambitious looking for a promotion, males searching for their virility, wives and mistresses looking for love, sick folk seeking good health. Her clients even included young people whom, the day before their civil service entrance exams, Mme. Esmondas had drink herb tea in which she had soaked whole pages of the Larousse dictionary or summaries from the Dalloz manual. Mme. Esmondas was a short black woman no taller than a ten-year-old child, whom everyone called "Madame" out of respect, without ever having seen a man on her arm. It was common knowledge that she inherited her great gift from her mother and grandmother, who had conversed with the invisible world before her, and could see as well in the dark as in daylight. But both these women had practiced their art in Vieux-Habitants,

Guadeloupe, the town where Mme. Esmondas was born. If you asked her why she had left Guadeloupe in the years when the BUMIDOM agency was in full swing she would answer with a little smile: "My blood would not stay still in my body!"

In France she had neither mopped nor scrubbed other people's floors. She settled at Savigny-sur-Orge, where she immediately made a name for herself and built a clientele. So much so that she divided her cluttered, claustrophobic living room in two, with its curtains permanently drawn, and converted it into a kind of consulting room. Lacking a companion—proof, you might say, that she couldn't keep love for herself—Mme. Esmondas did not have any children. She lived alone, and this was the great regret of her life. To whom would she leave her three-room apartment? Her heavy chain necklace? Her gold bead choker? The money she had saved up at the bank? Always quick to exaggerate, people whispered she had millions in her account. She had grown fond of Marie-Noëlle, whom she passed on the stairs lugging her heavy satchel, so different from the other children, always alone, always with a polite "Good morning" and "Good evening." At five o'clock she had her come into her kitchen, where, in between customers, she gave her a cup of steaming hot vanilla chocolate and crumbly LU cookies. When she could escape of an evening, while Reynalda was busy with her thesis and Ludovic immersed in his music, Marie-Noëlle would climb up to the sixth floor. During those moments Mme. Esmondas went back to being herself. Gone were the turban and flowing dress. In their place was a woman of uncertain age, her hair braided in tight little puffballs, looking benevolent in her faded clothes. Mme. Esmondas never asked questions, as if what went on on the third floor was none of her business. She never asked Marie-Noëlle to wash the dishes, sweep, or take the garbage down. She sat her down in an armchair like a princess and related to her in an unassuming way the most extraordinary cases in which she had demonstrated her powers. The time when she restored manhood to a man, cursed three times seven by his woman, whose penis had shrunk flabbier than a turkey's neck between his legs. The time when she cured a woman's tumor, wished for by a rival, that was eating up both breasts, climbing inexorably to her throat. The time she snatched from death a child who already bore the mark of a blue spatula in the very middle of his forehead. For let there be no mistake about it. The spirits migrate too. They follow hard on the heels of the Guadeloupean and swoop down on him wherever he may be. Marie-Noëlle took little pleasure listening to these stories. She preferred the moments when Mme. Esmondas talked quite simply about her life, her maman, and the time when she was a little girl.

✵

The town of Vieux-Habitants looked out over the sea. There were no canefields or factories on this side of the island. The church, the one-room school, and the huts lined up along the seashore. So in fine weather, when the sea was not in an angry mood, you could gaze on the jagged blue mountains of a blurred island in the distance. Mme. Esmondas's maman, whom everyone called Tanita, was a *dormeuse*—one of those people who merely have to close their eyes to see the life of others parade behind their eyelids. Which meant that she never slept like other human beings but spent hours sighing and lamenting at the tragedies looming. Until she was seventeen, Mme. Esmondas, who shared the same bed as her maman, had not slept either. She went to sleep amid tears and groans and woke up amid tears and groans. It was a little for that reason—the need for sleep—that she decided to live with Gertulien Gertule, a caneworker who was so good at dancing the *lewoz*. Alas! With Gertulien Gertule she did not sleep either. He made love to her like a bull, sometimes five, sometimes six times a night. It gave her great belly pains and three miscarriages. So in the end she went back to her maman. Insomnia for insomnia! It was Thérésa, a former classmate, who suggested she leave for France. She herself had gone there with her boyfriend, a carpenter, who soon left her for a white slut. Even so, she wrote letter after letter boasting of her happiness. She described her lodgings. Running water. Toilet. What she neglected to say was that all these wonders were outside on the landing, and her maid's room was not heated. But Mme. Esmondas did not regret having listened to her advice. If it hadn't been for Thérésa she would still be in Guadeloupe carrying a man's stillborn babies, whereas now she had property and respect. Of course there was the solitude. Harder still in winter! But, when all is said and done, you've got the Good Lord to keep you company. Mme. Esmondas was very religious and never missed a mass. Every evening, before she let Marie-Noëlle go down the unlighted stairs, Mme. Esmonda would explain to her how to defend herself against men. Marie-Noëlle was greatly surprised to learn that these very same men who never cast a look in her direction had, in fact, only one idea in mind: to pry open her body. Because of this she had serious doubts about Mme. Esmondas's credibility and, deep down, she pitied the clients who lined up in front of her door. Despite this, the moments she spent with Mme. Esmondas seemed blissful to her and were the closest thing to happiness.

The summer camps were always an ordeal for she loathed the physical exercise, the walks, the climbs, and the swimming, and very soon found herself ignored by the counselors, who always prefer the athletic types. That summer the municipality dispatched its flock to a village in the Dordogne, and the time was spent swimming in icy rivers, going on endless hikes in the woods, and climbing down to the bottom of caves where there was nothing to see. As soon as she got back to Savigny-sur-Orge she ran up to Mme. Esmondas's, to whom she had remembered to send a post-card and came face-to-face with a closed door. She went back up the stairs several times in vain and had to face facts. Mme. Esmondas had gone away. As she pushed open the door of their apartment with an aching heart, Ludovic placed a basket of wash-ing in her arms. While she hung out the pillowcases, towels, and socks, she never stopped asking herself, Where could Madame Esmondas possibly be? Her days were always meticulously worked out. She left her apartment only on Sunday mornings to go to church and on Wednesday afternoons to go to the supermarket. She did not dare confide her distress to Ludovic, who, she would bet, did not even know the name of Mme. Esmondas, living as he did like a savage, not caring about anybody in the apartments. The tiny scraps of joy she had experienced danced around and around in her head: Mme. Esmondas, motherly in a way her mother never was, the smell of hot chocolate tickling her nostrils, and the taste of the butter cookie in her mouth, freshly removed from its foil pack. If her only friend disappeared, she would have nothing to remember her by. Not a souvenir. Not a photo. Nothing but men-tal images that would not stand up to time.

After a few days, tired of her comings and goings, a neighbor finally half opened her door and told her that Mme. Esmondas had suffered an attack. An attack? An attack of what? Where was she now? The neighbor did not know any more than that. Marie-Noëlle armed herself with a dictionary. "Attack: 2. a sudden occurrence of an illness." Impossible! Mme. Esmondas prided her-self on never having had a headache.

The apartment on the sixth floor remained closed for months. In early spring it was opened. New occupants moved in. A family, Papa, Maman, and a litter of children, all boys. Since they kept to themselves nobody could get any answers. One had to be content with guesswork. They were probably relatives of Mme. Esmondas. There was a family look about them.

Deep down Marie-Noëlle kept up hope. She was convinced that Mme. Esmondas would not abandon her after all the friendship between them. She would convey to her a secret way of saying farewell, in a way she alone would understand. At night she waited for her in her dreams. But the months went by, and she never saw her again.

$\mathcal{B}$ uried among all this gloom, a memory, glowing like the promise of the sun in the predawn hours.

No summer camp that year. The month of July brought Rodrigue, Natasha, and their twelve-year-old daughter, Awa, to Savigny-sur-Orge: Rodrigue, a black, bearded giant, the very image of Melchior, one of the Three Wise Men; Natasha, blond, her looks already faded before middle age, a hint of her former beauty clinging around her eyes. Rodrigue and Ludovic claimed to be cousins because they were both children of Haitian emigrants to Cuba and, as small boys, had scratched and scarred themselves in the same sugarcane fields. But since then, their lives had gone separate ways, and Rodrigue had stayed on in Cuba with his family. This had given him the opportunity to study medicine at Moscow University and become somebody. It was in Moscow that he had met Natasha and he was now the director of a family welfare center in Upper Guinea, in a village set in the very middle of the dark green forest.

For lack of space they put Awa and Marie-Noëlle in the same bed, and on the very first evening, Marie-Noëlle, who never spoke because nobody ever listened, unleashed a litany of words that continued uninterrupted until morning, describing for Awa the sort of life she was leading. It was the first of a series of conversations that was to last for years and survive all kinds of setbacks. Immediately the flame of friendship crackled between the two girls and set them ablaze with its steel blue glow.

Awa and Marie-Noëlle were alike. They were the same height. Same weight. Same fairly light skin. Same eyes of ever-changing colors. Same gingery mop of hair, more curly than frizzy, always combed any which way. They swore they would be sisters and remained so for a long time.

On the second evening Awa in turn confided in Marie-Noëlle. She wasn't happy either. Her parents no longer loved each other. Her father was only interested in his welfare center, his patients, their dysentery, infected wounds, malaria, Guinea worms, and tuberculosis. Her mother, Natasha, was very lonely. On account of Rodrigue she had left her country, her parents, and those who spoke her language and buried her youth in a land of misery. So she never stopped filling his head with reproaches, accusations, and recrimination. She also knew that he kept an African woman and children as black as the devil in one of the village huts. She had tried everything to live her life to the full. Give Russian lessons? To whom? Nobody could read. Enroll in a correspondence course with the university in Dakar, Senegal? The mail was so unreliable. Have another child? She had put that idea into practice and had a son. Alas! The climate did not suit him, and he had died when he was a few weeks old. Now she never left Kouroussa so as to be always close to that little grave dug in the humus under the trees in the forest. Everything revolted her. The Africans in their wrap skirts as dirty as their skins, the few whites, storekeepers or teachers, gaunt and emaciated, ghosts of their former selves, the sky forever leaden and overcast above her head, and above all the forest, this forest that avidly opened its jaws wherever she looked.

Natasha spent all day long lying on her bed, crying and wailing for her mother, dead the previous year, recalling over and over again the splendors of Nijvorod, the suburb of Moscow where she had grown up and first fallen in love with Rodrigue.

At twelve Awa already showed an interest in boys that only intensified with the passing years. Certain people of mixed blood, said to be more sultry and sensual than others, are known for their sexual impulses. Marie-Noëlle was not entirely innocent either. At La Pointe she would suddenly awake to hear strange duets between Ranélise and Gérardo Polius and understood that what goes on between a man and a woman at night does not need the light of day. Her curiosity now focused on the physical relationship between Reynalda and Ludovic. Reynalda behaved in such a strange way with him. Never a meaningful gesture, a half smile, or an intimate side glance. Whenever he went to kiss her, she seemed to be in agony. Shrinking like a bed of sensitive grass. Yet Garvey hadn't turned up thanks to the Holy Spirit! Why was she playing so hard to get?

Awa dragged Marie-Noëlle far from these trivial considerations. All summer long the square in the Jean-Mermoz housing projects was filled with kids of various hues idly picking fights or kicking around a football. It provided, therefore, a limitless field of exploration.

Marie-Noëlle, paralyzed with envy, watched Awa as she set off to conquer these idle youngsters, engage them in conversation, and look them over, checking out what they had in their jeans next to their skin. Awa let herself be kissed and fondled in the stairwells and parking lots and in front of the washing machines in the basement. Then she adjusted her clothes and went upstairs to put on an angelic face at dinner. In the apartment little attention was paid to the children, for the atmosphere was generally razor sharp. Rodrigue and Ludovic, who had not seen each other for ages, had become like long-lost brothers and dreamed of starting over again side by side. They bombarded each other with questions. Was there a history of delinquency in Upper Guinea? Did they recruit doctors trained in the Eastern bloc at Savigny-sur-Orge? The women, however, ever since their meeting at Orly Airport, where their companions had forced them into a warm embrace, had shown a mutual mistrust. Now they were at loggerheads. Although Reynalda was content to avoid any contact by locking herself away in her study on the pretext of working on her thesis, Natasha had no scruples about making unpleasant remarks. About the way Reynalda dressed. Did not keep house. Ignored her guests. The way she treated her family. It was one thing the way she treated Ludovic. Ever since biblical times pearls have always been cast before swine. It was one thing the way she had so little maternal instinct for the adorable Garvey. He was a little man, and men are endowed with strength and courage from the cradle on. But nothing, nothing could excuse the way she treated Marie-Noëlle! So pretty, so gentle, so intelligent! Marie-Noëlle should have been the apple of her eye, the golden chain on her wrist! Sometimes God seems to act like a real ignoramus and bestows treasures on those who don't deserve them. In actual fact it's a trap He's setting them. When He summons them on Judgment Day, pray God they can defend themselves.

Natasha therefore set about repairing what could be repaired. Leaving Rodrigue and Ludovic to celebrate their Cuban childhood, downing beer after beer or chasing after a football like kids, she slipped on her dresses made from African fabrics, braided her blond hair, and took the two little girls by the hand. Carousels, fairgrounds, book fairs, shows for children, cartoons, musical comedies, and rock concerts, whatever. So that's how they got to listen in tears to Joan Baez sing on the square in front of Notre-Dame and dance frenziedly to the music of Ike and Tina Turner back from Ghana.

That summer Marie-Noëlle rediscovered the warmth of embraces, but also the heat of reprimands and punishments. In fact it wasn't wise to stay too close to Natasha, for you never knew what you were going to get, a kiss or a slap. But Marie-Noëlle relished the taste of chocolate eclairs and tarte Tatin in the tearooms on the rue de Rivoli and the ice-cream cones during the interval at the movies. She warmed herself from the glow of affectionate names. Her heart, numb in her breast, started beating again when Natasha called her "my pet," "my lamb," or "honey, dear," and she woke up at night in a sweat wondering whether the Good Lord, who had treated her so cruelly for so long, was not making a mockery of her.

Suddenly so much tenderness.

Shortly before their return to Kouroussa, while Awa moaned just thinking of their coming separation, Rodrigue and Natasha addressed a plea to Reynalda. Natasha had prepared a short speech in which, on the advice of Rodrigue and Ludovic, she refrained from sounding acrimonious or offensive. Awa and Marie-Noëlle adored each other, that was obvious. Like twins from the same womb. Marie-Noëlle got along with her as if she were her real maman. And with Rodrigue as if he were her real papa. Both of them loved her dearly. At Kouroussa the school was not that bad. She would help the children in their schoolwork, and Rodrigue would look after any illnesses. Why not let them have Marie-Noëlle?

Reynalda listened to their offer. She was in one of her rare good moods. At the beginning of the evening she had stopped hammering away at her typewriter and come to join them in the living room. She had tolerated the conversation, which did not vary much from one day to the next. Memories of childhood pranks by Rodrigue and Ludovic. Medical student stories from the time when Rodrigue was an intern at a hospital in Moscow. Stories describing the misery of Africans. Diatribes against neocolonialism, which was replacing colonialism. Finally, heated arguments. About the Cuban revolution. Was Fidel Castro really the "Lider Maximo" that some people worshiped? About Marxism, whose limitations Ludovic predicted. About Muntu, whose principles made Rodrigue laugh. That was an idea borrowed from the Americans, wasn't it? Reynalda listened, leaning against Ludovic's shoulder in a rare, relaxed attitude, with an open yet paradoxically impenetrable expression. When Natasha had finished, without a word she turned to Marie-Noëlle, who was trembling with expectation, holding Awa's hand, and looked at her. It was perhaps the first time she had looked at her in this way. Without shirking. Face-to-face. Straight in the eyes. And Marie-Noëlle knew what this look meant. It meant possession. She understood that Reynalda who had ejected her, abandoned her for ten years, for reasons known to her alone, that had little to do with love, no longer had any intention of letting her go. She herself, whatever she did, whatever others did, would never be free of her. She would spend her life imagining the unimaginable tenderness of times gone by when they had been joined together in the same flesh, and would spend her life regretting it and trying to relive it. But it would be a lost cause. She would never achieve her end and would be destined to wander alone in her desert. In despair she began to cry, and Reynalda, without a word or a movement in her direction, without a "Good evening" to anyone, stood up and went into her bedroom.

The two girls spent the remaining nights sobbing in each others' arms while Ludovic, Rodrigue, and Natasha quarreled among themselves, Natasha scolding both men for their lack of courage.

Never again was there mention of leaving for Kouroussa.

✦

The following year Marie-Noëlle, who had always been one of the top students, fell behind to join those who, class after class, teacher after teacher, heard themselves destined for a bleak future. Nothing interested her anymore. Life had become a series of mechanical gestures without rhyme or reason. Brushing her teeth in the morning with a mint-tasting toothpaste, bumping against the walls of the shower stall, eating her cereal, filling her school-bag with a ton of books, studying the tragedies of Racine, translating the poetry of Wordsworth, and dissecting the genital organs of rats and mice. Why not set sail once and for all to that shore planted with lotus flowers, cornflowers, and giant papyrus that the ancient Egyptians described? And amid the clash of sistrums greet her two souls, waiting for the moment to be reborn, praying that this time life would be less cruel?

Landing in this world of dunces, however, a world oblivious to success and hence devoid of the spirit of competition, Marie-Noëlle once again discovered friendship, that flower of lonesomeness. In the schoolyard, nobody wanted to go near the coal black little girl, her hair braided in rosettes, outfitted in the strangest clothes. Neither the Africans from north nor south of the Sahara nor the West Indians who made up most of the kids at school. Like Awa, Saran came from Guinea (not from Kouroussa but the capital), whose cohorts of refugees were starting to throng the highways of this world. Mandekuman, her father, had been a high-ranking officer in the regime, with two Mercedes-Benzes, and she had grown up behind a hedge of bougainvillea with a Mossi guarding her gate. Then the dictator changed his clique. Just as he was about to take flight across the rocky terrain of Malinke coun-try, Mandekuman chose Aminata, his third wife, for his exile—the wife who could read, write, and speak a little French—and left Saran's mother behind. From one day to the next the little girl's life underwent a radical change. In the unheated apartment the children, fed on sardines in oil and soggy rice, slept in their coats to keep warm. Saran was always the last to turn up at the school gate because she had a baby brother to change, some washing to do or ironing, and the sardines and rice to buy on credit from the Arab shopkeeper. Her boots leaked. Her fingers were peppered with blisters. Even so Marie-Noëlle maintained that her misfortune was no match for her own. At least Aminata, her stepmother, was a living person. A person who could laugh at her misfortune. A person who was never at a loss for words to describe the receptions in the flower-filled gardens of the president's palace, the women's gauze *boubous* and jewelry, the aroma of spit-roasted sheep by the dozen, and the shrill voices of the *griottes* from the National Ensemble singing the glory of the revolution. Saran thought otherwise, and, to prove it, she lifted up her blouse to reveal the bruises on her body.

Unlike Awa, Saran was not interested in boys. She could only think of her maman, gone back to her family, to whom she wrote letter after letter without ever receiving a reply. But there was a need for school supplies and the desire for potato chips, Mars Bars, and Smarties at recess. So she let herself be laid by the school's most strapping young students, those who were at least seventeen and repeating their last year in class. The rendezvous took place in an unused chemistry and physics laboratory. Marie-Noëlle was assigned to keep watch in the yard and look out for the janitor. But she preferred to glue her eyes to the windowpane. What went on inside the classroom terrified her, but also aroused in her a rush of blood. Recalling Awa, she would have given anything to be in her friend's place, splayed out, spread open, and yet all-powerful like a goddess dispensing pleasure to a line of supplicants. As for her, nobody desired her. The boys at school or in the projects passed her by without even a glance. Saran surprised her one day by revealing that she did not feel anything and only pretended.

Suddenly it became an obsession. Did Reynalda pretend? That would explain her behavior toward Ludovic. Saran also showed her some condoms, which she slipped on her partners in a most professional way. Did Reynalda and Ludovic, who no longer produced any children, use condoms?

From then on Marie-Noëlle became aware of Ludovic's body as he moved about the house, of his smell, his color, and the weapon he carried, standing at ease between his legs. She also became aware of her mother's body: somewhat thin and still juvenile despite her pregnancies. Two men at least had shoved her on her back. How had they gone about it? Had the first man laid her like a whore? Had he raped her? That would explain why she had wanted to kill herself. Marie-Noëlle woke up at night, listening to the silence, but could hear nothing except Garvey's breathing in the bed above hers. Tormented over and over again in her head by these unhealthy thoughts, she lost weight, her dresses became too big for her and in the late fall she had her first period.

✷

It was around the month of February when Saran told her of a plan. She was going to steal the jewelry that Aminata kept under her mattress, unknown to anyone, even her husband: necklaces as wide as pectorals, pendants as heavy as oranges, brooches in the shape of flowers and animals, and wrist and ankle bracelets, all made of platinum, gold, and silver carved by the best silversmiths in Guinea or encrusted with precious stones from South Africa and Zaire. Together with her memories, it was all that remained of her days of glory. Sometimes she would lock herself in her room and deck herself out, weeping all the tears out of her body. Saran would sell the whole bundle to a dealer—that shouldn't be a problem in Savigny-sur-Orge—and pay for two airline tickets. Then they would escape to the United States of America. Once there she would send for her maman. Perhaps Marie-Noëlle would like to send for Ranélise? And Claire-Alta?

Marie-Noëlle would have given anything to leave Savigny-sur-Orge far, far behind her. Nothing was keeping her. Except Garvey, whom she adored. He had just turned four, and he would cuddle up and hug her as if he understood her sadness. She would not miss Ludovic. Oh, no! Not him. The older she grew, the more she realized that his kindness hid nothing but pity. And who likes to inspire pity? In spite of that, Saran's plan was somehow unconvincing. It seemed to her childish, unworkable, simply crazy. So as not to hurt her, however, she made just one objection. Why go to the United States? Why not simply return to Guinea? Saran had thought the question over and come up with some arguments: "In Guinea the police will kill us like dogs, whereas America's the country of liberty."

Finally they decided to leave at the beginning of July, once school was over. Saran claimed that she had unearthed a dealer, an Algerian Harki from Tlemcen by the name of Tahar. She also claimed to have made arrangements with a travel agency. But the day she was supposed to lay hands on the jewels, she found nothing in the usual spot. Aminata must have changed the hiding place.

Marie-Noëlle could never get it out of her head that in actual fact Saran had never intended to leave. That she had talked a lot of hot air. And dreamed. Merely dreamed.

Chapter 6

ow many days stacked up to make weeks? Months to make years? How many years passed?

Marie-Noëlle's memory does not keep count. It keeps only the memory of this conversation with Reynalda, the only one they had throughout their entire life together. Marie-Noëlle must have been fifteen or sixteen. They were threatening to expel her from school. They had already expelled Saran. It was spring or summer since the windows were wide open and the screams of children rose up from the square. Reynalda had bared her shoulders, lighter than her face, and revealed the cleavage of her breasts, the same color, pushed outward and slightly drooping. Her locks of hair, reddish in places, stuck out in all directions like a gorgon's, without managing, however, to give her a fearsome air. She aimed her gaze at Marie-Noëlle, which, as usual, went straight through her to focus on a vague spot situated somewhere behind her, up to the right or left, perhaps on a strange print that Ludovic had pinned to the wall. She spoke as if what she said did not really concern Marie-Noëlle—as if she were not speaking to her but concentrating on some personal digression.

"It's hard work that put me where I am today. In an office on the

second floor of City Hall with a secretary at my beck and call. It's
hard work and nothing else. There's no master or mistress looking
over me. I do what I want, how I want, when I want. For years people treated me like a dog. They threw me their words like bones to
gnaw on and ordered me around: 'Reynalda do this, Reynalda do
that.' That's over with. You have to know what you want in life.
You have to decide for yourself because nobody lives your life for
you. You can't waste time sniveling and brooding over what happened. I realized that in the end. I've suffered more than anybody
else in my life. I don't know how many times I wished I were dead.
I can assure you I don't know how I'm still alive. It must be thanks
to Ludovic. But sometimes I wonder whether it was worth it.

"I was born on La Désirade. People from Guadeloupe have bad
feelings about Désirade because of the rogues and lepers they used
to send there, but also because nothing grows there. Nothing. No
sugarcane. No coffee. No cotton. No yams. No sweet potatoes.
But for me, as a little girl, it *was* really 'Desirada,' the desired
island, looming up out of the ocean in front of the eyes of
Christopher Columbus's sailors after days and days at sea. I knew
all its nooks and crannies. I breathed in its scent when the sun,
after baking it all day long, finally rested its head beneath the
water. I could lift up any stone and name the insect hidden underneath. I knew its undergrowth inside out. I lived on the
'Mountain' with Maman. No brothers or sisters. Just us two in a
rickety hut set on a desolate plot of rocky ground, hedged by cro-
tons, next to a *mapoo* tree. In the morning I fed crumbs of rice to
the birds I had trapped with glue and kept in a bamboo cage I had
woven myself. We had no electricity or running water. Every
morning I went down to the Cybèle gully with a bucket balanced
on my head. At night we lit candles that did nothing to lighten
the darkness. Like most of the other children I didn't have a papa.
It didn't bother me. Even so I often asked who he was. Whenever

I questioned her, Maman would give me a different answer. Sometimes she told me he was a fisherman who had gone to drag his net for tuna over Petite-Terre way and never came back. Other times she maintained that he raised fighting cocks in Baie-Mahault. And on other occasions he was a knife grinder in Saint-François over on the mainland. In actual fact I believe she herself did not know exactly who had given her a belly because so many men had climbed on top of her to take their pleasure. Probably not out of vice. She was simply a poor wretch, and poor wretches are up for grabs. Men have them and leave them and have them again whenever they feel like it. Maman didn't much like me. That I felt immediately. I won't say that she began to treat me roughly. It's just that she never had a kind word for me. She would repeat I was too black, too short, I had bad hair, not like hers, which was long and thick. She braided it in 'vanilla pods' to go to mass. She never stopped grumbling that I would never find a man to look after me. In the end she was mistaken.

"At home we didn't get to see much meat. We were lucky when Maman, who scrubbed the presbytery floors in Baie-Mahault, could pay for a skewer of fish that she fried in lard. Most of the time I soaked my slice of breadfruit or green bananas in oil. But I never let all that bother me. When my stomach rumbled too much, I poled down a mango. I scratched my hands picking hog plums among the clumps of logwood. But my biggest piece of good fortune was this: Wretched as I was, not a pair of shoes or a good dress to my name, only secondhand schoolbooks and tattered exercise books, I got top grades at school. The teachers took offense. They thought it wasn't right in some way. They would rather have given the pink grade sheets to their light-skinned little pets. Nothing doing. It was me, Reynalda Titane, who ran off with them all. It was as if I collected them. I put them away in a LU biscuit tin. I numbered them.

"I sang well too.

"However much the Sunday school teachers placed me in the last row behind the well-dressed children with their well-combed hair so that I couldn't be seen at church services, only *my* voice could be heard. It reverberated around the nave, it soared up to the ceiling in the shape of a ship's hull. It climbed even higher: up to the heavens.

"And that—strangely enough—was the cause of my misfortune. One August 15 the bishop of Guadeloupe landed on a pilgrimage to Désirade. In those days Guadeloupe was a distant, foreign land. Like most people, I had never been there. I had never taken a boat or traveled. Not even to Saint-François or the Pointe des Châteaux you could make out behind the cays and the open sea. That day everyone ran to the wharf as soon as it was light. Some merely to admire the launch with its flags and pennants of the Holy Virgin floating in the wind. Others because they had been told the bishop healed sick people. In Capesterre he was supposed to have healed two women and a small boy. The bishop climbed down leaning on two priests, one on his right, the other on his left. He wore a mauve robe, the color of his face. On his head was a gilded miter, and he made a blessing with great gestures of his hands. A choirboy was swinging an incense holder. Everyone went down on their knees. Then we filed up in procession to the church for high mass. The children's choir was at its usual place at the foot of the high altar. I was behind. As usual, only I could be heard. It seems the bishop wept. Afterward he asked to see me, and the Sunday school teachers felt obliged to take me to him. The bishop was sitting in the great hall of the presbytery with all the priests, the mayor and notables of Baie-Mahault around him. He was quite fat, sweating, with a kindly face, it must be said. He gave me his ring to kiss. He asked me my name. He wanted to know who my papa was, who my maman was, if I liked school and if I worked hard. Everyone was looking at me, but I wasn't frightened. I answered his questions and then I went back into the kitchen where my mother was helping out the priests' servant girls. I remember we ate a ton of things I never even imagined. Foie gras. *Vols-au-vent*. Duck conserves. I even tasted some sweet white wine.

"One evening a few weeks later, in comes Father Rousseau, the parish priest, all out of breath. He had received a letter. A letter from the bishop, whom I had already completely forgotten. The bishop was of the opinion that I should not stay on Désirade eking out a life of misery, but should come to La Pointe, where there were so many possibilities of social advancement for intelligent black people. By studying hard one could even become an elementary schoolteacher or principal. He had found a position for Maman as a servant with an Italian jeweler on the rue de Nozières, a man of great integrity and kindness, even though he was a Jew, whose wife was always laid up, and consequently he needed someone trustworthy to keep house. The man's name was Gian Carlo Coppini. He would provide food and lodging. More important, he pledged to send me to school until I was sixteen.

"I thought Maman would refuse. Why go and work as a maid for a white man, and an Italian no less? Why leave Désirade, where we had the sea as far as the eye could roam, the sun above our heads, and hummingbirds quivering over the tops of the acacias? To my great surprise she jumped at the offer like a sick person presented with a bowl of chicken broth. The priest handed her some hundred-franc bills as an advance on her first month's wages, and she began to dash from hut to hut boasting of her good fortune: 'Neighbor so and so, I've found some work in La Pointe, I have!' 'Neighbor so-and-so . . . '

People were amazed at her good luck and badmouthed her behind her back. 'It must be men she's after, since none of those around here want anything more to do with her.' She piled our wretched things into a wicker basket, turned the key in the lock, and we were off. I was in agony. The day before we left I opened the cage and freed all my birds. I went and said farewell to all the places I loved: to the cool spot down in the Cybèle gully, to the stream that babbles under the blanket of duckweed, to the trees— the *mapoo*, pink cedar, and *ti-bonbon*—and to the sea, especially the sea, where I would never again jump in feet first."

D

"It was Arcania who told me about Gian Carlo—Arcania, always bedridden and as beautiful as the Madonna, whom we the children of the house called Maman because we worshiped her. She hated him as much as I did. But she too was powerless. She had crossed the ocean with him. At that time, cheated and mistreated, women did not even think about divorcing.

"Gian Carlo Coppini was the only boy in a family from the region of Como, where the men had been jewelers from father to son. At the outset they had been Jews from Poland. But they italianized their name shortly after they arrived and no longer bothered with the business of the Sabbath. Even after they converted they didn't bother with the Good Lord's business, and everyone took them for heathens. At the age of twenty-two Gian Carlo did something so serious—Arcania did not know what— that his papa and maman banished him, even though he was their only son. After having wandered throughout northern Italy, finding work easily because he was a good craftsman, skillful at filigreeing gold and mounting cameos, he appears to have settled down in Milan with the renowned goldsmith Paolo Renucci. The heart of the matter was that Paolo had a daughter, just one, the angelic Arcania. Paolo Renucci slept with a loaded gun under his pillow, swearing that the man who would mount Arcania was not yet born. Wicked tongues even whispered that it was obvious he wanted her for himself. When Gian Carlo gave Arcania a belly, there was only one solution: Get as far away as possible from Milan and Paolo. Of course there was the United States of America. In those days the ships were full of Italians emigrating. But Gian Carlo and Arcania hesitated. Friends of Gian Carlo in New York wrote him distressing letters describing the beast of winter as it raged through the streets.

"One day, while he was leafing through *La Stampa*, he came across an advertisement:

> Rendezvous with the sun in the blessed islands of Guadeloupe and Martinique. Regular crossings on luxurious liners, comfortable hotels, picturesque itineraries.
>
> —Compagnie Générale Transatlantique

"That made up their minds for them.

"Gian Carlo and Arcania, pregnant with Ira, her first daughter, who was to die at the age of six months, arrived in Guadeloupe on board the steamship *Allier* at the end of the Second World War, the very year I was born of an unknown father on Désirade. Guadeloupe had greatly suffered from the blockade. A good many mothers were mourning their sons who had left to join the Resistance and General de Gaulle and had been killed or reported missing. Gian Carlo, who knew how to bargain, bought the house of a penniless white Creole for next to nothing. It was in need of repair but well situated on the rue de Nozières: two wooden storeys plus an attic built on top of a ground floor made of concrete, where he opened the jeweler's shop he christened Il Lago di Como. Very quickly his business prospered more than he had ever imagined.

Folk in Guadeloupe had never laid eyes on jewels of the sort he made. Of course they had already seen cameos. Gian Carlo introduced them to the intaglio, which is something else; it is engraved with a sunken design. Women from the upper classes came from as far away as Basse-Terre, Saint-Claude, and Matouba to place their orders. Gian Carlo could no longer keep up with demand and was obliged to pay for the passage—in third class—of two of his sisters. Both were on their way to becoming old maids. So he had them believe that with their skin the color of milk and their blond curls they would have no trouble finding a husband among the white Creoles. In reality as soon as they landed off the ship he tyrannized them. He made them work without paying them a cent in wages. He rationed their rice and codfish. The poor women were so ashamed of their dresses, patched up again and again, and of their shoes, which could no longer be soled, that they never set foot out of doors. Except to go to confession and eight o'clock mass and sometimes sit with mantillas lowered on the Place de la Victoire on the Widows' Path. We felt pity for them, Aunt Lia and Aunt Zita. But their misfortunes never altered the goodness of their hearts. They were two saints who deserved paradise.

"This was the house I entered on September 10, 1955, when I was ten years old.

"Maman Arcania, as everyone called her, even her husband, even her sisters-in-law, was as white as lard. In ten years she had had ten children. Out of the ten she had buried five. Fortunately she could not have any more, since she had suffered an internal hemorrhage that had put her at death's door. As a result Gian Carlo made life extremely difficult for her, because he had not had his son. She spent most of the day lying in bed reading novels, listening to records, daydreaming, and crying. Occasionally, once the sun had gone down, she stretched out in a chaise longue on the second-floor balcony to take in the cool of the evening. On some

Sundays she found enough strength to walk as far as the Cathedral of Saint-Pierre-and-Saint-Paul on the arm of Gian Carlo, and instead of praying and reading their missals, people would steal a glance at her as if she were an oddity. At other times—but this was very rare—she went down to the shop, sat for a few moments at the cash register, then went back up again, exhausted. Her voice was so soft, like church music, that you had to get right up close to hear what she was saying. Her clothes smelled of arnica, tincture of benzoin, and the perfume Soir de Paris, and underneath all that was another smell, more acrid, of the blood she was slowly losing.

"As soon as she started work, Maman set about looking after her in a way she had never looked after anyone. Least of all me. She dipped into the little money Gian Carlo gave her for the week and bought her eggs, milk, brioches, and fruit. At noon she fried beef's blood for her, cooked chicken breasts, fish fillets, and mashed potatoes with hearts of lettuce; in the evening she made pumpkin puree. She washed her, dressed her, perfumed her, greased her hair with Roja brilliantine, and made her lie down in her shuttered room, which she decorated with arum lilies. She would not tolerate the children knocking on her door, sitting down beside her, kissing her, embracing her, and telling her stories about their day at school. Even if they did not make any noise, she would shoo them away: 'Off you go! You'll tire her out!'

"It was as if she were jealous. As if she wanted to keep her all to herself, like Arcania's father, Paolo Renucci.

"Even so, this did not prevent her from doing what she did. Maman and me, we slept in the attic in two cubbyholes separated by a wall as thin as cigarette paper.

"Evening after evening I could hear Gian Carlo climb into Maman's bed and manhandle the mattress springs. I could hear him groan like the pig he was as he came to a climax, noisily clear his throat, fart, and piss straight into the earthenware jar. I never heard Maman and that was more hideous still. Had she shouted, cried out, and struggled like a victim I would have felt sorry for her. Had she expressed her pleasure I would have thought of her as a beast in heat. But this silence turned her into an inert object, maid for all things. I don't think Maman had been there a week before they started their affair. I don't know how it all began, and I can only imagine it. I imagine Maman scouring the floors like she did so well. She must have been down on both knees in dirty water, beside the pail holding her scrub brush, with her dress tucked up. He entered the room. Saw her buttocks in the air and, without even taking the trouble to say hello, stuck in his rod. In the evening he came back to find her again. I hated him. I hated Maman. I don't know which one I hated more. I dreamed of killing them. In the most bloody, atrocious way. I imagined a thousand ways of torturing them. They had to suffer, they were monsters."

At that moment Reynalda, who looked like someone in a coma, seemed to regain consciousness. She suddenly stopped. She looked around her, at the window behind which dusk had fallen. She looked in astonishment at Marie-Noëlle who, petrified, was drinking in her words, and then stood up. She made a strange movement with her entire body as if she were shaking off something, then went back into her study.

$\mathcal{D}$

A few weeks, months(?) later, a routine medical check-up at school showed that Marie-Noëlle had tuberculosis in her right lung.

Chapter 7

In its 250-acre park filled with deer and rare trees, the sanatorium at Vence formed a closed world, a world apart. It had its own laws, its own way of thinking, and an architecture all to itself. The rhythm of every weekday was punctuated by the pills to be swallowed, the temperature charts, the infusions, the injections, the naps outside on the terraces or inside (depending on the inclination of the sun), the X-rays and the CAT scans. Time was measured by how long the hundred or so schoolgirls and female students were confined to their beds. After three months, if their Koch bacillus was not too resistant, they had permission to leave their room for a few hours, strictly timed by the nurses, and to have their dinner in the refectory on the ground floor. After six months they could start preparing for their exams under the guidance of teachers, former TB patients themselves, from the nearby schools in Nice, Grasse, or the university at Aix-en-Provence, which wasn't too far away either. After a year they were authorized to spend one afternoon a week wherever they liked, staying clear, obviously, of such extremes as immoderate drinking, drugs, casino gambling, and especially sexual intercourse. After three years they could, in the best of cases, say their farewells to the institution, and if they were careful, they could hope to continue their lives without a relapse. Like a prison, the sanatorium was a place of violent passions. All the patients were in love with the doctors and the interns who cared for them. They hated the nurses and invented a thousand ways to complicate their job. Roommates adored each other or, on the contrary, from one day to the next, loathed each other and became sworn enemies. Marie-Noëlle spent two years and nine months at Vence, and over the years, with the help of her memory, embellished this episode in her life with the colors of a golden age. It was there that she resumed her studies and prepared for her baccalaureate. Except for the faithful letters from Ranélise and Awa, she received neither packages nor visits. Once a month a money order with the same words came: 'Affectionately yours, Maman.' Every two weeks, a call from Ludovic, giving her news of home. According to him Garvey never stopped asking for her. Her Maman had finally defended her thesis on social psychiatry and been unanimously congratulated by the jury. On Sundays and holidays, when the sanatorium filled with the chatter of worried relatives, she remained alone in her room, which did not bother her. This way she could pretend, as everyone around her firmly believed, that her family, Maman, Papa, brothers, sisters, and cousins lived abroad. This way she could imagine that those years spent at Savigny-sur-Orge had no place in reality. That Reynalda had never sent for her to treat her the way she had treated her. That they never had that conversation, fortunately interrupted, for she feared some horrible confession. Marie-Noëlle had come straight from La Pointe. She had left Ranélise sobbing on Claire-Alta's shoulder at the airport. But soon, in good hands, she would be cured. She would be able to go back home to Guadeloupe. Take up her life again where she had left off in the Vatable Canal district.

Marie-Noëlle was happy at Vence for another reason. She had

made two friends: Leïla, a seventeen-year-old Tunisian girl, who, after three relapses and two operations, had only one lung to breathe with. Araxie was an Armenian of the same age, hardly any stronger, who had already done the rounds of the country's sanatoriums. The others could not understand why Marie-Noëlle felt she had everything she could wish for and had no need for anything else. Seeing that she had nobody for company they persisted in pitying her and showered her with well-intentioned but unnecessary kindness. The doctors and interns rivaled each other with reassuring predictions about her condition. The nurses stuffed her chest of drawers with crystallized fruit or else candy from Aix. The teachers insisted on giving her individual lessons in every subject.

Marie-Noëlle never tired of hearing Leïla and Araxie describe their family life and the reunions around the table for birthdays, weddings, and baptisms. She imagined the laughter, the quarrels, the taste of the crème Chantilly, the aroma of liqueurs, and the sticky warmth of affection. She did not understand their recriminations or what they were complaining about. Their papa was too strict, their brothers overprotective, and their maman too possessive. What she would have given to know these tyrannies of love!

Once a week all three of them went down to Nice. Leïla and Araxie refused to take the sanatorium's comfortable minibus on the pretext that they needed to escape the atmosphere of sickbeds. No sooner were they sprawled on the backseat of the bus that rattled along the kilometers of winding road than they began all sorts of pranks. Singing saucy songs, telling dirty jokes, giving men the eye, making nasty remarks about the women and shrieking at every curve in the road. It was as if a fury possessed them. The other passengers smiled forgivingly at their commotion. They probably knew where they came from, and at the bottom of their hearts felt sorry for these youngsters. Getting off the bus, they went and joined a group of unemployed Arabs, West Indians, Turks, whatever—young half-castes like themselves, with no family to speak of, smokers of hash and drinkers of alcohol. Together they man-handled the slot machines in the bars of Old Nice, downing beer after beer and, more than half drunk, spent the remainder of the afternoon making love in the Nuits de Tlemcen, a somewhat shab-by hotel-restaurant owned by Laakdar, an Algerian Harki. Marie-Noëlle regularly slipped away when it came to going up to the rooms. It was easy because the boys never actually asked her to go with them. Had she been present they probably wouldn't have hesitated to lay her, individually or as a gang. But they barely noticed she'd left. While Leïla and Araxie were having their flings, she hung around the flower market, strolled as far as the seafront, and dipped her feet into a Mediterranean so cold and colorless compared to the Caribbean of her childhood. Sometimes she sat in deserted churches or nearly empty movie theaters, almost without caring what was flickering past on the screen. Then she went and joined her friends, deadbeat and disheveled, suddenly worried about their health.

𝔇

In June 1978, like the ten other candidates submitted by the sana-torium, Marie-Noëlle passed her baccalaureate. It was a great honor for the institution. It was a reason to celebrate. So they had a party. The doctor in charge gave a speech in which he congratu-lated not only the patients but also their devoted teachers. Then the nurses handed out cakes and white wine. Those in better health danced in the refectory, and disco music echoed through the corridors until midnight. Contrary to what you might think, Marie-Noëlle did not have a joyful heart that evening. Alone in her room she never stopped crying. Her latest X-rays had been excellent. In fact the doctors had declared her cured, and she could leave Vence at the end of the summer. What was to become of her? Was she going to enroll at the university? Start her higher education? She could no longer imagine being dependent on Reynalda. Or going back to live with her. So wouldn't she do better to look for a job and settle down somewhere far away, as far away as possible from Savigny-sur-Orge? A job? Who would get her a job? She couldn't do anything with her own ten fingers, and the worthless diploma she had just obtained did not prove otherwise. It was Leïla's and Araxie's turn not to understand her. Her tears were insulting. What wouldn't they give to regain their health and go back to a life without pills, a life without afternoon naps, a life without losing weight, a life without scales!

One day when they had gone down to Nice, a newcomer turned up. The boys spoke to him in an unusually respectful way because he was the only one in the group who had a job and could pay the rent for a furnished room. They nicknamed him Bob Marley because of his dreadlocks. In fact his name was Stanley. His parents came from Trinidad, but he was born in London. Very black, stocky, and well built, he gave the impression of strength. He was voluble, a real chatterbox. The entire afternoon he never stopped smoking and drinking and telling stories about himself. As a boy he had been a child prodigy who, with a razor-cut part through his mop of hair and dressed in a velvet suit, played the piano at his brothers' birthdays. Then he had said farewell to his family and learned on his own how to play the saxophone, the recorder, the flute, the classical guitar, the electric guitar, and the banjo. Now he headed a band of five musicians, a pianist, a double-bass player, a drummer, a trombonist, and himself on the saxophone, playing at the Ramada, a jazz club on the Riviera. But he had no intention whatsoever of wasting his time in this club. Within a year he would be in America. And once there, he would make a name for himself. Marie-Noëlle listened to him with a lot of surprise and a little envy. So much determination in this boy hardly older than herself. Whereas her life stretched out before her without a marker or a beacon like a wasteland, he knew what he wanted. Yet these dreams reminded her of Saran's—childish, unattainable, and crazy. Once again she hazarded just one objection. Always the same one. Why the United States? Like Saran, Stanley had prepared his answer: "It's the only country where a nigger can succeed in life!"

In the middle of the afternoon, Marie-Noëlle was about to sneak away as usual when the time came to go upstairs. But he firmly held her back.

D

Strange, how strange that Marie-Noëlle has no memory of that afternoon! Because nothing memorable happened. No *griotte* watching at the door to proclaim the untainted blood. No extraordinary pleasure. No pain either. They groped across a moist landscape and then fell asleep, one against the other. The next morning, however, Stanley asked Marie-Noëlle to come and live with him.

D

Ludovic grabbed his pen and wrote Marie-Noëlle a detailed letter. He said he was writing to her as a man who was familiar with every dirty trick life liked to play. He was not preaching, but where did this Stanley, who was keeping her in Nice, come from? He was a musician, so she said. Beware, music seldom feeds its man: He knew from experience during the years he had strummed a guitar in Brussels. Succeed in life in the United States? He had slaved in New York, unloaded ships in the port, driven the number 9 subway, and he could assure her that the American dream was long dead and gone. In fact nobody had ever seen it alive. Today only the stench of its corpse terrorized the nostrils. He asked her to reconsider what she was doing. By wanting to escape her maman, whom she had never tried to understand, she was running the risk of building herself a future of suffering and disillusionment.

Of the entire letter, only the reproaches of the last sentence stuck in her memory. Ludovic thought she had never tried to understand Reynalda. How can you understand someone who is elusive? It was true she wanted to escape her. But wasn't Stanley the ideal opportunity to get a life without her, far from her? Marie-Noëlle was not in a position to analyze herself clearly. After so many years standing watch for her friends—Awa, Saran, and Araxie—here was a man showing interest in her body. Here was a man prizing what all the others had despised. It was true that during the day Stanley ignored her. In the morning, as soon as he managed to drag himself out of bed, he clasped his precious saxophone in his arms and went off to never-ending rehearsals. He reappeared in the early evening and disappeared again to go to the Ramada, where he played nightly. At first she thought it her duty to join him and stay listening to him until the early hours of the morning. Every time she felt more and more out of place in this temple, where the only passion permitted was music. Amid the smell of smoke and liquor, the regulars would nod their heads, clap their hands to the beat, then suddenly, as if in a trance, utter shrieks and applaud frantically. Stanley did not seem to notice her presence. He was far away, blind and oblivious to everything except the sounds of his instrument. While playing, he looked like a suffering martyr. During the intermissions, he drank constantly, clasped the hands of his admirers, and grinned at them. In the end she preferred to wait for him in their furnished rooms on the rue des Fleurs, listening for his step on the stairs and anticipating the pleasure he would give her. In fact he was a capricious and irregular lover. Some nights he would hurl himself onto her, shower her with kisses, and make love to her ravenously. Other times he seemed to have no desire and spent the night talking, separated from her in bed by the immensity of his dreams. In the dark he described in detail their radiant future in America. For several months now he had been in touch with the Full Moon, a jazz club in Boston. It was an unusual place, devoted to the avant-garde. It was there that Cuban music had first been heard in the United States, long before Dizzy Gillespie contracted Chano Pozo to play in Harlem. It was here too the greatest reggae musicians, except for Bob Marley, had played before they had become famous outside their tiny island home. He insisted he could not have his music played just anywhere. It was unlike anybody else's. It was likely to grate on the ears of the unsophisticated, too naive to catch its subtlety. These conversations generally continued until morning, and Marie-Noëlle fell asleep rocked by this babbling stream. And then there would be nights when Stanley would bluntly turn his back on her in bed and sleep like a log, without a thought for her once his head hit the pillow. Yet, if you had questioned Marie-Noëlle, she would have assured you she was happy. The only problem was money. Stanley did not seem to understand that money could be used for other things besides smoking and getting drunk with the other musicians from his band. He did not trouble himself with any of the things that make life what it is: to eat three meals a day, wear decent clothes, take the bus, and so on. He did not understand that he was responsible for Marie-Noëlle, and she had no way of providing for herself, except now and then with Reynalda's money orders. Devoid of logic, he would buy her expensive presents: perfumes, silk scarves, and handbags. She never used the perfumes, finding them too strong and heady, or the scarves or the handbags, which were too luxurious. Yet he couldn't see she needed a coat and was shivering in the mistral.

Marie-Noëlle had never been deprived. Ranélise, poor unfortunate soul that she was, had brought her up like a princess. On Sundays she had been dressed in organza and patent leather shoes. At Christmas she had received sumptuous presents. As for Reynalda, she had rationed only her affection, and in the school recreation yard Marie-Noëlle often had the most expensive schoolbag. Since she never dared ask Stanley for anything, she went through his pockets. But all she found were the remains of some marijuana, some snuff, and pieces of paper scribbled with music notes. When, on several occasions, she felt herself faint with exhaustion and saw her wretched reflection in the mirror, she had no other solution but to look for work.

To her great surprise, she found some.

The boarding school of the Immaculée Conception looked very much like the sanatorium in Vence. It was similarly surrounded by a many-acred park filled with deer and rare trees. Its visiting room also smelled of wax polish, disinfectant, and that inimitable smell of communities living in isolation. The nuns who ran it did not object to the years Marie-Noëlle had just spent at the sanatorium. They merely took it as a pretext to halve her pay. Marie-Noëlle was put in charge of teaching French to the sixth grade. Her students, thirty or so young girls aged around ten, came mostly from well-to-do families in the area. The nuns were very proud of having the daughter of a wealthy perfume maker from Grasse in tenth grade, and the daughter of a restaurant owner cited in the Gault-Millau guide in eighth grade. But Marie-Noëlle very quickly noticed that, in spite of their elegant kilts and matching pullovers, the boarders all suffered from the illness she had been exposed to, an illness more widespread than tuberculosis—the absence of love. These poor children had been exiled to the boarding school to humor a stepfather or stepmother who could not put up with them, so as not to cast a shadow over the brothers and sisters of a second or third marriage, or not to encumber the life of parents busy earn-ing more and more money or treating themselves to the good life in far-off places. So she did not bother teaching them about the agreement of the past participle. All they needed was affection, for which there was little room in the discipline at the Immaculée Conception. Marie-Noëlle catered to their desires. Instead of teaching them La Fontaine's *Le Chêne et le Roseau* or Molière's Monsieur Jourdain's monologue, she read them stories that had moved her to tears at the same age or told them Creole tales, the very same ones Ranélise and Claire-Alta had delighted her with. She handed around pictures whenever they wanted and had them taste coconut cakes she had baked in the oven from one of Ludovic's recipes. She organized singing, drama, and even dancing contests to give the less gifted the opportunity to do well. It was no surprise when at the end of the term the mother superior piously gave her her notice. They had felt sorry for her, but she was not doing her job. The class average had dropped. The children cried a lot during her last class. With their pocket money they bought her an Hermès scarf that she added to those Stanley had already given her.

After that Marie-Noëlle was employed in a group medical prac-tice. She did not stay long because she was too slow on the telephone. Then she found a job in an Interflora shop that spe-cialized in tropical plants and flowers. This young Guadeloupean, who matched flamingo flowers with birds of paradise and gerberas, seemed to be a find. Unfortunately here again they could not keep her. She had no sense of color. And then she was so sulky. She never smiled.

Yet she was so pretty when she did smile!

Chapter 8

*S*ometimes, waiting for Stanley at night, Marie-Noëlle imagined her mother. She imagined her with affection and pity. She forgot where she was, the time and the moment. In Nice. In furnished rooms with no modern conveniences, lost in a bed with somewhat gray sheets. Her imagination carried her away completely. It was as if she left her body behind, shedding her skin like a *gajé*, and was back in a strange Guadeloupe, some twenty years earlier.

Reynalda had arrived in La Pointe when she was ten, a frail little girl who went unnoticed and immediately hated La Pointe and the life she led. No trees or greenery. Buildings pressed one against the other. A tangle of streets. The suffocating smell of dust.

Although the house on the rue de Nozières was huge and well situated, it dated back to the beginning of the century. As a result it had none of the modern comforts. It was Gian Carlo Coppini who, at little cost, had installed electricity and running water. In order to wash themselves the family crammed into a rudimentary bathroom containing a zinc bathtub, basins, and pitchers, wedged between two bedrooms on the second floor. As for Nina and Reynalda, they washed downstairs in the so-called washhouse, a shack made of corrugated iron, cluttered with buckets, brooms, and brushes, where a tap dripped over a sink. Each morning Reynalda would lather the *savon de Marseille* and slowly rub her entire body for ages in the hope of purifying herself of the night. Then she went up to dress, and since Nina was already bustling around Arcania, she went looking for Aunt Lia, who was in charge of combing the hair of all the children in the family. Aunt Lia and Aunt Zita occupied the same room and slept in single beds like two teenagers. While Aunt Zita kept her eyes closed, her head on the pillow, Aunt Lia, in her cotton nightgown trimmed with a lace collar, sat in a straight-back armchair and leaned over the girls sitting in turn between her legs. She combed the heavy, velvety locks of her nieces as gently as she combed Reynalda's picky hair. She ended each operation with the same kiss on the forehead, as light as the brush of a bird's wing. Reynalda, cheered by this ritual, went back down to the kitchen, quickly swallowed her cup of light brown chocolate, and went out, leaving the house behind her. At that hour Nina had scrubbed the sidewalks to shine like a new penny. José, the underpaid shop assistant, dressed in stained khaki shorts, was raising the steel curtain of Il Lago di Como. The seven o'clock mass had released its stream of sanctimonious churchgoers wending their way home, their mouths pursed, still in raptures over the host they had swallowed.

In her mind's eye Marie-Noëlle followed the little ill-dressed silhouette hurrying along the still silent and almost deserted streets as far as the Dubouchage school. Soon they would be crowded with a throng of schoolchildren, hunchbacked from their bags. They would echo with all those noises that scared her: the hooting of bicycle horns, the revving of car engines, and the cries of the street merchants touting the merits of their coconuts. Rather than cross the Place de la Victoire, where often ragamuffins hung out behind the sandbox trees, Reynalda made a detour by way of the Darse to breathe in the smell of the sea. The forest of schooner masts blocked the horizon, but the breeze that blew in from the open sea salted her lips. She stopped, hopped from one foot to the next, then once again hurried on to get to school. Some students already had their foreheads glued to the gate. It was like a ritual. At seven-thirty exactly the old janitor, grousing about his hernia, emerged, jangling his bunch of keys, as big as Saint Peter's.

"*Ban mwen lè souplè!*" he shouted.

The students moved aside, and he pushed the gates wide open. The children then surged in, uttering all sorts of animal cries. For a few moments the boys seemed to go crazy, running and elbowing each other, violently playing catch-as-catch-can or leapfrog, while the girls, less turbulent, whispered secrets to one another. Then the bell rang, silence fell, they lined up two by two, and filed into class.

The lepers that used to be exiled to Désirade got more attention than Reynalda. She would have turned out like one of the many losers at the Dubouchage school if she hadn't prepared for her education certificate in Madame Lépervier's class. Despite her hawkish name, Madame Lépervier was goodness itself. Until her untimely death, her mother had sold fish in the Saint-Antoine market. The eldest of eight children, she had raised them all. So there was no mistake, she had hit rock bottom during her child-hood. As an adult she was determined to help those in need. Her husband too was an elementary schoolteacher, who wore his heart on his sleeve and was a very active member of the Communist Party. The day term started, after a quick inspection of the class, Madame Lépervier noticed Reynalda. She immediately under-stood what lay in store for this frail, forlorn little girl and took her under her wing. It must be said too that she reminded her of a lit-tle sister who had been laid to rest in the cemetery at the age of fourteen. Three times a week, after school, she took her home with her. She made her eat her own children's yogurts and cottage

cheese, had her do her homework, and went over her math problems with her, marveling deep down at her intelligence. Even so
something bothered her: Reynalda refused to answer any questions
about herself or what went on in Gian Carlo Coppini's house. She
could not even get out of her one of those heart-rending stories
that a deprived child so easily blurts out to someone she trusts. She
herself had heard nothing good hawked around about Gian Carlo
Coppini. Although everyone was full of admiration for the enamelwork and cameos he fashioned, as for his character, that was a
different matter altogether. It was said he was unusually miserly.
And irascible and lecherous on top of that! He was quick to kick
people in the ass and put his hand up his servants'. For a while,
before the police got wind of it, he kept a black girl on the Morne
à Cayes. Well, "kept" might be somewhat exaggerated. All he gave
the poor wretch in his generosity was a series of blows. Every time
Madame Lépervier tried to broach the subject with her—"Are you
being well looked after at home? How are those white folks treating you? Especially the boss they say is like Satan himself?"—
Reynalda would close up. Her eyes begged to be left alone. Her lips
trembled. Then she picked up her things and went out of the door
stammering apologies. What was she trying to hide? Did the miser
beat her like they said he beat his wife, his sisters, and his daughters? Did he treat her like a servant?

When Reynalda left Madame Lépervier's house in the Faubourg
Alexandre-Isaac, La Pointe was beginning to dress up for the night
like a lady of easy virtue. Oil lamps glowed on the sidewalks and
codfish fritters perfumed the frying fat. The Place de la Victoire,
now deserted by the nursemaids and their charges, rustled with the
babble of schoolboys in love. First pledges of love. First kisses. First
embraces. First quarrels too, behind the trunks of the sandbox
trees, witness to other wars. In order to avoid these scenes
Reynalda began to run, taking time to cross herself even so as she

passed in front of the Cathedral of Saint-Pierre-and-Saint-Paul.
Bats nested in the trees and in holes in the stonework. On the
presbytery veranda, the priests walked up and down reading their
Bible. She shot looks of hatred at them. Wasn't it because of them
that she found herself where she was? Wasn't it Father Mondicelli
who had had the bright idea of securing Nina's services? This son
of Italian immigrants, who had not forgotten the race of his ancestors, visited Arcania every day the Good Lord made. Did he know
where the so-called kindness of his heart had gotten them? He
arrived at the rue de Nozières on the stroke of four, just after
Arcania's afternoon nap. Sometimes he stopped by the shop to
greet Aunt Lia and Aunt Zita but usually he went straight up to
the second floor. There he sat at Arcania's bedside and read her
the *Nouvelles de l'Episcopat* from cover to cover, a hand-printed rag
published in Basse-Terre by his friend the bishop. An hour later
Nina came in, and without a glance in his direction, for she could
not bear him, she set down the tray of chocolate and marble cake
on a low table. Then she tied an embroidered napkin around
Arcania's neck. What did Arcania and Father Mondicelli say to
each other once the door was closed? Did Arcania confide her misfortune? Did she complain of her heartless husband, her
hypocritical and depraved servant, and the bleakness of her entire
life in this country so far from her own? Or was she well above such
petty thinking, already musing on her afterlife? The visits always
ended by their reciting two sets of ten rosaries together.

Often, at the corner of the street, Father Mondicelli passed
Reynalda coming home with her schoolbag on her back. Each time
he blessed her with an air of compassion. How much did he know?

When Reynalda reached the house, José was lowering the steel
curtain on the jeweler's shop. He tried to chat with her, for he was
always ready to badmouth the boss and his family, but she dashed
into the stairway. Gian Carlo was not at home. Every day at the

same hour he would grab his cane and announce he was taking the air along the wharf. His absence lasted two and a half hours by the clock, then his step could be heard hammering the sidewalk. To tell the truth, nobody bothered about where he spent his time. It was the only, all-too-brief moment of happiness. The children crowded into Arcania's room. Aunt Lia and Aunt Zita sat down beside her on the bed and told her all the gossip and tittle-tattle in La Pointe, stories about people she did not even know, but that made her cheeks flush and her lips redden. They listened to a record, always the same one, of Mario Lanza singing *O Sole Mio*. Panting from having dashed up the stairs, Reynalda joined the group. She threw her bag into a corner and made room for herself against Arcania's shoulder. Arcania pushed her children aside, put her arm around her, and whispered in her angel's voice: "What did you do at school today?"

But Reynalda had no inclination to talk about school, math, French composition, or even Madame Lépervier, however kind-hearted she was. Closing her eyes, she pressed her cheek against this soft, silky skin that smelled so good. How she would have loved to be an infant again, a baby at her mother's breast gorging herself with milk and lying sated and immersed in the comforting silence. Arcania knew everything, she was sure of it. Through her unwavering gentleness she signified that she absolved her. Alas, the time was all too short. Nina, who had finished banging the dinner pots, pushed open the door and angrily chased everyone away.

"You'll tire her out!"

Without a word of protest Aunt Lia and Aunt Zita went up to their room. The children glumly set about doing their homework. Shortly afterward Gian Carlo's steps could be heard pounding the sidewalk. In the dining room Nina dished out lentil soup.

The night was already jet black.

𝕯

Amid this desolation Reynalda had made a friend: Fiorella, the eldest daughter of Gian Carlo and Arcania, born one year after her.

At first sight Reynalda and Fiorella had nothing in common. People agreed admiringly that Fiorella was the prettiest creature alive. When Aunt Lia and Aunt Zita used to push her baby carriage around the Place de la Victoire, passersby would stop and comment on the infant's perfect features. A few years later, when she was three, Gian Carlo forbade her to come down to the shop since the customers would admire her so much they forgot to place their orders. At ten her hair, let loose, wrapped her in a rich mantle of black velvet. Her eyes were like two panes of washed sky between a break in the clouds. Her skin was diaphanous, delicately flushed around her cheekbones. Her mouth was like a hibiscus bud. As a result the nuns at the Saint-Joseph-de-Cluny boarding school she attended designated her year after year for the great ceremony celebrating August 15. Dressed in a white alb, with two wings of the same color fixed to her back, she piously climbed the steps leading to the cathedral's high altar; then, as the choir sang, she placed a crown on the statue of the Virgin Mary. For the same reasons, the lovesick haunted Il Lago di Como and tried to hand love letters to Nina. Aunt Lia and Aunt Zita worshiped Fiorella because as the years went by she resembled their deceased maman more and more, and they could never set eyes on her without wanting to hug her and shower her with kisses. Arcania tried in vain to hide her preference for her from the other children. Even Gian Carlo, so indifferent, sometimes brutal with his daughters, occasionally brought her back from his walks some small white potato *topi tamboos*, a cornet of powdered corn *kilibibi* or grilled peanuts, and forced a smile at her.

In spite of that Fiorella was melancholic and taciturn, and her eyes brimmed with tears for next to nothing. It was because she had seen her three little sisters, her beloved playmates, carried off in quick succession to the graveyard. She knew that the death of Ira, the firstborn, seven months prior to her own birth, had inflicted an inconsolable wound on her maman's heart. So it seemed she had grown up amid grieving like the grass between tombstones. Add to that Arcania's illness, the submissiveness of her aunts, the vices of her father, and the *laisser-aller* around the house, and it was easy to understand that her mood matched Reynalda's. The two girls had grown fond of each other from the very first day when Reynalda had finally emerged from Nina's printed calico skirt and shown everyone her tearful, swollen face. Fiorella had dried Reynalda's tears with her cambric handkerchief, then taken her into the room she shared with Donatella and Beatrice. From then on they had told each other everything. Fiorella was the only person Reynalda told about the nightmare she lived night after night. Their fury was aggravated by their feeling of powerlessness. They could do nothing against Gian Carlo. They could only imagine. Frantically they dreamed of a thousand ways to do away with him. And how about stringing him up by the feet over a tub and slitting his throat, like the pig he was? They would skin him. They would hack him into two chunks with a cutlass. They would slice him to pieces. And how about slowly roasting him? His flesh would sizzle and crackle and ooze a foul-smelling juice. How about cutting off his head, then stamping it into a ditch of nettles? Fiorella, who was good at drawing, embellished these imaginings in charcoal sketches that she kept in a folder melodramatically labeled "Hell." The two girls also put their heads together to write tales marked by the same vengeful and bloody nature. In this Reynalda excelled. So Fiorella proposed having the texts published by Lardenoy, publishers of *La Guadeloupe illustrée* and the works of winners of the local poetry contest. To this Reynalda protested loudly.

She did not want her immense shame to be flaunted for everyone to see.

※

Marie-Noëlle emerged from her daydreams only when Stanley returned. For a second she wondered what man was this who had power over her body. She was about to push him aside when her memory returned and she made room for him beside her.

Chapter 9

To Marie-Noëlle's great surprise, Stanley's plans, which she had always thought unworkable, worked. They had not been living together a year when the Full Moon sent a formal contract to his band, the MNA. This engagement was the start of great upheavals. First of all Gus, the pianist, and Freddy, the trombonist, had no intention of living in exile in Boston and left for Tangiers, where at least the sun shines for a good part of the year. It wasn't a great loss, and Stanley quickly found Amandio and Nando to replace them, twins of Caribbean parents from the Cape Verde Islands, who were so much alike you could only tell them apart when they began to play their instruments. Then, one morning, he took a swig of alcohol as he usually did, lit his joint, and asked her to marry him. It should be said that the proposal had nothing romantic to it. He had enquired about immigration into the United States, and marriage seemed to him the best way to avoid hassles with the authorities. Even so Marie-Noëlle was bowled over. Living with Stanley, she had the feeling they communicated in languages as different as Greek and Japanese and were following diverging paths in life. She was dragging herself from one wretched job to another, refusing to make any plans for the future. One week she worked as a checkout clerk for a supermarket; the next she was a lunchtime monitor for squabbling high school kids; and then she was clocking in at a shoe factory, only too happy to be able to pay for her meals. She read nothing except for the newspaper headlines and went to the movies as much as she went to church. When she looked at herself in the mirror, she shuddered. Was this wizened face hers, she who was not yet twenty? Two vertical furrows outlined her mouth. Her eyelids drooped over lackluster eyes of an indefinable color. Where had her youth gone? Though her young years lay ahead of her, they were already far behind her. Every one of her features bore the mark of wear and neglect. Stanley, on the other hand, glowed with the expectation of tomorrow, a radiant tomorrow that would bring fame and fortune. Oblivious to everything around him, to the filth and wretchedness of their furnished rooms, to the landlord's angry expression when the rent was late, to the faces of the tenants in the other buildings, crusty old folks who had turned their backs on bohemia, he only found room in his head for his dreams.

He was very proud of his first record; he would explain the title *Melba* to whoever was willing to listen with the wealth of detail reserved for describing the subject of dreams. Melba, he said, was the name of the first woman who had made love to him. He was fourteen or fifteen at the time. His school had taken him to Amsterdam. While his classmates were wasting their time in the Rijksmuseum, he had wandered around the red-light district. In a window, larger than life, a jet-black prostitute under a blond wig, dressed in red satin pajamas, with a cabalistic sign tattooed on her left breast, had motioned to him to enter. She had received him between her thighs and made no mockery of his virginity. Fearful of her pimp, an Indonesian tough guy whose pockets were stuffed with knives, she had kept him from venturing outside. When she received her customers she hid him under the bed or in the wardrobe, and he lost count of the number of nights he had lived drunk with love in this poky little room smelling of paradise. Finally the police on the alert had found him and sent him back to London. Despite its magical name, *Melba* had gone unnoticed on its release, except for one or two lines in a music monthly. Even so Stanley did not lose hope. He was positive that things would be different for his second record.

Marie-Noëlle confessed she did not have much of an ear for a music that, according to the experts, was unlike any other. She had sent *Melba* to Ludovic, but his only reply was a lukewarm comment that shed no light on the matter.

Marie-Noëlle was in agony then and blamed herself for having misjudged Stanley. The man she thought was farther and farther removed from her, indifferent and self-centered, was actually concerned about her. He was in fact the only person on earth to feel that way. He wanted to protect her. These feelings so moved her that she tearfully accepted his proposal. Stanley spent the night dreaming up plans. Okay, the engagement at the Full Moon was only for a few months. But he was certain it would be extended. If not he would find a gig in another club. And the famous Newport Jazz Festival was not far from Boston. And then New York, with its Blue Note and all the Village jazz clubs, was just a few hours away. Marie-Noëlle tried not to interrupt him and ask the questions that wanted to flow out, sounding like calls for help: "And what about me? Am I just swapping the desert of Nice for the desert of Boston?" Stanley ended up dropping asleep right in the middle of a sentence. To Marie-Noëlle's great regret he hardly ever made love to her any longer.

The wedding ceremony took place hurriedly two or three weeks later, the time it took to publish the banns. Marie-Noëlle remembered an icy wind was gusting, but the sky was a sharp blue, a metallic blue over the sea that also had been washed for the occasion. Her euphoria of the previous days had quickly been replaced by the familiar anxiety. Yet all the faces around her dutifully put on cheerful expressions for the joyous occasion. Laakdar the Harki, who had made them feel at home so many times in the past, went out of his way to play the older brother. He paid for a sheep to be barbecued and hung multicolored garlands on the walls of the Nuits de Tlemcen. Standing in the middle of the table, at which a dozen places had been set, the birds of paradise, lilies, and torch ginger that Ranélise and Claire-Alta had sent spoke of exotic shores. Nando, who was also a master on the guitar, strummed away, while Amando sung *mornas*. The nostalgia of these tunes reminded Marie-Noëlle of those rare interludes of serenity during her childhood, when Ludovic had allowed her to place the records she liked on the player. Was it surprising she had become what she was? The love she had felt for Reynalda and that she had buried deep inside her, since it served no purpose, had left a dry, stony spot where her heart had been. It was Reynalda's fault that she had lost interest in everything and everyone, that she drifted aimlessly through life. She had hoped Stanley would cure her, but he was a poor physician, and, in any case, her sickness was incurable.

Squeezed between Leïla and Araxie, out on special permission, she wondered why happiness was an island she would never reach. The following morning she was to take the train to Paris, from where the band would fly to Boston. She would take this opportunity to say her farewells to what served as her family. Stanley had decided not to accompany her, as he detested anything by the name of family, having left far behind him Papa, Mama, brothers, and sisters.

𝔇

Four years since she had set eyes on them. Reynalda, Ludovic, and

Garvey, Garvey who must have been close to ten or eleven. In actual fact it was Reynalda who occupied her thoughts. What did she look like now? Worn out and wizened as well? She would probably avoid looking her in the eyes. She would be reluctant to speak to her. And she herself would be pathologically embarrassed in her presence. Marie-Noëlle also thought about Ludovic, already anticipating the disappointment his attitude would cause her but not daring to admit to herself what she expected of him.

At the end of the afternoon, everyone squeezed into a car rented for the occasion to drive Leïla and Araxie back to the front gate of the sanatorium. Behind the iron gate, the trees in the park still stood as straight and rigid. Stretched out on the terraces the bedridden patients breathed in lungfuls of air in the hope of purifying themselves. Leïla and Araxie scolded Marie-Noëlle for never coming to visit them. She realized now that she had not wanted to spoil the only memories of happiness she had in her life: When the future boiled down to a temperature chart. If, at the time of parting, Marie-Noëlle cried her heart out, it was not for the same reasons as her friends. Leïla and Araxie wept at the thought that their friendship was over and that they would probably never see one another again. Marie-Noëlle wept for herself and the future she believed lay ahead.

𝕯

In order to put off the moment of confronting Reynalda, Marie-Noëlle began by dragging her feet around Paris. To be honest she hardly knew the city. She had visited it with Natasha and Awa during that unforgettable summer, sometimes in the company of Ludovic, who for years always bought his records from the same shop in the Latin Quarter. She and Stanley had checked in to a cheap hotel on the Left Bank. They were staying in a dismal,

corridorlike room with no modern comforts, whose window, however, looked out onto Notre-Dame and the banks of the Seine.
Despite a gloomy sky and a biting wind, the tourists were joyfully
piling into the *bateaux-mouches* that plied the river like floating
aquariums. For some life was like that: a ride on the river in a
dream city.

When she went out, everyone seemed to her well dressed and
well groomed. The women looked elegant, at ease with themselves. Couples were window-shopping; buying books, newspapers,
and candy; strolling arm in arm, and stopping to kiss each other.
And all this time the man she had gotten herself as a husband was
asleep, wrapped in thin cotton sheets. He would sleep like that for
hours and hours, deaf and oblivious to the calls of daylight. He
would finally open his eyes, fill his stomach with two or three
glasses of liquor, then, forgetting about his wife, he would disap-
pear until morning with the other musicians. She went into a café
merely to feel the warmth of other humans, ordered a croissant and
a tea with milk, lit a cigarette, and opened up a newspaper, simply
to be like one of them. A man soon moved over to her table. But
he was drab, already bald, wrapped in a raincoat. Birds of a feather flock together: She only attracted the down and out. Shortly
before noon she made up her mind to catch the bus, a green cater-
pillar that crawled through the streets. The students were
streaming out of the Sorbonne and heading for the cafés and the
student restaurants. At Vence the teachers all agreed she was highly gifted. She too, like these young students, could have completed
a degree in classics, modern literature, or history. She could have
written articles. Published a book. Become a writer. Why not?

It had been two years since Reynalda had stopped working as
a welfare assistant in Savigny-sur-Orge. She now worked for
some organization or other in Paris. These blurred details that
she got from Ludovic came into focus when she found herself

standing in front of a brand-new apartment house in the XIIIth Arrondissement. Entry phone. Hallway decorated with modern sculptures. A fast, silent elevator. Only then did she realize with amazement her mother's social ascent. While she was sinking to the lowest depths of society, the woman who had given birth to her was soaring toward the sun. It was Garvey who opened the door on the tenth floor. A very different Garvey. Somewhat stocky. Almost as tall as she was, which wasn't very tall. At first glance nothing distinguished him from the other little bullies of his age, except for his uncombed mop of hair, which fell in irregular, ragged bangs over his forehead. His light brown eyes showed more curiosity than friendliness. Only after visibly hesitating did he offer a cheek. Fortunately Ludovic was there. Besides letting his hair grow, he was growing a beard and a mustache, and in the middle of all this untidiness he was smiling radiantly. He hugged Marie-Noëlle, and with her head on his shoulder she felt so much emotion she almost burst into tears. While she was trying to gain control of herself, he scolded her affectionately. All these years with scarcely a word from her. And Stanley, where was he? He would very much have liked to look him straight in the eyes and have a few words with this musician who was taking her so far away! Boston, the capital of winter and prejudice, she would soon see for herself! She dried her tears and defended herself as best she could. Despite her semblance of gaiety, she knew her happiness at meeting him again was threatened. Reynalda would emerge, and this happy atmosphere would end. Around them the living room was poorly furnished. Four places were set at a trestle table, for despite their social rise Ludovic and Reynalda seemed no more interested in refinement and comfort than they had been in the past. The furnishings were hardly different from Savigny-sur-Orge. Old pieces mixed in with new ones, and she recognized them like familiar faces in a strange crowd.

Reynalda finally appeared, and Marie-Noëlle came face to face with the bulge of her misshapen belly. Reynalda was pregnant. At least eight months by the look of the bomb shape she was pushing in front of her. Feeling really nauseated, Marie-Noëlle recalled that one of Ludovic's letters had mentioned a surprise. Was this it? Obscene surprise! Painful surprise! This pregnancy that could be considered the climax of sexual fulfillment was the final blow below the belt. She was already excluded from the family territory. This coming infant would occupy the place that never would be hers. Worse still, she took stock of the paucity of her affections. She was the one who should be flaunting a belly, looking for christening names, and thumbing her nose at Reynalda with the stamina and fertility of her youth! Instead she was standing there, old before her time, badly dressed, teetering on worn-out heels. Reynalda lightly touched her cheek as she had in the past, nothing more, nothing less, as if they had parted the day before and not four long years ago. Then she sat down opposite her. Except for her rounded belly, she was thinner and visibly very tired. Her veins coiled and twisted down her neck and over her hands. She now wore her hair in an Afro, the new fashion, which revealed her forehead and the rest of her features, and made her look almost childlike. Once again Marie-Noëlle could not make up her mind whether she was pretty or ugly. In the meantime Ludovic was talking for both of them. He did not like Paris, and he missed his juvenile delinquents.

Furthermore Muntu had died a natural death. The young guys in the West Indian association that employed him were interested only in girls and showing off. Nothing serious was planned. The mere words "Revolution" or "Marxism" made them yawn. Africa, Cuba, Fidel Castro, and Sekou Touré interested them far less than Stevie Wonder or Marvin Gaye. They worshiped the music of Fela

Ransome Kuti but did not bother to translate the words of his songs. Ludovic encouraged Garvey and Reynalda to speak up and engage in the conversation as if he were dealing with two unsociable children. Garvey was too absorbed in a television program to bother about anyone else. Reynalda uttered monosyllables or brief phrases from time to time, as if what was being said was of little interest. She too missed Savigny-sur-Orge. Her work had not really changed, in fact. She still worked with women from the so-called underprivileged class. The only difference was that she conducted surveys and wrote reports for the Ministry of Population. What was the point of these surveys and reports? Nothing. Except to provide the underwriters of such research with a clear conscience. Toward the middle of the afternoon Garvey, once again glued to the television set, announced he was going out with his friends and left without saying good-bye to anyone. Shortly afterward Ludovic too excused himself. It was obvious that he wanted to give mother and daughter the chance for a tête-à-tête, something Marie-Noëlle had been dreading since she had gotten up.

For a few moments the silence was unbearably heavy. The sun that flooded the living room finally found its strength and warmed the room before disappearing again. Through the bay windows the gray slate and pink tiles of the rooftops of Paris could be seen. Reynalda lay sunk in the cushions on the sofa, with her head slumped back as if she had fallen asleep. Marie-Noëlle thought she could get up and steal out the front door, when suddenly, without opening her eyes or moving, Reynalda said:

"I never wanted this child. It was Ludovic. I'm not made to be a mother, as you know all too well. And that's why you're not happy. Garvey's not happy either. You think I don't worry about you? You're wrong, but I can't give you what I never received myself. One day, you remember, I started telling you my story. I didn't have the strength to go to the end because the words tore at my throat. I'll try to go on, sparing you the details. Otherwise you'll think I'm exaggerating. That's all I can give you. The truth. In the hope you'll understand and that way you'll start to live your life."

Chapter 10

udovic was right: Boston is the capital of winter. When Stanley and Marie-Noëlle arrived in mid-January, the snow that had been falling for weeks was piled up on the squares and along the streets in cliffs as black as soot. The branches of the trees sparkled in their sheaths of frost, and on the frozen river skaters drew arabesques. At every hour of the day and night the wind tore along open-mouthed, blowing a frigid blast and swallowing everything in its path. The headlines in the papers or on television were full of schools closed, trains derailed, and flights canceled. The Full Moon was no bigger than a handkerchief but had a tremendous reputation. On weekends the line went three times round the block. It was owned by Luis and Leo, a couple of homosexuals, one of whom was in a wheelchair, though there was little reason to pity him since he was the one who mercilessly managed the finances. By clever deductions he managed to pay Stanley and his musicians less than half of what they expected. So much so that Jerry, the double-bass player, a skinny guy who merged into the shadow of his instrument and voiced himself only through his playing, decided to go back to Europe. It wasn't too serious a setback, and Stanley replaced him within a week. For Boston is not only the capital of winter, it is also the capital of music. More musicians come out of its countless schools than loaves of bread from its bakers' ovens. Terri, whom Stanley unearthed in a club in Cambridge, was born in Léogane. But he had left Haiti as a baby clinging to the breast of his tearful mother, and could speak neither French nor Creole. His only language was American and the nasal accent of Brooklyn, where his mother and his three aunts had brought him up. Unlike Stanley, who without ever getting drunk never stopped imbibing all kinds of liquor, he neither drank nor smoked. He seemed to have a great appetite for women and immediately started flirting with Marie-Noëlle. She couldn't believe her eyes. It had been such a long time since a man had desired her. Her last sexual contact with Stanley dated back to their stay in Paris. Coming home one morning, he had found her crouched on the bed in tears, shattered at having relived Reynalda's tale of agony, and he saw it was the only way to console her.

Since Stanley had no practical sense, Amandio, the trombonist, decreed himself the band's banker. He began by renting a fairly comfortable apartment just next to the club. So that neither snow nor hail nor ice nor freezing rain would prevent the musicians from going to work. Unfortunately once the rent was paid there was no money left over for food, even less for heat. The cold was so penetrating through the brick walls that the instruments went out of tune all on their own, and they had to wrap themselves in old newspapers under their clothes to try to keep warm. Amandio therefore leased a house in Camden Town. It was enormous, with first and second floors, an attic and a basement, all in all about fifteen rooms. There was enough space to house them all as well as room for rehearsals. But Camden Town was far out in the suburbs and had a bad reputation, so bad that the police patrolled in pairs and certainly not after 9 P.M. At first, when Marie-Noëlle remained alone in the house, after the musicians had left for the Full Moon and the streetlamps lit up the surrounding desert of snow, she would bolt herself in and lock herself up. She would jump at the slightest noise and thought of hiding a sharp knife or a loaded gun under her pillow. She imagined beasts of prey breaking in, despite the locked doors and windows, and devouring her alive. In this nightmare she invariably ended up thinking of Reynalda, her maman, who also had waited in fear, watching in the night and imagining violence and murder. She wept while waves of tenderness surged up to her heart. She got up, ran to her table, and wrote letters she never sent. She knew that even if Reynalda received them they would remain unanswered. Nothing would ever change between them. Love is something you learn at birth, and the ways of the heart never alter.

Gradually, however, she noticed that in Camden Town violence was not blind. It struck certain individuals, those who drove Lincoln Continentals with black-tinted windows and conducted their traffic in bars off limits to the uninitiated. These were the ones who turned up stiff as corpses at the intersections of deserted streets or on plots of waste land. In fact Camden Town was very much like Savigny-sur-Orge. It grew on you. It was inhabited by African Americans, Africans, immigrants from every island of the Caribbean or country of Latin America, hardworking, law-abiding people, whose extreme poverty, however, made them suspect. In the shops Spanish or Haitian Creole could often be heard. In the middle of winter the shop windows overflowed with avocados, plantains, peppers, and papayas, while at mealtimes all the cheap restaurants had pork with rice and beans on the menu.

D

Marie-Noëlle cannot remember exactly when she and Terri began to make love. Very early on, probably, because she had desired his desire from the very first day. They were quite open about it. When Terri came back from the Full Moon, he joined her in the room she was supposed to share with Stanley, who in fact never set foot there, preferring to go down to the basement, play softly on his saxophone, and fall asleep in a corner fully dressed. In certain ways Terri reminded her of Ludovic. His open face contrasted with Stanley's, which was increasingly masked and foreign. His body was tall and featureless, like that of an adolescent who had shot up too quickly after an illness. All his strength was concentrated in one place, and when he made love he lost the polite manners of a boy tenderly raised by a quartet of women. Night after night Marie-Noëlle hoped tremblingly for a metamorphosis. He would knock politely on her door, undress, gaily recounting the events of the evening—the packed room, Stanley's incredible improvisation, the standing ovation he got—and then, without further ado, he threw himself on her as if he were one of those voracious creatures she had dreaded. Before losing herself in sleep, she thought again of Reynalda, but now it seemed that her pleasure had betrayed her. Even so this adultery, which was having no tragic effects, tormented her. What did Stanley feel? On the surface nothing had altered. He had not changed his attitude toward Terri. He still seemed to prefer him over Nando and Amandio or Pacheco, the drummer. He listened to him, took into consideration what he said, and spent hours improvising with him. He had not changed toward her either. Sometimes he even noticed she was present, inquired whether she was not too cold, if she was going out, and on her twentieth birthday had twenty roses delivered. When he was not playing at the Full Moon, rehearsing in the basement with the other musicians, playing cards or eating with them, the only moments when he was accessible were when he snorted like a water buffalo in the bathroom. She went in and gazed at him, as muscular as a boxer in his threadbare bathrobe or else completely naked, with no visible desire for her, cutting his nails or trimming the hair in his nostrils. He launched into his plans for the future, without letting her get in a single word. Thanks to some enthusiastic reviews that had made it down to the Caribbean, the MNA band had been invited to the jazz festival in Santo Domingo. It would be the first time he had set foot in the Caribbean, and he had every intention of visiting Sangre Grande, where his family came from. When he was a little boy, his maman, who had Indian blood, had told him of the Shango cult. He was intrigued to know what kind of music they played in the temples. He would go to Cuba too, and discover the Afro-Cuban music that his papa had danced to in his youth. Since he had been in Boston he had nurtured the idea of composing his "Symphony of the New World." He dreamed of a musical rendering of the contribution of immigrants who alone could breathe new life into America's stale and sluggish blood. Without the defiance of the Latinos, the Chicanos, the Haitian and Cuban *balseros*, risking their lives at the borders and on makeshift rafts, the United States would die from gulping down the vicious broth of fear and hatred. Marie-Noëlle listened to him in admiration. Ashamed at her lack of grandiose ideas, she was left with her trivial thoughts, turning them over and over again in her head.

As in Nice, hunting for a job forced her to face the outside. With her feet frozen in her flimsy shoes she splashed through the snow and the mud, slipping on the ice, stumbling to La Rosita, the Puerto Rican restaurant where she worked as a waitress. The people there had had no trouble adopting her since she'd learned to speak a little Spanish and gently rap the roving hands of the men. Yet, deep down, she felt guilty. Had Reynalda struggled valiantly for her child to lead this sort of life in her footsteps? It seemed she was following the road her mother had refused to follow. That she was becoming like Nina, her grandmother, who could never do anything else but spread her legs, be taken by men, and pocket pitiful wages. What had become of Nina? In her hatred and bitterness, Reynalda had never bothered to find out. Yet she must still be alive, as she could not be more than sixty. Did she still hire herself out to Gian Carlo Coppini's family? Had she returned to La Désirade in her old age? Marie-Noëlle imagined her sitting in front of her door, her white hair braided in rosettes, her body racked with pain, wrapped in a loose-fitting, faded cotton dress, waiting for a sign, waiting for forgiveness. There were moments when she got the urge to entrust Ranélise with the job of finding her. Then she told herself that too would be pointless. In time she would make the journey herself back to Guadeloupe.

One day in a bus shelter she noticed an advertisement. A single mother was looking for a young woman to look after her five-year-old daughter and teach her French. The wages were generous.

$\mathcal{D}$

Anthea Jackson lived in a somewhat more respectable neighborhood of Camden Town, in a house that thirty years earlier had appeared on postcards. Nella and Earl, her grandparents from Alabama, had built it with their own hands. They had made their fortune as undertakers. Their company was the first in the region to be owned by black folk. They were skillful at giving the deceased the skin color he or she would have liked to have had in life. They dutifully chose the gospels that a choir in mauve alb and white surplice performed with gusto. For category one services they added the Requiem by Berlioz. Nella and Earl had raised their only son, Cornell, as if he were of royal blood. They had steered him into law, making him the first black lawyer to open a practice in Boston. Cornell was happy with his life, his clientele, his Cadillac,

and his light-skinned wife. Nevertheless he harbored one regret.
He could not forget how the forbidding walls of Harvard had eluded him. He did not rest until Anthea, his daughter, had been
admitted, after getting her B.A. at Yale. Anthea did not like being
reminded that she had begun her university career by writing her
Ph.D. dissertation on the novels of Jane Austen. It was a mistake
of her early years, which she made up for by becoming the leading
specialist in female slave narratives from the early ninteenth century. She had also written prolifically on Nella Larsen and Zora
Neale Hurston and had the reputation of being one of the most
caustic feminist pens on the East Coast. Her marriage to a former
Harvard lawyer had not lasted, and she had decided to come back
and live in Camden Town. A political statement at a time when
the African-American middle class was deserting the black neighborhoods, the same way their parents had fled the cotton fields in
the South in the 1920s. While teaching for a year at the
University of Kumasi in Ghana, Anthea had adopted a little girl
by the name of Molara. Obviously it was gossiped around that
Molara was well and truly her daughter, and she had simply gotten
herself a belly in Africa. But all things considered it was highly
unlikely. Molara was as black as Anthea was light skinned and
short as she was tall, with the distinctive features of an Ashanti
mask. Biological or adopted child, it did not really matter. Molara
had just spent a sabbatical leave in France with her maman and
spoke French like a little Parisian.

Anthea's appearance was extraordinary. She wore her hair in a
crewcut like a man. She wore necklaces as wide as pectorals, pendants so heavy that they stretched her earlobes, and under her coat
clothes of unusual design cut from her own patterns in African fabrics. It was said that she terrified her students, and throughout her
classes not one of them dared contradict her. Yet, if you were not
turned off by appearances, you realized that beneath the surface

beat the heart of a vulnerable, indeed fragile person. It wasn't long before she told you of the sadness of her life. Her childhood dominated by an arrogant father. Her marriage to an unfeeling bully. Her countless affairs with men whose sole preoccupation was to destroy her. Now, like a Hindu arrived at the end of her cycle of reincarnations, she no longer desired anything on this earth. She had two objectives for the remainder of her life: to raise her daughter, her little Molara, and, through her work, rehabilitate her race. In a certain way, these two objectives were the same. She had saved Molara from the indifference of a father and a mother who were vegetating in the poverty of an African shantytown. She would dress her in so much grace and virtue that everyone would bow down in front of her to worship her black perfection. This surprising blend of strength and weakness reminded Marie-Noëlle of Reynalda and was perhaps the reason for her affection for Anthea. She confided in her, which was unusual for her. Answering Anthea's questions, she gradually pieced together the blurred parts of the puzzle that made up her life. She thought she could guess the circumstances of her own birth. Like every child on this earth she had a papa. She could name him. Had he cared about her? And Nina? What had Nina felt? Fear? Remorse?

She thought she could guess what had happened.

The evening Reynalda disappeared, Fiorella ran looking for her through every street of La Pointe. She even ventured into the neighborhoods where the people of no reputation lived. The drunkards came out in front of the rumshops to watch her dash by at the speed of a kite over the sidewalks. Astonished, they commented on her speed. Without exaggeration, she ran faster than a fisherman's boat speeding over the sea on the August 15 holiday.

When she got back, stammering in tears, Aunt Zita and Aunt Lia, who had been waiting for her, spoke of calling the police. Then fear held them back. Who knows what bundles of dirty linen they would find in the cupboards of this house? In fact they only made up their minds to alert the police much later. The police quickly dismissed them but kept Nina for questioning and took down her statement. Going by her hardly affable expression it would have surprised nobody if her daughter had run away with no hope of return. When day after day went by, proof that Reynalda would not come back, Arcania fell into an even deeper languor. Did she have the secret conviction that Gian Carlo had had a hand in this drama? She confessed her distress to Father Mondicelli. But he shrugged his shoulders: She wasn't going to fret about a little slut who was learning the trade of loose virtue. He had always been convinced from her poker face that Reynalda was not at home in a Christian household. At present she was probably getting her pleasure with a nigger as depraved as she was.

Arcania's health continued to deteriorate. Soon she no longer left her bed. She could not keep down her food. A burning fever raged through her body and despite Dr. Malenfant's treatment, Nina's attentions, the prayers of her sisters-in-law, and the tears of her daughters, she passed away one morning in September. Soft and melancholic, the rainy season had begun. Before putting their noses out of doors, the old folk made sure there was a break in the clouds. The night of Arcania's wake, as well as the day of her funeral and all the following week, the rain never stopped filling the storm channels. The flowers, engorged with water, shot up like trees while the fruit did not wait to ripen and fell with a soft thud. It was surely the sign that nature was lamenting the departure of a tortured soul. From the moment she got back from the cemetery, Fiorella refused to speak to her father. Through the intermediary of Father Mondicelli she made it known she wanted to be admitted to the Sisters of Compassion boarding school in Basse-Terre. One Saturday she climbed into a rented car and, in spite of her deep mourning, her beauty glowed like the sun. She was never again to set foot in the rue de Nozières. Three months after Arcania's death Gian Carlo married the seventeen-year-old daughter of another Italian jeweler with whom he did business. But the girl died giving birth to the son she was carrying. Everyone saw in this epilogue the long arm of God.

⚷

Anthea Jackson did not treat Marie-Noëlle like a servant or even like an au pair. Rather like Molara's older sister, whose virtues she intended to foster as well. On her own initiative she enrolled Marie-Noëlle in the university's general studies program, which unlocked the door to a degree. When she invited her friends over, all African-American women like herself—university professors, literary critics, artists, and sometimes writers—she had her sit at the table with them. These intellectuals were cheerful and lively. Not the least bit arrogant or uptight. They knew how to launch into bursts of laughter, as surprising as improvisations on a trumpet. Yet when coffee was served—reverently taken without sugar—their mood darkened, and the conversation unfailingly turned to racism. Each of them had her own sad story to tell about the refusal of the whites, the Caucasians, to recognize the value of those with a different skin color. They warned Marie-Noëlle about their cruelty and deceitfulness, predicting for her all the obstacles they would place in her path to prevent her advancement. Marie-Noëlle was not moved. First of all she doubted she had any enviable career in store. And then where was this world of white folk, Caucasians, they warned her about? Quite unreal. As unreal as the world of werewolves. She was used to a very different world. A world of blacks, half-castes, mixed-bloods, the exiled, the displaced, and the uprooted. Most of those she knew could hardly speak English, did not read newspapers, and only watched TV programs in their own language. They had been born elsewhere and, through the grace of God, hoped to return there, since there was no love lost between them and the place where they were forced to live—these United States of America, whose dollars, the color of hope, they did not see much of but intended to hoard as many as possible of before going back home, richly laden with material goods.

The only cause for disagreement between Anthea and Marie-Noëlle, though slight, was that the latter refused to accept any gifts of clothing.

Chapter 11

hen Marie-Noëlle thinks about it, after the festival in Santo Domingo the roles she and Stanley played began to change. As if right in the middle of an act, or even a scene, a director decided on a whim to stage his play and direct his actors in a totally different way. For lack of money she did not accompany them to Santo Domingo, and had no desire to. She needed calm and solitude to think. She felt so melancholy deep down! It wasn't the chaos and discomfort of the house she lived in. She had scarcely known anything else, except for the blissful time at the sanatorium. It wasn't the ugliness of Camden Town either, the dismal façades of buildings destined for demolition but never demolished, the mean little houses behind their front yards that the snow covered in mud or hardened with ice, the launderettes, the Pizza Huts, the Wendys, the Vacancy/No Vacancy motels, Essos, Shells, Amocos, and the homeless housing themselves on the sidewalks in old cardboard boxes. She had gotten used to all that. No! It was a devastation and monotony that came from within. Even her adultery had become routine since it was tolerated by everyone, and Terri's sexual cravings almost made her regret Stanley's abstinence. Stanley at least had other desires in his head than the craving for a woman's body. Her occupations were meaningless. The only pleasant moments were those spent at Anthea's, partaking of a life so different from her own. Apparently Anthea was solely preoccupied with matters of the mind. When she was not teaching at the university she was busy working at home. She was regularly up before dawn. By the time Marie-Noëlle arrived for Molara's breakfast she was already in her study. She would lock herself away for the morning and a good deal of the afternoon, eye to eye with her computer, clicking away on her keyboard. On no condition was Marie-Noëlle or Molara to disturb her. While she distracted the child with a thousand things, Marie-Noëlle was reminded of the time when Ludovic asked Garvey not to make a noise as "Maman was writing her thesis." The mystery of her labors and her stubborn determination were puzzling. She walked over to the study and spied on Anthea through the half-open door, ashamed at wanting to imitate her, fascinated by the golden characters of her thoughts that scurried over the screen like lines of marching ants. When she joined them at the end of the afternoon, Anthea still did not stop her intellectual activities. She would strike a red pen through her students' homework. Sometimes she listened to music, always the same records. Marie-Noëlle had been tempted several times to ask her what she thought of the MNA's music. Then she stopped herself. Could someone who loved Johann-Sebastian Bach's *Vergnügen und Lust* appreciate the harmonies of Stanley Watts?

One afternoon, although she was not expecting them home for another week, the musicians returned from Santo Domingo with gloomy expressions, dragging their feet. Even so she could get very little out of them. She had to wait until nightfall for Terri to tell her what had happened. He had still not gotten over it.

For him and the rest of the band it had been their first visit to an island in the Caribbean. His immigrant parents had filled his head since childhood with the same old stories of dictators, repression, poverty, and inevitable exile. But when they arrived everyone had given them a wonderfully warm welcome. After the gloom of Boston, the sky, decked out in blue, was smiling down at them. They had been housed in a five-star hotel nestled between the sparkling promenade of the Malecon and a garden laid out with a mass of flowers and plants. On one side the enchantment of the sea that washed against a line of rugged isles. On the other a tangle of bauhinias, frangipanis, orchids, and bougainvillea that brushed up against the mountains. Never having given a moment's thought to their past, convinced that their history of conquest and defeat held no interest, the musicians' eyes had been opened to the myths and splendors of the palace of Diego Colón and the stone houses with patios splashed with azure. Beyond the walls of the old town, rusty ships' hulks lay dormant at the mouth of a river. Throughout the flight Stanley had drummed into the band the credo of the MNA. Yes, their music was the music of tomorrow. Yes, it was the symbol of this New World that was constantly changing and mutating, defying any definition. There was no doubt their symphony would conquer the universe. It would be heard in England. It would be heard in Europe and the Caribbean, and everyone would recognize the expression of his or her voice. The misunderstandings began, however, during their first radio interview. It was obvious that nobody in Santo Domingo cared about these speeches on migration, the future, and the New World, and Stanley came over as a bore. They hardly listened to him. They interrupted him in the middle of a sentence. Because of his dreadlocks one journalist took him for the likes of Bob Marley, which he vehemently denied. Did this mean he rejected Bob, the master of masters, as a model? Stanley stammered out an explanation and talked about Dvořák. Behind his back some technicians made fun of his suburban London accent. He heard them and made the mistake of showing his temper. Yes, he was born in Wimbledon, and he had studied at the Royal Academy of Music. Was that a crime?

The MNA's first concert was to be held in the courtyard of a former piano factory called the Mambo Palace. Due to a programming mistake, hundreds of fans had turned up to hear Chico Alvarez—one of their own, friend of Carlos Chavez—who had made a name for himself at the Cabrillo Festival in California. On learning they were going to hear, instead of their idol, a totally unknown band, three-quarters of the audience left, leaving the floor strewn with empty beer cans and dirty paper napkins. The rest left in equal pandemonium as soon as Stanley and his musicians struck up the symphony. The bad publicity spread to such an extent that the second concert took place in a virtually empty hall. A few idlers manifested their disapproval with violent whistles. For lack of an audience the third concert had had to be canceled, and the MNA had returned to Boston earlier than planned. By a sad coincidence their engagement at the Full Moon ended at the same time. The Benga Boom ensemble was arriving from Kenya with ten musicians, including the famous Daniel Owino Misiani, and a good many bookings had already been taken. From that moment on Terri took over as impresario as best he could. But the MNA musicians could only find one-night stands here and there, one evening in one spot, two evenings in another. Sometimes miles from Boston.

In spite of this bitter disappointment, the "Symphony of the New World" caught the attention of an enterprising producer, who invited the MNA to record in New York and wagered on their success. Marie-Noëlle did not hesitate. She felt it her duty to accompany Stanley. As usual he did not ask for her opinion, but for the first time during their life together she felt him to be less self-reliant, closer to her, almost vulnerable. She was able to imagine that he needed her. Often of an evening he entered her room, and without taking offence at Terri's presence, he lay down beside them and described his plans for the future. But he spoke in a muffled voice. It was as though he were impersonating himself and did not believe a word he was saying.

D

For five hours the train rolled through hideous towns and neighborhoods that looked like they had been destroyed by napalm. One wondered where the stamina of America was. New York, however, surprised her. The producer owned a recording studio in a formerly Jewish neighborhood bordering Harlem, close to Columbia University. The area had been taken over by Hispanics. Beauty salons and botanicas rubbed shoulders with synagogues. People sat on folding chairs on the stoops of their houses. This city, so reviled and feared, had the look of a village inhabited mainly by women dragging children behind them, university professors, and harmless students, totally oblivious to violence and the ravages of drugs. On the Saturday a street fair sprawled down Broadway. The cars kept their distance and clowns in three-cornered hats juggled multicolored balls. Marie-Noëlle had no interest whatsoever in the sights, the museums, the skyscrapers, and the yellow cabs, all those things the tourists rush to take pictures of. She sat on a bench in Riverside Park with the mommies, the babies, and the dogs and watched the changing landscape of boats and houses on the other side of the Hudson while her head filled with muddled thoughts.

D

It was around the middle of the second year in the United States that Awa turned up in Boston. Winter was over, and the rowers in striped T-shirts, straining at their oars, had replaced the skaters on the Charles River.

Awa's life had been turned upside down. From one day to the next Rodrigue had been arrested in Kouroussa for so-called counterrevolutionary activities and he had gone to join the thousands of men wasting away in the country's prison camps. As a result Natasha, stripped of her resources, had returned to Moscow with Awa and survived there on the generosity of her family. She who had hated Guinea suddenly began to paint it in the glowing colors of a lost paradise, and her unfortunate family had to put up with never-ending descriptions from morning to night of the Africans' virtues, the splendors of the tropical forest, and the vitality of their cultural traditions. She had been living in Moscow for three years when the rumor got back to her that Rodrigue had died. Nobody knew whether he had been killed during an operation by a commando of Portuguese mercenaries hired by the rebels to overthrow the dictator and open wide the prison gates. Or whether he had died of hunger and ill treatment in his jail cell. Or whether he had tried to escape and had been gunned down by his jailers. Once again taking Awa with her, Natasha left Moscow and returned to Guinea. She hoped to cast light on the disappearance of her husband and bring back his body. On her arrival in the capital the Sisters of the Visitation took pity on her. They gave her a room in their dispensary in the middle of a rundown neighborhood and generously shared with her their daily lot. Every day Natasha dashed from ministry to ministry, from one government agency to another, to such a point that she became a *cause célèbre* for some, an object of ridicule for most. When they saw her arriving dressed all in black under the glaring sun, limping with fatigue, her feet gray with dust in her sandals, her hair streaming behind her like dirty snow, her eyes wild and teeth yellowed, the civil servants crowding the windows doubled up with laughter. They demanded all sorts of documents and proof, proof of her identity, proof of Rodrigue's identity, proof he had been a doctor, proof they had been married, proof they had lived at Kouroussa, and proof he had managed a family welfare center. They inflated the number of permissions, authorizations, seals, and stamps, which meant that after two years of languishing in Guinea, Natasha had gotten no further than when she first arrived. One morning Awa could put up with the suffering no longer. She gave herself to a truck driver who hid her in his truck full of kola nuts bound for Sikasso, on the border with Mali. From there she had walked to Bamako and slept in the streets with the homeless, eating out of garbage cans. After a few days her constant comings and goings in front of the U.S. Embassy had caught the eye of a marine stationed at the gate. He had been moved by her sad story and got her a plane ticket to join Marie-Noëlle in Boston, the only person left on the planet who cared about her.

Despite this reversal of fortune, Awa remained lovely and vivacious, with radiant smiles and laughter that rang out in perfect harmony. She brought warmth to the sadness of Camden Town and gave a sense of direction to a house without one. In Camden Town everyone was used to doing as they liked. Henceforth twice a day the musicians sat down to savor the meals she cooked from mildewed beans, overripe plantains, and substandard meat, paying no attention to the constant harping of her obsessions. Dictatorship. Shortages. Moral and intellectual distress of the African people. The ravages of every version of Marxism throughout the world. Corruption and incompetence of civil servants. Excessive red tape. Whereas they lacked everything, Awa found enough money to rent a TV set and so instead of drinking their cheap liquor to the last drop, the musicians now sat down quietly to watch the sitcoms and soap operas. She bought a washing machine on credit and set about doing the laundry. She did much more. She paid with her person and dispensed pleasure to everyone. In fact her childhood tendencies had not been refuted. She put as much zeal into making love as each musician put into playing his instrument. Marie-Noëlle did not have time to be hurt by her escapades with Stanley and Terri, since she had no sooner finished experimenting with them than she decided to move into the beds of Amandio and Nando. She said it excited her not being able to tell which of the two was fondling her. Moreover, with them she could share her nostalgia for Africa and her dream of returning one day, once the wounds of colonialism and neocolonialism had healed. This did not stop her from falling in love with Dave, an African American who came to repair the TV, and devoting a growing number of nights to him each week. Dave was the key that unlocked black America for her, and she began to reproach Marie-Noëlle for her apathy and indifference to the country they lived in. What did she know about it? What did she understand about it? She was living there like a parasite. Because of Dave, Awa began attending services at the Bethlehem Baptist Church, watching for the moment when worshipers and pastor would fall into a trance amid the frenzy of the organ. She attended political meetings where white folk were called Satan, and church bazaars where the kids smeared their mouths with barbecue sauce. She became an ardent fan of baseball, basketball, and football and learned the nicknames of the sports heroes who made the boys from the ghetto dream. Awa never failed to accompany Marie-Noëlle to the university. But whereas Marie-Noëlle was busy studying the French authors on the program, Awa, determined to improve her knowledge, armed herself with a dictionary and endeavored to decipher the works of African-American theoreticians. This idyll ended, however, the day Dave's wife turned up with a commando of female buddies and threatened her with a revolver, which she would have certainly fired if the musicians had not intervened. The result was that, from one day to the next, there was no more ferocious critic of black America than Awa.

Awa and Marie-Noëlle, who had never stopped writing letter upon letter to each other, became inseparable again. It was as if they had never been parted since that beautiful summer memory at Savigny-sur-Orge. Sometimes at night they managed to forget their companions. Sitting opposite each other in the living room they never tired of reliving their childhood and reminiscing about their mamans. In the end they merged into a common vindictiveness. Awa had taken to hating and criticizing Natasha. According to Awa, Natasha had returned to Guinea only to spite the family of her co-wife. For Rodrigue, tired of her morosity and constant lamentations, had not made love to her for years and had taken a second wife, a Kissi from the forest. Awa had met her on several occasions, as well as her little brother, the spitting image of Rodrigue, and praised her generosity, her warmth, and sensitivity, all the virtues that Natasha did not possess. It was as if she bore a grudge against her mother for being alive on this earth while the body of her beloved papa was rotting who knows where, without a funeral or a grave. Marie-Noëlle, who had just been informed by Ludovic of the birth of her little sister, Angéla, had tears in her eyes when she thought of this innocent child who had not asked to be born. It was not difficult to see what future lay in store for her. Like her older sister she would go adrift in life. She was eager to introduce Awa to Anthea.

Marie-Noëlle chose to close her eyes to Anthea's failings and odd habits, to her intellectualism. She knew what they masked and wanted to remember only the way Anthea had transformed her life. Without her she would still be serving plates of *bacalao* and *frijoles negros* at La Rosita, only too happy when she managed to fill her stomach with a little rice and beans. Anthea agreed to meet Awa one afternoon over one of those cups of vanilla-flavored

Sumatra coffee she frequently drank. From the very outset it was a fiasco that even the simple songs—"Frère Jacques" and "Savez-vous planter les choux"—duly drummed into Molara by Marie-Noëlle—could not save. It was clear from the start that Anthea did not appreciate the purple prose, the pièces de résistance, of Awa's conversation. Every one of her words irritated her. Awa had no sooner turned her back than Anthea advised Marie-Noëlle to be on her guard, for she saw nothing but narcissism and vanity in this false friend.

As for Awa, she thought Anthea arrogant and dogmatic and accused her quite simply of being jealous of a youth she had lost.

relis di Ferrari did not look like Mme. Esmondas. She had a mass of hair as black as the night, pulled into a Spanish chignon and pinned with an openwork tortoiseshell comb. Her complexion was ivory colored and in the depths of her eyes flickered the memories of her gilded youth in Buenos Aires. She lived in one of the most imposing houses in Camden Town, a folly of brick and white stone, with a Studebaker that was gathering dust in her garage. Yet they both practiced the same trade. Clairvoyance. Like Mme. Esmondas she too had visiting cards that she left at the drugstore, told fortunes from the cards, and read palms in the most traditional way. The highlight of her séances was when she switched off all the lights in the room at once and spelled out the future in the trembling flame of a candle. These were moments of high theatricality, when her deep voice announced tragic encounters, dire ordeals, fatal illnesses, and unspeakable tribulations. For Arelis the future hid in its shadows a succession of catastrophes as fateful as natural cataclysms, such as earthquakes or hurricanes. Unless . . . Unless . . . Here she suddenly switched the electric light back on and placed in the hands of her frightened clients a ten-dollar vial with a foul-smelling liquid they had to spray themselves with three times a day. Nobody had the courage to refuse, and Arelis, having nimbly snatched up the dollar bills, stood up and indicated that the séance was over.

One morning while Arelis, loaded down with her shopping bag, staggered along the sidewalk, Awa and Marie-Noëlle had taken her by the arm and delivered her safe and sound back home. From then on they did her a thousand small favors. Sometimes they did her shopping for her. They took turns waxing her floors. They polished the frames of the countless photos arranged just about everywhere around the house, depicting Arelis at different stages in her life. Above all they brought her back, carefully snuggled into brown paper bags, her bottles of Smirnoff vodka.

For Arelis was a hard drinker.

She would start in the early morning under one pretext or another: the never-ending winter in this wretched America that turned your body to a block of ice; a pain that wouldn't let up around the heart; a weakness in the kneecap. This went on all day long after every séance, ending with a stiffer drink at nightfall to help her get to sleep. The truth was that Arelis had so many bad memories to drown in her head. She had coped with the impoverishment of her family, ruined by misguided investments; she had coped with the fact she had never been able to complete her education; she had coped with the men who, one after another, had left her in the lurch. But she had never coped with the fact that her son—her sweet handsome Anthony, the apple of her eye, whom she had had with an Australian, her third husband—had been riddled with bullets at the age of twenty-four on a corner of Lenox Avenue. The sinister business had never been cleared up. The police had dared to state that ever since high school they had had their eye on Anthony, who was dealing in drugs with others of his kind, and that it was quite simply a settling of scores. People in the neighborhood would have been of the same opinion, for the only time they met Anthony was around midnight, dressed to kill under his fur coat, gloves, and hat and accompanied by strapping guys with the forbidding appearance of bodyguards. As for Arelis, she swore, calling as witness one of the many portraits of Jesus Christ that adorned her room, that Anthony was in fact the sweetest, the most affectionate of sons, loving his mama as they all do and destined for a bountiful future. Up to the age of ten he had slept in her bed, and she could remember the warmth of his young body pressed up against her side. He had showered her with jewels and dresses made of silk and lace. He was the one who had bought her this imposing mansion. This garden big enough for deer to frolic in, but where only tame squirrels scampered. These two floors, from which Arelis had sold the best of the furniture and which she now rented out by the room, in order to try to make ends meet, to noisy Latino couples, always quarreling or listening to music and incapable of paying their rent. Arelis hated Hispanics, Caribbean islanders, Peruvians, Costa Ricans, Mexicans, all those half-breeds whom the United States were weak enough to let in with wideopen arms and who grew bolder by the day demanding that Spanish be declared the offical language in certain states. She boasted that she had never let a Hispanic soil her sheets, for although her family had been living in Argentina for generations, they came from Italy and could trace their bloodline intact to Padua. One day when she was feeling particularly melancholy, Marie-Noëlle told her that her own father might have been Italian. This had sealed their friendship. When Awa left to explore Boston on her own, the two of them remained behind to keep each other company, drinking together—though Marie-Noëlle never drank excessively—smoking marijuana, and listening to Arelis's favorite operas by Verdi. Marie-Noëlle was no match for her companion's torrent of tales. About her parents. Her friends. Her lovers. An inexhaustible treasure trove proved to be the heroic deeds of her angel and martyr, her son. Then there was life in the United States. Arelis had lived in America for more than thirty years and had never stopped hating it. Nothing found favor in her eyes, neither the language nor the climate nor the food—the fruits and vegetables and cheeses in the supermarkets—neither the television nor the movies nor the fashions. But she hated Argentina even more. Once again it was not the foreign or domestic policy that shocked her—none of the major reasons, such as the dictatorship or the disappearances—but rather the wickedness in the hearts of the Argentinians, who reveled in slander and gossip. Hadn't *El Pais*, the leading daily in Buenos Aires, devoted an entire page to Anthony's death, underlining the point so that it was plain to everyone what a respectable family his mother came from?

Often in the evening, when the flow of customers dried up, Arelis tried to communicate with Anthony. She would burn sweet-smelling herbs in all four corners of the room. Then she would turn off all the lights and passionately recite in the dark the prayers that would bring back her son. Such exhortations could go on for a very long time. Anthony did not respond. So Arelis would collapse onto the pedestal table she had been unable to turn, drunk with disappointment and vodka. Without too much difficulty, for she was as light as a feather, Marie-Noëlle would undress her and slip her into one of the lace nightgowns Anthony had given her. She laid her in her vast bed, as deep as a boat, and left the bedside lamp on.

As she went out she turned the key in the door and threw it into the letterbox. In the badly lit entrance hall she usually bumped into the Diaz brothers. The Diaz family, four children, two adults, were squeezed into two rooms on the second floor. The parents paid their rent on the dot on the first of each month. Even so Arelis would have very much liked to get rid of them, for evening after evening they quarreled like furies and screamed and swore the most terrible obscenities. Marie-Noëlle did not exactly feel reassured on meeting the Diaz brothers, over six feet tall, frightening to look at, and ill-kempt, wearing woolen hats pulled down level with their shifty eyes, and padded overcoats. At the same time she was ashamed of herself. Was it their fault they were poor and undesirable, their sole distraction being the slot machines and the cheap beer in the bars? Even so! Despite her reasoning, she shook with fear as she crossed the garden sparkling with frost, expecting them to grab her from behind and slash her with the switchblades they carried in their hip pockets.

She then had to walk two or three blocks along North Avenue, dark and deserted, lined with gutted building façades behind which who knows what species found refuge for the night. In the distance a police siren wailed, speeding towards the scene of the crime. Suddenly the memory of all these rapes, robberies, and murders that the tabloids fed on flooded her mind. When the house finally came into view at a corner, she ran as fast as she could, dashed up the steps to the porch, and barricaded herself in. Everything was silent. The musicians would not be home for a long time. Where could Awa be hanging out again? In the freezing kitchen she made herself a cup of chocolate and put herself to bed. Freezing as well.

D

That night was like any other. No premonition. No nightmare.

She had gone home earlier than usual, for Arelis, glutted on too much Smirnoff, had soon given up trying to communicate with Anthony. She had quickly collapsed over the pedestal table, and Marie-Noëlle had put her to bed. She had kissed the old face that hinted of lost beauty and cleaned up the glasses and empty bottles.

Back home she had made herself a cup of hot chocolate and plunged into a treatise of literary theory. Literary theory was the hot issue at the University of New England, recently introduced by two professors who had been enticed away from Yale to the tune of many dollars. Marie-Noëlle concentrated hard during their classes but had to confess she did not understand very much. Awa got home around midnight, all excited and beside herself with laughter. She had been to a political meeting in a black neighborhood. Fiery orators, one after another, had taken the floor for hours to hammer out the obvious. America was not changing. America would never change. Sure there were pomaded black guys and girls dashing everywhere, looking pleased with themselves, holding leather briefcases. But for most the daily lot remained poverty, underemployment, arbitrary convictions, prison, and death. To a certain extent this painful situation was only just retribution. For the black community had neglected God. It had forgotten the traditional values. It drank. It fornicated. It committed sodomy. It was addicted to drugs. Young people killed each other for a pair of Nikes. Adults, for material goods that were just as foolish. It had to stop. How? Through a common cleansing. Churches, temples, mosques, and all kinds of places of worship must be erected in every city, every neighborhood, and the child must take care of its parents, the father must take care of his mother, the brother his sister, and the uncle his aunt. Whereas the exploited worldwide were preaching violence and strikes and taking management hostage, these people were prescribing prayer. How true; America had not changed since the time when the slaves invented the gospel under the whip. *In the upper room.* Awa was still denouncing this näiveté when the musicians returned home. For once they were exhilarated. Not one table empty at the Last Resort. Emotional curtain calls. And a standing ovation at the end. By way of celebration they drank a few glasses. Then Stanley had gone down into the basement with his instrument. Awa retired for the night with Nando and Amandio. Terri and Marie-Noëlle lay down next to each other and made love.

The house was still asleep when the police came hammering on the door.

🝆

For months and months Marie-Noëlle made a wide detour to avoid going anywhere near Arelis' house. Her face loomed up in front of her as if in reproach. What had she been guilty of? Of not having known how to protect her? Of not having sweetened her solitude? She had done everything that had been in her power. Obviously it had not been enough. It was not only the remorse that tortured her. It was the knowledge that once again, like Mme. Esmondas, her friend had left her without saying good-bye. She would have nothing to remember her by. She should have grabbed one of her countless photos while there was time. The one of Arelis as a boarder in a religious institution in Buenos Aires. The one taken at her first wedding—the marriage hadn't lasted six months—to a white American, as WASPy as they come. The more recent photo of her as a radiant mother cradling little Anthony in her arms.

The police reconstructed the events. Her killer, entering through a window, must have murdered her in her sleep, which explained why there was no trace of a struggle. Then he wrecked the apartment. He did not know that Arelis, artful as she was, kept nothing at home. She would dash to the bank as nimbly as she could to deposit her days' takings. In his frustration he had hauled off the silverware, the chandeliers, and everything that remained of her past bourgeois splendor.

Like the other tenants, the Diaz brothers were quickly cleared. At the time of the crime a hundred witnesses saw them at the

Monsoon getting drunk and manhandling the slot machines. The police quickly gave up the investigation. One of those sordid crimes committed a hundred times a day in the big cities and seldom solved, involving a sixty-year-old woman, slightly cracked, living alone, whom nobody would miss on this earth. Did she have any family in the United States?

Some six months later, a remaining sister in Chicago, whom Arelis had never mentioned, showed up and put the house up for sale.

Part Two

Chapter 1

The funeral was over. The priest and the two choirboys swinging the incense holders like yo-yos hurried back to the Church of Saint-Jules. The congregation scattered, wearing the poker-faced expressions suitable for mourning but really in a hurry to get the sadness over with. It had lasted long enough. It was now time to let Ranélise sleep her sleep of eternity under the casuarinas. Only the closest family friends walked back to the house to embrace the family one last time, drink a glass of star anise, and above all finish off the remainder of Claire-Alta's thick soup that had embalmed the house the previous night. So much grief! It would be talked about for many years to come. Death had swooped down on Ranélise without troubling to announce itself, without even a drumbeat. On Tuesday, coming back from Tribord Bâbord, renamed La Belle Créole, where she still worked as cook, she had complained of pains in her chest. On Friday, feeling the pain shoot into her forearms, she had talked about going to see the doctor. But what was the point? Those charlatans never find anything wrong with you and give you a clean bill of health when you are already at death's door. She had been content with a strong broth of *carouge* leaves, three aspirins, and had gone to bed early.

On Saturday she had collapsed in her yard, uttering the name of the girl who had always been in her heart, but whom she had not seen with her own two eyes for eighteen years. By the time two neighbors had carried her to her bed, she had passed from this life to the next. The Vatable Canal neighborhood had gone into deep mourning. In every house the mirrors were covered with mauve shrouds and consecrated palms placed under the holy images. For four days and four nights people never stopped filing past and sitting round the glass-topped coffin where she lay. Eyes brimming with tears, they reminisced about her generosity, her words of comfort for those afflicted with misfortune, and the food and drink always on her table. Gérardo Polius turned white haired overnight. The year before he had buried his wedded wife, and so he found himself twice widowed. He could not find room in his heart for Marie-Noëlle. First, because she was the daughter of Reynalda, who had rewarded Ranélise's goodness so badly. Second, because the daughter did not seem any better than the mother. For years, season after season, she had promised Ranélise that she would come and warm up her old age. So he had cabled her an ultimatum. There was no going back on her word this time; she would have to keep her promise to the deceased—which she did, announcing her arrival as quickly as she could. Géraldo and Mano, Claire-Alta's husband, went to fetch her at the airport, and they had to confess how surprised they had been on greeting her. She did not look at all like the person they had imagined, who lived and earned her living in the United States, the land of every dream.

Marie-Noëlle was no bigger or taller than when she left. Not very well dressed or well kempt either, her hair cut any old way. Her eyes just as melancholy and languishing, set in large circles that looked as though they had been outlined with makeup. Her jeans and flowery shirt were no different from any other

"Negropolitan" or "white trash" you met thumbing a lift by the side of the road. She was awkward and spoke in monosyllables. She had not cried—everyone noticed it—when she knelt down beside Ranélise's coffin. She had remained holding her head in her hands without looking at anyone, and then she went and locked herself in one of the rooms built at the back of the yard. Claire-Alta had never wanted to leave her older sister, who had raised her like her maman, but ever since she had a husband and two boys to look after, Ranélise's four rooms had become too small. So Mano, one of the few men who still knew how to work with his hands, had built two rooms under the papaya trees, complete with full bathroom; a far cry from the time when you used to wash as best you could under a sheet of corrugated iron. Now there was hot water, bathtub, shower, and a bidet. Behind the shutters Marie-Noëlle had slept for a long time, such a long time that the people around Ranélise's bed started to take offense. Some had commented out loud on the bottomless sea of children's ingratitude. Shouldn't Reynalda have been present at such a moment? She too had been cabled but had merely sent via Interflora a mass of white flowers that filled vases and pitchers. Even so, it wasn't right. Flowers? When the woman who had saved her from drowning and accommodated her in her misfortune was setting off on her longest journey! People could not get over it. Without Ranélise, where would she be today? Everyone remarked that although Marie-Noëlle had eaten nothing, she had, on the contrary, drunk quite a lot. Swigs of star anise and one rum punch after another. She had neither prayed nor sung, as if the words of the hymns and psalms no longer meant anything to her. She remained seated, eyes lowered, both hands clasping her knees, as rigid as a statue. During the church ceremony she had not shown any emotion, and anybody who was expecting her to shed a tear from the corners of her eyes during the priest's homily would have been in for a disappointment. Her same dry eyes had watched the coffin as they lowered it to the bottom of the grave to lie for eternity, then as they shoveled in the earth. Now she was dragging her feet back up the hill, squeezed into an ugly, rumpled black dress she had slipped on the night before. Claire-Alta had lent her a hat she carelessly stuck on her head, and for those who saw her she inspired something like fear they did not quite understand. They sensed she came from elsewhere, an elsewhere for them as deep and mysterious as the dense forest. They guessed they would be unable to fathom the stories she told, if the inclination took her, or to join in the jokes that made her laugh. Consequently they avoided speaking to her and kept their distance.

The mournful September weather the past few days had suddenly cleared up. Big, ragged, leaden clouds sailed over to Dominica and let through the setting rays of the sun. Soon, blackness would ensnare La Pointe with its nighthawk claws. And then the glow of daylight would return. A new day would dawn, and tomorrow would take over from today, little interested in knowing whether Ranélise would be there to admire it or not.

The little group of mourners reached the house draped in black by the undertakers, where, beneath the perfume of tuberoses and white lilies, death had hidden its unmistakable smell. Once they crossed the doorstep, Claire-Alta and Géraldo both realized that their life with Ranélise was over. They would no longer see her drinking her coffee in front of the window. They would no longer hear her peals of laughter or her bursts of anger. They would no longer see her get out of bed, complaining of her aches and pains. Suddenly they began to weep and Mano hugged them to his ample chest. Mano, in fact, never had occasion to complain of his sister-in-law. He could not recall one sharp word between them, not one word louder than the next. But there were times he thought she took up a lot of room between his wife, his boys, and himself. So he was close to feeling a sense of liberation that curiously showed through his grief. The attitude of Claire-Alta and Géraldo, on the other hand, was simple and clear-cut. It was an attitude that could be summed up in one word. "Regret." All those present, especially the women, felt for them in their grief. With the compassion of a Greek chorus they sympathized and urged them not to cry and to take courage: *"Pa pléré! Pwen kouraj!"* After a while Claire-Alta pulled herself together. She sniffed, dried her eyes, and headed for the kitchen. She set out glasses of star anise on a tray and heated up the thick soup—one of Ranélise's recipes of oxtails with marrow, pumpkin, turnips, cloves, and garlic—and the aroma of this familiar dish that she had so often shared with the deceased started filling her eyes with tears again.

D

Marie-Noëlle was at a loss to understand. Ever since she arrived she had tried to remind herself she had spent the happiest moments of her life in this place. To keep her warm over the years her memory had provided her with picture postcard images of multicolored, one-story wooden houses, trees reaching up to the canopy of the sky, clumps of pokerlike barbaric blooms perched on the end of their stems, and warm, welcoming faces. Instead all she could see around her was poverty and ugliness. On the outskirts of the airport the building façades were peeling and faded. The streets were ill paved or riddled with potholes. Garbage cans and heaps of refuse stood guard at intersections. If the sun had not cast its generous rays over everything, the decor would have seemed as desolate as Camden Town or Roxbury, where she taught. In her memory the house where she grew up was out of a fairy tale. It now looked like a ridiculous shack, cluttered with furniture too big for the rooms and cheap consumer trappings, such as a television,

VCR, stereo player, and cordless phone. Her ten-year-old face smiling out of a gilt frame on the chest of drawers left her cold, and the smell of reheated soup, the scraping of spoons, and the sucking on marrow bones like a hollow tooth, turned her stomach. Yes, she had loved Ranélise, but after a while love fades like perfume, something she did not realize. While they emptied their plates, the remaining friends went on wrapping the deceased in her virtues and mummified this hot-blooded creature who had been so fond of life and men. You could feel her entering the world of the invisible and that already she no longer belonged to the real world. The real world was Marie-Noëlle, whom they were dying to talk to. They did not dare, however, and watched her in silence. Once they had paid their respects and filled their stomachs, they all rose together and took their leave amid a noisy round of kissing. Mano drove Gérardo Polius home in his brand-new Toyota, and Claire-Alta and Marie-Noëlle remained alone. They carried the plates back into the kitchen, which was not lacking for home appliances, then they sat down on either side of the table covered with a cross-stitched cloth. Claire-Alta switched on the television, and for a moment surrealistic pictures of massacres in the Middle East filled the screen. Women and children were screaming. Shells were ripping open human flesh. But neither of them paid any attention and Claire-Alta asked self-consciously: "Have you any news of your maman?"

Ever since she arrived Marie-Noëlle's shoulders had felt the weight of reprobation that Reynalda's indifference and ingratitude deserved, and could not think how to shrug it off.

"She never writes, you know," she stammered. "I only get news of the family through Ludovic. He says everything is fine."

This was not true. In his letters Ludovic openly described how Garvey, now a teenager, was giving him all sorts of trouble. After years of his laziness and bad behavior, they had finally expelled him from college. Ludovic talked of an apprenticeship, but all he wanted to do was hang around and stir up mischief with his gang. Once Ludovic had to go and get him at the police station. When Marie-Noëlle thought about her little brother, rebellious, cut to the quick and deeply unhappy, as she once had been for the same reasons, her bitterness toward her mother flared up again. Soon it would no doubt be innocent Angéla's turn. Nature fails her duty. Women who have gone through Reynalda's experience change from victim to tormentor. They turn into those woody stunted trees in the savanna, nothing but trunk and bare branches, giving neither blossom nor fruit.

"So you're a schoolmistress?"

Marie-Noëlle jumped. For a moment she wondered if the question was addressed to her. Schoolmistress? The expression conjured up pictures of caring teachers and studious pupils lined up in single file under the plane trees in a recreation yard. It had nothing in common with her work. The college where she taught was located in the very middle of Roxbury, a district as wretched as Camden Town, likewise inhabited almost exclusively by blacks and Latinos. Those enrolled with the intention of graduating were white-haired and old enough to be grandparents. After a lifetime of discipline in unrewarding jobs, they allowed themselves the luxury of studying for a degree that would procure them nothing but the vanity of not finishing their lives as imbeciles. The rest of the students, those of school age, were all up in arms. Seething with rage. They only came to class to band together and revile a system that, after having destroyed their parents, was bent on destroying them.

The boys' outward appearance was intentionally intimidating: tall and threatening with unkempt dreadlocks, box cuts, or shaven heads and a ring in one ear. Boys and girls alike stuffed their pockets with firearms or sharp-edged knives. They shared their alcohol and drugs. As for their language, they seasoned it with the most terrible, obscene swear words. Yet, as Marie-Noëlle soon realized, all this was a sham. Appearances were deceiving. Deep down this young generation was scared stiff and at a loss as to how to fend off the viciousness of life. An understanding gesture, a considerate word, or a compassionate smile took them so much by surprise that even the most raging bulls turned into lambs. Marie-Noëlle, who had not forgotten the pitfalls of her own adolescence, went to the trouble of listening to them and, wherever possible, endeavored to satisfy their needs. So there was no doubt her courses came as somewhat of a surprise. Appointed to teach French literature in a place where nobody cared, she did not attempt to impose the Fables of La Fontaine or the classical tragedies or the moralists or philosophers from the eighteenth century, nothing of what is usually taught. The only writer she returned to year after year was Jean Genet. He had enormous appeal. Generally speaking the students forgave him everything except his homosexuality. He was a pretext for unending sparring matches on the subject of exclusion, colonialism, theft, prison, love, sex, and virility that could be considered a far cry from literature. Thanks to her students Marie-Noëlle found in Jean Genet the subject of her doctoral thesis, and with the help of Anthea she published some articles in university journals. She was even making a small name for herself.

"Have you got any children?"

Marie-Noëlle vigorously shook her head. Good Lord, no thank you!

There was of course Molara, whom she teasingly fought Anthea over for possession. Molara was growing up graceful and well behaved. Her mother had enrolled her in a school for exceptionally gifted children, and at age nine she could speak four European languages: French, Spanish, German, and Russian. Soon it would be time for the African languages. She played the piano as well as the recorder, and her little compositions were a delight to the ear. When she went with Anthea and Marie-Noëlle to visit museums, her questions amazed them. Yet she was not at all a show-off; she was happy and agreeable, a real pleasure around the house. Apart from this child she had chosen, Marie-Noëlle had been spared motherhood. In her case nature had decided for her and wanted her sterile.

"You're all alone then?" Claire-Alta insisted.

The tone was one of pity. Only normal. What would you expect from a woman with her house full with a husband and two unruly boys? Marie-Noëlle nodded. She lived alone in her bare apartment, fortunately just a few doors away from Anthea's house. When the MNA broke up, she did not have the heart to leave Camden Town, whose ugliness and squalor were as dear and familiar to her as the graceless face of a favorite relative. She had grown fond of the dilapidated façades scorched by fire, the gaping windows nailed up with planks, and the plastic garbage bags piled up on the sidewalks. Yes, she was alone except for the neighbors' cat she had inherited, who regularly gave birth to litters of six; the runaway female student who slept on a mattress in her office; and the men encountered here and there who shared her bed. Stanley and Terri had left her, each in his time, each in his own way.

It's strange! Now that the only memory of Stanley was a few unsold records in the stores, she seemed to understand his music better. Moved to tears, she would listen to his "Symphony of the New World," and the complexity of its harmonies no longer put her off. She closed her eyes, and her imagination flew from chord to chord and went back in time. It was after the festival in Santo Domingo that Stanley's ideas had become dogmatic. By way of an introduction to his concerts he would launch into never-ending speeches on his favorite subject: the beauty and creativity of migration and its promise of a better future. Some evenings the exasperated audience would leave the room before he had played a single note. All this did not fool Marie-Noëlle, who sensed full well that deep down inside him a light had gone out. In the end he lived beside her like a zombie. He wore himself out composing what he called an oratorio, while working on symphonic poems. On his death all that remained unfinished: merely some cluttered staves of scribbled notes she had laid to rest in the chest of drawers.

High-pitched children's voices could be heard. It was Mano returning home with his sons, Randy and Kevin, who had been kept out of death's way.

*M*arie-Noëlle awoke amid the full glare of the midday sun. Daylight was sticking daggers into the louvered shutters, and the steel of their blades shimmered in silence. It had been years since she had slept for so long. Even so, she had had a dream that was still haunting her like a violent nightmare.

She had no idea where she was. It was nighttime. The moon was on its back in a cloudless, luminous sky. Its beams lit up a pitted, vermiculated limestone plateau that ran down to the sea she could hear screaming with the voice of a madwoman. Not a house in sight. Only a cabin bathed in moonlight. It might have seemed abandoned had it not been for the presence of a hound, one of those ferocious, famished Creole dogs that the kids like to pelt with rocks. Marie-Noëlle knew she had to draw closer and go in. But her legs refused to carry her as if weighed down by an enormous swelling. After a while the door creaked open. Nobody came out, and it remained ajar on a darkness as terrifying as the starry void. Then it creaked shut again, offering up its hard wooden face.

Marie-Noëlle ran over to push up the shutters and look outside. She had forgotten these colors: the green of the papaya leaves, the darker green and gold of the fruit perched at the top of the trunk, and the deep blue of the sky up above. Her youngest son clinging to her skirt, Claire-Alta was hanging out a dazzling wash. Children's clothes, men's and women's underwear, were flapping in the wind like kites. Marie-Noëlle caught herself envying such a carefree life, filled with the simple things: weddings, births, the two boys' first day at school. She had arrived in Guadeloupe with a definite mission. To demand justice for Reynalda. But suddenly she was afraid and shrank back. She had no idea how she would introduce herself at the Lago di Como or how she would be received. In order to put off the fatal moment she almost went back to bed and buried her head in the pillow that smelled so sweetly of vetiver mingled with another childhood smell she had difficulty identifying. Yet she managed to force herself.

Rue de Nozières, her heart missed a beat. Claire-Alta, however, had warned her. According to her Il Lago di Como no longer existed. The old upstairs-downstairs house, hunched over its secrets, had been replaced by a building in the ubiquitous concrete that was all balconies and striped awnings. The site of the jeweler's shop was occupied by an ultramodern pharmacy where the customers' silhouettes were reflected in the glass cabinets and the polished lacquer of the medicine drawers. The store lacked for nothing. From cornflour for infants, baby food, and dog biscuits to diet teas for guaranteed weight loss. Monsieur Théodore, the pharmacist, had a soft spot for women. It was obvious immediately. Il Lago di Como? The Coppinis? They belonged to the Guadeloupe of long ago. Long dead and buried. Finished, the Italian jewelers. And the Lebanese hawkers. Today's immigrants were from neighboring Haiti, Dominica, or Santo Domingo. Not to mention the homeless and drug addicts who brought with them their vices and weird accoutrements from metropolitan France. Monsieur Théodore was convinced that Gian Carlo Coppini had been dead for ages. When his parents had bought this ground-floor shop, it was already a pharmacy: the Delétang Pharmacy. Marie-Noëlle managed to venture a few questions. What had become of the rest of the family after the death of the father? Monsieur Théodore was unable to say. But, seeing her air of dismay, he promised to find out. Could he have her telephone number?

☙

Marie-Noëlle emerged into the bustling crowd of passersby hurrying about their business or strolling for strolling's sake. The din of cars and motorcycles deafened her. She was oblivious to everything going on around her. She had the feeling she had just been the victim of a robbery. Fate, which had already run off with her childhood and her mother's love, had dispossessed her once again. In fact she wasn't expecting anything from Gian Carlo that one has a right to expect from a papa. Neither affection nor moral nor material support. No dramatic recognition, no *coup de théâtre*. Simply she wanted to imprint on her mind the features of his face and hear the sound of his voice. Only once had she found herself in his presence. She had been barely eight or nine years old. So she pried the maximum of details out of her memory of that brief moment. He was handsome, that she remembered. Not lecherous, not brutal. Just a little conceited. She remembered his silvery hair curling over the nape of his neck, and his large eyes. Apart from that she did not know whether he was tall or short. He might have been wearing a drill suit, a stiffly starched white shirt, and the pith helmet men wore in those days. She had the vague feeling that the jeweler's shop was filled with women. Of a pale complexion. In rather shabby clothes. They concealed their braids under white mantillas. Little girls were doing their homework or playing in a corner. No doubt her half-sisters, who knew nothing of her existence. Nobody knew she existed in this family of hers. She was the forgotten offshoot.

Suddenly the heat pounced down on her neck in one swoop. She almost fainted and entered a café. It must have been close to a high school, for the place was filled with young boys and girls. With their backpacks, their Nike trainers, T-shirts and jeans they were decked out like her students in Roxbury. But the resemblance stopped there for they were kidding around in Creole. Creole, the forgotten language, the language that had shaped a world where she did not belong, which at times she hankered after. Remembering her childhood, she ordered a cane juice, heard a voice sullenly reply they did not sell that, and made do with a Coke like her neighbors. She was on her first sip when someone invited himself over to her table. It was no stranger. Judes Anozie. She had been introduced to him at the wake and remembered his name because he reminded her a little of Terri. This was no chance encounter. He must have questioned Claire-Alta and followed her. She wondered what he was after. Couldn't he sense she brought bad luck?

Terri had sensed it and had been the first to run from her. Without a word. The only evidence he left was a long letter for Stanley on the dining room table. He told him he shouldn't get him wrong. He had great admiration for the MNA's music and considered Stanley a genius. But he was tired of their sordid existence. He was leaving for Toronto to join the band of a Haitian friend. Nothing wrong in that, playing dance music for immigrants' associations.

After Terri left Stanley took up his rightful place again in Marie-Noëlle's bed. As if all those months had been a digression to which she alone attached any importance. As if for Terri and Stanley she had been nothing but a consenting body they had passed from hand to hand. Then Stanley had left her. Not a word either. Despite their efforts the police had never arrived at a satisfactory conclusion. The Last Resort, the jazz club where Stanley liked to play solo after his musicians had left him and he had found himself all alone with Marie-Noëlle in their big Camden Town house, had a wide terrace that extended down to the Charles River. In summer, barges floundered through the swamps, tangling their prows in the reeds on the bank. In winter the river froze as far as the eye could see and moonlight polished its hard, smooth surface. The theory went that Stanley, who evening after evening drifted about in a haze of alcohol, must have accidentally gone too far, and the treacherous ice had collapsed under his weight. Or else he had deliberately walked beyond the safety limits. Whatever the case they had fished his frozen body out several yards downstream. It was the second theory Marie-Noëlle knew to be correct, for Stanley no longer had the words in his mouth, no longer had the dreams in his head, to embellish his life. So what was the use of living? When he lay on top of her he froze her with the chill of a corpse. And all that was her fault. Anthea's psychiatrist could do nothing to convince her of the contrary.

She looked at Judes Anozie sitting opposite her, a real nitwit. If he had known what was good for him he would have run as fast as he could. Instead he chattered on without rhyme or reason.

"Here, you know, a woman must always have a man on her arm. It's the custom. Otherwise they disrespect her. I'll give you my arm. I'll accompany you everywhere. I'll help you discover what you want to discover. Tomorrow I'll take you to my granny's. She can neither read nor write. And yet everything that's happened in this place is engraved in her memory forever."

ⅅ

Claire-Alta did not get along too well with Marie-Noëlle, whose long line of rebuffs included her refusal to accompany her to high mass on Sundays on the excuse that she had nothing to wear. Her refusal to do the rounds of Ranélise's friends, who had all seen her when she was a baby in arms, then later as a little girl, on the excuse that she no longer remembered them. Her refusal to go with her to the supermarket on the excuse that she hated that. They had nothing to say to each other. When they had breakfast together, they sat in silence on either side of the table while their coffee lost its aroma and went cold in the cups. At lunchtime Marie-Noëlle pecked about at her plate, then went and locked herself away in her room for a siesta without waiting for the obituaries on the radio. In the evening Mano was there to show off as usual whenever a woman was present. He had her listen to the latest hit music on the stereo. He practically apologized for the family mourning, which prevented him from taking her dancing, and he would describe the island's nightclubs to her. But it was obvious that none of the above interested her. She did not like excursions. One Saturday they had taken her to the beach at Deshaies. She had not gone swimming and sat on the sand looking bored at this bay that tourists from all over the world went into raptures about. Nevertheless Claire-Alta was glad the way things were turning out. Okay, Marie-Noëlle could not find her papa. But she had found a man. This return home that Ranélise had so hoped for— right up to her deathbed—looked as if it might work out. It's true that Judes Anozie was not the ideal match. He was a math teacher, slightly cracked, who was president of an association for the protection of the environment. According to him Guadeloupe was disfigured. Marred by the raging stream of cars and the constant tramp of tourists, wrecked by concrete, roads, highways, traffic circles, intersections, and link roads, sullied and soiled by garbage of all kinds. Whenever he was given the opportunity, he would launch into anathemas on television, and people would shrug their shoulders on hearing him. What had gotten into him? He was a dreamer who wanted to go back to the time of oxcarts and makeshift shacks on four stones. Guadeloupe's good old days were gone. Despite what some people thought. It was progressing like the rest of the world.

No need for Judes and Marie-Noëlle to go through City Hall or the Church. Today everyone put Easter before Lent. The Church no longer reserved Saturdays for illegitimate children. Even the upper classes were living together as husband and wife, and nobody cared whether blood had flowed between the thighs of the young bride on their wedding night. Claire-Alta would have given anything to know what Marie-Noëlle and Judes had said to each other when they met that afternoon. Marie-Noëlle's somewhat disinterested look, however, discouraged her, and she was afraid to ask questions. Without a word she watched her undress, revealing a body more bone than flesh, more hollow than rounded.

Hardly had she laid her head on the pillow and pulled the sheet up to her chin, as if they weren't stifling from the heat at this late hour, than she pleaded in a childlike voice:

"Tell me about Maman."

About Reynalda?

The question caught Claire-Alta off guard. What was there to say? They had occupied the small room behind Ranélise's, sleeping in the same bed. Reynalda was taciturn, self-centered. Even so, they had become more than sisters. What belonged to one, belonged to the other. Everyday dresses. Sunday dresses. Plastic or leather sandals. Sunday shoes for mass. Rosaries. But there was one treasure Reynalda did not share: a missal with a white lacquered cover, engraved with the gentle face of the Infant Jesus, gilt edged and as thick as a dictionary. Every other page opened to a religious picture. An angel with wings spread, a chaste Holy Mother, an emaciated Christ. Reynalda wept regularly leafing through it, but never revealed the name of the person who had given it to her. The folk in the Vatable Canal district had little sympathy for

Reynalda. So much fuss over a belly. Through her silence they believed she was trying to cover up a terrible secret. A secret that gave her nightmares. At night she cried like a small child, screaming: "No, no!" Once her baby had come out into the light of day, it was obvious it was the child of a fair-skinned man. The infant was as white as milk. But there's no lack of fair-skinned men in Guadeloupe. Especially at that time, when the streets were filled with the French riot squads running after the independence fighters with their billy clubs.

Claire-Alta had been deeply affected when Reynalda had left for metropolitan France. Especially as it had happened so suddenly. One morning she woke up with this idea of BUMIDOM. According to her, she had made inquiries at their offices without telling anyone. She had filed an application and got hired as a domestic. As simple as hello. Gérardo Polius claimed it couldn't be done because it required an investigation of good character from City Hall. They didn't need criminals or good-for-nothings in France. The entire household waited in expectation for news from Reynalda. Every day Ranélise stood watching for the postman. In vain! Nothing! Not a letter. Not a card. Claire-Alta, however, never took offense. She had never considered Reynalda ungrateful or heartless like everyone else. She had understood that Reynalda was stuck in a bad dream that she was trying to erase from her memory. Up to this very day she did not forget her in her prayers. At that moment Claire-Alta noticed that Marie-Noëlle had fallen asleep like a child in the very middle of a story she had begged for. She lowered the shutters and left the room. The house was plunged into darkness. The boys were asleep. Once he had bolted down his dinner, Mano had gone out again to join his buddies—or mistress?—and would not come home until the first light of dawn. Crossing the yard, Claire-Alta repeated to herself the proverb that had become her life's motto: *Sa zyé pavwé, kyé pa-w fè mal*— "If the eyes don't see anything, the heart is not hurt." At the foot of the hill, one of the last that the municipality had not yet razed to make way for low-cost housing projects, La Pointe slept. The unremitting heat of the night air carried the hot sounds of *zouk* music. Claire-Alta, however, kept a soft spot in her heart for the Haitian music that had livened up the dances when she was still in love with Mano. It was to the sounds of the *Shleu-Shleu* they had danced locked in each other's arms, lost in love. Suddenly, for no reason, she burst into tears.

That night Marie-Noëlle had the same nightmare: the bare cabin on that high, devastated limestone plateau.

*N*obody knew what ill fortune haunted this family. It was as if they were paying for some infamy one of its members had secretly committed. After the death of their beloved sister-in-law Arcania, six months had not gone by before it was the turn of Aunt Zita and Aunt Lia to set off for the Briscaille cemetery. They both departed the same week during a terrible epidemic of typhoid fever. Folk had not seen anything like it since 1937, when it was introduced by the oxen from Puerto Rico, those snorting mastodons who in those days were coaxed off the boats along the wharf with great whiplashes. They were laid out under the same tombstone, side by side, the way they had lived, and every Sunday the hands of their nieces weeded the grave and covered it with lilies and arums. Shortly afterward it was Gian Carlo's turn to depart, in a way that left its mark on people's imagination. His double widowhood had not darkened his disposition, and he still ordered around his servant girl, his apprentice jewelers, and his daughters like a tyrant. The sound of his fits of rage echoed as far as the Place de la Victoire. It was said that his children were so afraid of him they were struck with a stutter that made their words incomprehensible. One lunchtime he was finishing his meal with a mango. No doubt annoyed by the flies that were attracted by the sweet sticky juice on his mouth and cheeks, he overreacted with a sharp clumsy movement and stuck the knife in his left eye. Blood spurted out onto the white tablecloth. He was rushed to the General Hospital, where the doctors treated him the best they could. However, he lost his eye and from that day on, he had to wear a black leather patch—which, to tell the truth, suited him quite well, giving him a sort of pirate look. But imagine a one-eyed jeweler! He could no longer tell one gem from another, or twist the gold filigree or mount the cameos. His reputation sank. One by one his customers deserted him, and as a result, he began drinking far more rum than was good for him. One evening when he was drunk, he set fire to his sheets and perished in the fire. Folk in La Pointe were quick to point out the short distance between these flames and hellfire. For them the name of Gian Carlo Coppini was synonymous with Satan himself. From one day to the next, therefore, his daughters found themselves orphans, without Maman or Papa, and worse still, without resources. For Gian Carlo left behind so many fake invoices and debts from risky or phony investments that they had to auction off the house on the rue de Nozières and the contents of the jeweler's shop to pay for them. The sale drew a crowd of buyers, outbidding one another for the enamelwork and cameos, brooches, pendants, and chokers. Fortunately there were compassionate relations in Milan who had not forgotten the offspring in Guadeloupe. Crying their hearts out and leaving behind their dearly departed, whose graves nobody would flower on All Saints' Day, the girls boarded a plane for Italy; and only the eldest, Fiorella, had remained in Guadeloupe.

When Fiorella decided to stop speaking to her father and asked to leave for the boarding school of the Sisters of Compassion in Basse-Terre, the diocese found her a guardian. The Démonicos. In spite of their name, they were not Italian, but a family of mulattos, fairly dark skinned despite their grand airs. They were raising a brood of seven or eight children in a villa on the ramparts road with the uninspired name of Villa Mélodie. Their garden was a forest of lychees. Monsieur Démonico was a magistrate at the Appeals Court in Basse-Terre. His wife was a nursery-school teacher. Both of them realized that Fiorella was hiding a terrible secret that was preying on her mind. They questioned her and questioned her and finally she let out snippets of her secret. Reynalda's disappearance had been Nina's fault. She had mistreated her child from very early on. She was going to take her out of school to place her as a domestic, and Reynalda feared that more than death itself. Monsieur Démonico used his authority then to reopen the inquiry in La Pointe. To no avail. By some extraordinary coincidence, the day Reynalda had disappeared the police registers recorded nothing of note. No suicides. No runaways. Just the usual batch of battered women kicked out in a fury, brawls in the rumshops for a draft of rum, and quarrelsome neighbors slicing body parts with a cutlass. There was one incident involving eight children who, in their mother's absence, had been burned to a cinder in a shack near the canal, but it had nothing to do with her case. Two or three newborns had been thrown into the refuse carts to rot, but Reynalda was not pregnant, and if she had been, Fiorella was absolutely certain that she would never have committed such a monstrous act. At Monsieur Démonico's insistence Nina was summoned again to the fourth district police station. She walked in without giving anyone the time of day and looked at the police officers like a horse that has thrown its rider. Then she shrugged her shoulders.

"It's all a mystery to me. I've no idea what could have gotten into her head. Reynalda never told me what she was doing. She was somewhat secretive, I'd even say sly and underhanded. She only confided in Fiorella, a shameless hussy like herself. All I can tell you is that she'd been taking in men for some time. She must have gone off with one of them. By this time she's probably walking the streets in Dominica."

Learning of the mischief that Nina had let loose, Fiorella first wept buckets. Then she went into a great fit of anger and got the whole story off her chest. Monsieur and Madame Démonico were dumbfounded. Madame Démonico, wishing to protect her innocent-minded daughters, made her swear never to talk about such horrors to anyone. Monsieur Démonico got doubly serious. She was making a terrible accusation. Enough to send the guilty parties to jail for a good many years. Was she really sure of her story? Fiorella sobbed even louder, adding details she said she had from Reynalda. The very next day Monsieur Démonico traveled down to La Pointe, which was unusual for him. Like most of the inhabitants of Basse-Terre, he disliked this noisy, frenetic little town that robbed the capital of its commerce. He arrived at Il Lago di Como at the height of the daily rush. Having made the journey from the far corners of the island, the women customers were crushed up against the wooden counter, and the two aunts, mantillas askew, did not know which way to turn. Looking even more like Jesus Christ, Gian Carlo lorded it over all this commotion. Monsieur Démonico left as quickly as he had come in. What should he do? Set in motion the legal machine? Open an enquiry? Sully the reputation of a reputed craftsman going on the tittle-tattle of a teenager? Somehow he couldn't help thinking that Fiorella had told the truth and nothing but the truth, yet he could not come to a decision. He wandered over to the presbytery, where he learned that Father Mondicelli, Arcania's former confessor and friend of the family, had left to become chaplain to the new leprosy clinic in Pointe Noire. Dissatisfied with himself, he lunched badly at La Belle Créole and in the middle of the afternoon left for Basse-Terre. And that's where matters stayed.

After her papa died and her younger sisters returned to Italy, the Démonicos adopted Fiorella for good. She moved in with them as one of their children. She ended up getting a belly for herself and marrying one of their boys, the third son, Aristide, who had done very little at school and worked as an employee at the Préfecture. It wasn't a very successful marriage, for Aristide kept a number of mistresses and, what's more, liked living it up too much. Fiorella never left him, but spent long vacations in France with her youngest daughter, who despite her marriage remained under her thumb. She no longer spent more than six months of the year in Basse-Terre.

And Nina?

Nina looked hard for another position. But vague, shadowy rumors circulated about her. Folk in La Pointe were frightened of her and considered her Gian Carlo's creature. She did not stay long with the Lebanese who hired her as a nursemaid to his children. They complained that she pinched them to the bone in her fits of anger, and to prove it showed their arms dappled in red. She did not stay any longer either with the pensioner in a wheelchair who hired her to do his cooking. She deliberately left the saucepans on the stove and served him burned pumpkin mash. She had no other choice but to return to La Désirade, her native island, where she hadn't set foot for more than ten years.

Was her cabin still standing?

D

Marie-Noëlle felt so discouraged that she almost started to cry again, something she never did nowadays. As if in a bad dream she saw herself in pitch darkness roaming the rugged landscape of La Désirade, holding a lantern, looking for Nina Titane everywhere, and finally stumbling on a solitary grave in a cemetery by the sea.

She made a rapid calculation. Nina, who before she was twenty had given birth to Reynalda, who had given birth to her at the age of fifteen, could not be more than sixty-five. In all likelihood she was still alive and as fit as a fiddle.

Like Judes' granny.

Judes' granny was an old woman no taller than the clump of vetiver in front of her door and hardly any bigger, but was sturdy enough—you could feel it—to live to be a hundred. She had begun her tale in Creole. Then she noticed that Marie-Noëlle was lost and had difficulty following. So she painstakingly brought out her rusty school French, dropping a heavy grammatical mistake here and there like a rock. In either language she had never had a moment's hesitation, balancing squarely on the stepping-stones of her memory. Like Claire-Alta she imagined all sorts of things going on between Judes and Marie-Noëlle. It was obvious from the way she mothered her, as if, in this place, a man and a woman could not be seen together without them being imagined immediately in the same bed. But Marie-Noëlle, who had put that theory into practice too often, especially after Stanley's death, had no inclination to go to bed with anyone.

She felt comfortable with herself where she was. The clocks no longer marked the hour, and time had stopped. It seemed as if she had dreamed her recent calvary in Boston and all the months of mourning she had just gone through. Her heart wondered whether it had really felt all that pain.

∅

It had rained the day Stanley was laid to rest. A cold winter rain like melted snow, that lashed the few friends present. Nando and Amandio. Awa. A few MNA fans. Terri had sent a wreath from Toronto. The ground squelched underfoot with greedy sucking noises, and the horizon was curtained off. Stanley's parents, whom he never mentioned, had been notified by Marie-Noëlle for form's sake and rushed over from Wimbledon, father, mother, and an older brother. Marie-Noëlle had trouble making the connection between these well-dressed, God-fearing West Indians and the rebel musician who had shared her life. She had to accept it. Stanley was the son of a well-to-do family, who—for reasons she would never know—had strayed down that wrong path on which she met him. Out of the three members of the Watts family the father seemed the most inconsolable. In his grief he called on the services of an expensive undertaker who spared them neither gospels nor Mozart's *Requiem*, neither sturdy walnut coffin nor candles dripping tallow for three days and three nights. The mother endeavored not to show any emotion except for a dignified grief. But beneath the tears in her eyes, Marie-Noëlle could read the animosity she felt for this unknown daughter-in-law and the suspicions she had concerning her. Well-deserved suspicions, since everything that had happened to Stanley was her fault. She had never been able to make him feel that she loved and needed him. She had not understood he had genius and deep down took the liberty of not liking his music. The night he was drifting on the river in a drunken stupor, it was Reynalda she was thinking of, over and over again. In a word, she could not stop thinking about herself.

Ð

Judes' granny lived in the Grands Fonds on Grande-Terre. No magnificent view over the ocean or the volcano. Behind the curtain of sugarcane, a savanna as smooth as an English lawn, hollowed out in the middle by a pond where the Indians led their oxen to drink of an evening. The cabin was modest in appearance. The curtains were made of cretonne dotted with small flowers.

Half-sun openwork patterns ornamented the walls. Portraits of the infant Jesus and the Holy Mother smiled piously next to profane advertisements for Coca-Cola and Lucky Strikes. In her flutelike voice Granny, who had already finished with the misfortunes of the Coppini family, was describing the day the hurricane of 1928 struck—which, she was proud to say, was also the date of her birth. Carefully locked away in her chest of drawers she kept a yellowed copy of *Le Nouvelliste*. When it began printing again several weeks later, it listed the names of the babies who had braved the wrath of nature to emerge into the light of this world. Anastasie Séphocle, there she was. After describing in great detail the cabins blown away, the zinc roofs ripped off, and the ocean waves rearing up to the sky, she rambled on about a childhood deprived of shoes and lace dresses, but lavish with affection. In those days Guadeloupe lived with doors and windows wide open, and life slipped past, as limpid as water in a river. Then, without taking a breath, Granny launched into her version of the Second World War: the good old days of Governor Sorin, as she put it, a golden age when folk from Guadeloupe made their own soap. Listening to her you forgot the usual references in European history. Six million Jews had resumed their works and days. No Nazis, no victims. Paris was no longer burning. From Judes Anozie's bored look, Marie-Noëlle could see he knew these stories by heart like a picture book whose pages had become dog-eared. As for her, she let herself be charmed and realized that Guadeloupe's merit did not lie in its present, under constant threat, but in its past, a legend repeated over and over again, for the benefit of young and old alike, to calm their fears. She started when Granny returned without a blink to the present and began questioning her about the United States. Never leaving home—not even going to mass, for the Good Lord lives everywhere and prefers the houses of those who have always respected Him—she watched the American news on her color TV. One of her grandchildren had paid for her to have cable TV, and she recited the names of singers, movie stars, government officials, and the president. Marie-Noëlle did not know how to talk about America, apart from the myths it secreted: race relations, puritanism, sexuality, and violence. She did not know how to speak of her experience nor explain her attachment to a country which she had accosted by chance like her illustrious predecessors, but that nevertheless kept a firm hold on her. She had made no decision to live there forever. Yet she could not see herself living anywhere else, a woman with no husband, no lover, no child—in short, no family, except for Anthea and Molara—and nobody she cared for except her students. Despite Awa's constant invitations to come and join her in Mexico City, where she had recently found the love of her life, Marie-Noëlle had no plans to leave Boston. The United States was made for people of her sort: the defeated, the dispossessed, without country or religion, perhaps a race, who slip anonymously into its vast shadowy corners. Nowhere would she feel as safe as in Roxbury.

Without their noticing, Granny's chatter had lasted the entire afternoon. The bullfrogs had started up their din and the Indians' oxen were sauntering down to the pond, swaying their muzzles. It was time to set off back to La Pointe. On the way home Marie-Noëlle fell into a deep contemplation. She had decided to continue her investigation with Fiorella in Basse-Terre. But she felt it was Nina who held the key to her family tree. If she delayed the moment of encountering her, it was because she was scared. Scary Nina crouched on her deserted rock. Marie-Noëlle could not figure out how to go about naming the name of Reynalda and naming her own name. She had no idea whether Nina would open her arms to her or disown her, and whether she would find herself rejected. Once again.

Someone who was disappointed to see them return home so

quickly before nightfall was Claire-Alta. The more the days passed, the less she understood Marie-Noëlle. She ended up asking herself why she had come back. It was not to make amends for the long years of indifference, ask forgiveness from Ranélise, and lay her to rest, as everyone thought. It was to run after her own fanciful schemes. Here she was giving herself an Italian father to suit her fancy. Claire-Alta dug deep into her memory and could not remember Reynalda mentioning Gian Carlo Coppini even once. It was true that every time Il Lago di Como was mentioned she burst into tears as if she were being reminded of a place of torment and torture.

What really annoyed Claire-Alta was Marie-Noëlle's behavior toward Judes Anozie. For Marie-Noëlle he was an old man's walking stick, a blind man's dog. That was not the way to treat a man. She had no real respect for him.

Chapter 4

Once again Marie-Noëlle looked out through the shutters.

Up above the meadow of sky was still strewn with tiny pieces of moon and stars. Yet you could sense that darkness, which for hours on end had smothered La Pointe with all its weight and stifled it in its grip, was loosening its hold. Until then it had held fast. But suddenly it was about to relinquish its quarry to the sun, defeated as always by the stronger of the two. Marie-Noëlle tossed and turned on her warm pillow, dampened with sweat. Once again she had had the same bad dream, the rickety cabin, standing with door ajar on its limestone plateau, and she tried to find the key. What was approaching her in the darkness of the future? She realized too there was a chapter missing, several chapters to the story she was compiling inside her. The middle chapters were missing, for Reynalda only ever spoke about the beginning. About her childhood. As if only that period mattered to her. As if all those years that had lapsed between the time she left Guadeloupe and the time she sent for Marie-Noëlle in Savigny-sur-Orge did not count. Yet they can't have been very radiant or very heartwarming either, those years in Paris. The Paris Reynalda landed in at the end of the fifties was not the Paris of today, the capital of color, the second generation, the Negropolitans, the Harkis, and the Beurs, the French-born Algerians. It was the white Paris of the *"Y a bon, Banania!"* poster. The red tarboosh and the "Yes, massa" smile were spread shamelessly over every wall in the Metro. On the trains and buses a circle of empty seats set apart the black woman of the wrong color. Small children pointed at her as she huddled in her corner, whereas grown-ups casually voiced their comments out loud. After ten days of seasickness, being tossed around by the ocean's waves, Reynalda had taken the maritime train, more commonly known as the "nigger train," which at that time shuttled the overseas emigrants from Dieppe to the very center of Paris: the Gare Saint-Lazare. Every arrival was a major reunion. Parents, relatives, and friends who had not seen each other for years threw themselves around one another's necks in tears. Exchanging kisses, gossip, the latest news from Guadeloupe, Martinique, Guyane, and addresses, they formed an escort and promised to see each other as soon as possible.

Nobody was waiting for Reynalda, a little silhouette slipping into the crowd. She took a letter out of her case and, following the directions, arrived without difficulty at the boulevard Malesherbes. Her eyes looked neither right nor left, but only upward at the numbers on the façades of blackened stone.

Jean-René Duparc was a stomatologist. A stomatologist in vogue, who refurbished the smile of politicians and movie stars. Marie, his wife, had abandoned her career. She had too much on her hands with her three children, especially as Jean-René was very fond of entertaining. Despite their frivolous and extravagant ways, Jean-René and Marie were staunch Christians, working closely with Catholic Relief and sometimes inviting the homeless from the Emmaus Association to their table. For this reason they took the future of their domestics very seriously. Besides Reynalda, in charge of the three children, the couple hired the services of a cook, a cleaning woman, and a chauffeur. They gave Reynalda a room without running water on the sixth floor under the roof, but authorized access to the children's bathroom. Three times a week Marie dropped her off at five for evening classes and, between two baby feeds, left her time to do her homework. For her general education she bought her the novels she had liked when she was her age: *Le Grand Meaulnes*, *The Great Gatsby*, *To the Lighthouse*, and *L'Ecume des Jours*. Sometimes she took her to the movies with Nathalie, her eldest daughter, who was nine. One half-day a month she made her go out on her own, after having consulted *La Semaine de Paris* and suggested what exhibitions she should see and what walks to go on.

Reynalda took note but did exactly as she pleased. Besides, she always took the same walk. From the boulevard Malesherbes she went down to the Seine and strolled along the banks as far as the Latin Quarter. Once there she did not go anywhere near the forbidding Sorbonne or enter the bookstores and cafés. She was content to breathe in from afar the smell of liberty and high spirits of the students. How she would have liked to be one of them instead of spending her time always serving. "Yes, Madame. Yes, sir. Thank you, Madame. Thank you, sir. Of course, as you say." Instead of wearing a maid's mask over her face day and night.

Summers were spent in the Dordogne, where Jean-René had renovated an old farmhouse by himself.

In short the Duparcs felt themselves beyond reproach. That was why they were so upset when four years later an educational counselor came calling at the door and treated them in a most indignant way. She accused them of exploiting their hired staff and ordered them to look for another nanny, since Reynalda had won a scholarship and was going to take the entrance exam to the school for social workers on the boulevard Brune. Jean-René went into a fit of rage, and Marie wept on hearing such an undeserved altercation. They summoned Reynalda. Why hadn't she told them she wanted to leave? Didn't she like their little darlings? But Reynalda stood with her head down and had nothing to say in her defense. It should be said that Jean-René and Marie had been good masters. But everyone knows that since slavery the good master has been the most hated. That during the slave revolts he was the first to have his throat slit. His spilled blood anointed the baptism of liberty.

The fact remains that Reynalda left the boulevard Malesherbes with her case a little less empty than when she arrived, stuffed with old pullovers and faded scarves that Marie had given her. The other domestics did not miss her. Neither did the children. The former thought she put on airs. The latter had never seen her laugh or smile, and when she gave them their bath in the evening her expression made the water freeze over.

🖎

Marie-Noëlle imagines Reynalda in the heart of Paris in a cheap boardinghouse on the rue Lhomond run by nuns of the Order of Saint-Esprit. Three stone steps, worn down in the center, encircled by a black wrought-iron balustrade, lead up to the low door. In the refectory permeated with the lingering smell of cauliflower, a coal-burning stove has great difficulty heating up winter. The boarders are of all ages. Reynalda is not the youngest. Or the oldest. They include a sales assistant in a bookstore and a bookbinder's apprentice. She is the only black girl and the only one continuing her studies. Behind her back they good-naturedly nickname her "Snow White," because of her color, or else "Mamzel Docteur," because of her studious look. When asked to be more specific the mother superior, Sister Tharcisius, her face as wrinkled as an apple under her starched winged coif, is somewhat at a loss when it comes to the "young black girl." Nothing to report. Only those without family or affection board together under the roof of the rue Lhomond. Reynalda was only a fleeting visitor to the boarding-house, for at the end of the first year she passed the entrance exam to the school for social workers. Sister Tharcisius ponders hard, but can only think of one or two things worth mentioning. As soon as she had a spare minute Reynalda would run off to the municipal showers on the place Mouffetard and stay there for hours. In the narrow cabin with wooden walls she would lose herself in her thoughts amid the stifling steam. She would scald herself with hot water, then shiver under the nip of the ice-cold jets. As if she could never get clean enough. At night she was prey to nightmares and disturbed her roommates. They ended up putting her in a room with a Jewish woman who had survived the Holocaust. Apart from that Reynalda never went out in the evening and had no friends. Neither male nor female. Let's skip the three years Reynalda spent at the school on the boulevard Brune. They are not very enlight-ening either. A photo of the class of 1967, three rows of young girls dressed in identical white overalls, gives an idea what her physique must have been like. Nonexistent, you might say. Little skin on her bones. Sitting in the front row, she was so small, eyes lowered, hair smoothed back as best she could into a tiny chignon. The job of social worker that had just been created was still in need of a def-inition. It consisted of being a pediatrics nurse, a legal counselor, and a religious sister all rolled into one, with the iron rule of a chief warrant officer. Strangely enough Reynalda excelled at it, and at the age of twenty-three she was given her first job, at the city hall of Savigny-sur-Orge. At school she was told she had a promising future.

The real secret Marie-Noëlle would have liked to pierce was the relationship between Reynalda and Ludovic. A love as unexpected as stepping out into a clearing after the thick tangle of deep woods. Like the light after hours of total darkness. Basically Marie-Noëlle is terribly jealous. What is wrong with her? Why has nobody ever loved her like Ludovic loved her mother? Neither Stanley nor Terri. Or any of the multitude of men who passed through her bed.

She will never know how Reynalda and Ludovic met. How he managed to get close to her, she who lets nobody up close, how he untied one by one the tangled knots of her mind and healed her gaping wounds. There they are walking hand in hand down the avenue Gabriel-Péri without a glance at the cheap clothing stores and watchmaker's shops. They sit down under the chestnut trees in the Danièle-Casanova Park amid the curly-headed Arab children, and she tells him about her childhood. No sweet smell of sugar or cinnamon for me. No Creole tales or carousel music. That's why I've become what I am. At one point he mentions Muntu, the association he belongs to. He takes her along to their meetings. One day they go up to his room. Under the gaze of Malcolm X and Bob Marley, his gods, he takes her in his arms like a sick child. He clasps her to his chest. His hand, his mouth, draws close to her tortured genitals and she submits to him. He dispenses pleasure to her suffering body.

D

Marie-Noëlle had never been to Basse-Terre before because when she was a child it was a journey you only undertook for a good reason, and Ranélise had none.

Shortly after Petit Bourg she entered into a strange new realm of greenery and banana plantations. On both sides of the road the landscape flashed by like a series of what-you-would-expect postcards that somehow managed to amaze. Marie-Noëlle realized the danger of giving in to the magic, but also the danger of rejecting it outright, seeing only the human element behind it, crouching frightened and fragile, under the zinc roofs and the concrete. Whatever the case beauty is worth the detour.

Marie-Noëlle and Judes Anozie had no trouble finding the villa of Aristide and Fiorella Démonico under the mango trees on Ramparts road. It had formerly belonged to their parents, but they had renamed it Villa Arcania. Villa Arcania. By virtue of these white letters painstakingly engraved on a wooden rectangle painted black, the members of the Coppini family no longer belonged to the realm of ghosts, shades haunted by memory, but had now become flesh and bone irrigated with nerves and blood. This history of origins, this family history that was founded only on hearsay, somebody's word against another's, was now emerging. All it needed was the hand of a scribe to fix it in writing and thereby give it the authority of truth. Yet at the moment of taking over the role she had been preparing herself for, perhaps unconsciously, perhaps since the beginning of her life, Marie-Noëlle faltered. She was about to wake the zombies, pour salt on the tip of their tongues. Whereas she had no claim to this history. She belonged there only because she belonged to Reynalda. Reynalda who had wrapped herself in silence, who had broken every tie that moored her to the island. Wouldn't writing be tantamount to betraying her, to wounding her once again?

The somewhat unkempt garden of the Villa Arcania was akin to the jumble typical of this region of rain and humus. Vines hung from the trees and the golden cacao pods gleamed among the foliage. Looking bored, Aristide Démonico was waiting for his guests on the terrace of a house made of concrete (yet again). In Marie-Noëlle's eyes all the houses on the island had a family look about them. Bloated with verandas, attics and additions, they remained extensions of Granny's cabin which was the original blueprint. The Villa Arcania endeavored to give itself the importance fitting its master. Aristide Démonico. A square-built mulatto with curly, graying hair. Standing there in his old-fashioned drill suit, he seemed to be waiting for a photographer.

Not at all mortified by approaching old age he inspected Marie-Noëlle from every angle. He could not have been entirely displeased with what he saw, for he changed expressions and ventured a smile. Like Granny, he talked nonstop, without letting anyone else get a word in. But his legends were different from hers. He was crazy about the area and would never live anywhere else. He recalled the nightmare events of 1976 when the Soufrière's bad-tempered eruption forced him to take refuge with a cousin of his father's on Grande-Terre. With his gift of the gab he described the chaos on the roads and the unending line of country buses bristling with mattresses, children, and paltry possessions piled on in the rush to evacuate. At the time he was a young civil servant, and for six months he had been obliged to shut himself up in the sous-préfecture of that stuffy, overpopulated town by the name of La Pointe. Despite the machinations of metropolitan France, determined to put an end to the island's tale of two cities, Basse-Terre had survived. It had even flourished. When he was a small boy the Rivière aux Herbes that divided the town in two had been nicknamed Rivière Caca. From sundown to sunrise people would come and empty the contents of their chamber pots into it. Its muddy waters would churn down to the sea its cargo of excrements. The cabins huddled together on the ledges of the Saint François district and stacked up the hills of the Carmel neighborhood. Only ships carrying packaging materials for the banana plantations docked in the harbor. Today Basse-Terre was one of the most up-to-date cities in the Caribbean. Like the rest of Guadeloupe it was modernizing. Had she driven over the Route de la Traversée, which cuts straight through the mountains?

So she was looking for her family? (He laughed.) For her identity? (He laughed even louder.) Identity is not like some piece of
clothing that is lost and found and then slipped on hoping it will
fit. Whatever she did she would never ever be a true
Guadeloupean. At that moment Judes Anozie, who up till then
had kept silent in his corner of the terrace, managed to get a word
in. What did that mean, being a true Guadeloupean? The question
irritated Aristide Démonico, who did not take the trouble to
answer. He merely turned his back on Judes Anozie in contempt.
And turned to face Marie-Noëlle. Pity, neither he nor Fiorella
could be of much use to her. As he had told her over the phone,
his wife was on a cruise with their youngest daughter. She was the
one who never tired of filling people's heads with the same old
questions without an answer. Nobody would believe him if he said
that this obsession of Fiorella's had in some way ruined their marriage. When he came to take her in his arms she murmured the
name of Reynalda. She had transformed their marriage bed into a
psychiatrist's couch, with fits of hysterics and tears thrown in as a
bonus. All her sentences began the same way: "When we were little we did this, when we were little we did that!" How many times
had he heard her rant on about her dead papa who, according to
her, was a sadist and a rapist, and about Nina, the wicked servant,
who, she said, surrendered her own daughter to him! It was quite
easy to see why. She hated them because they slept together and
betrayed her beloved maman, Arcania, bedridden on the second
floor. A common case of filial jealousy. And Judge Démonico, who
took the matter so seriously! Who made inquiries about Gian
Carlo, a craftsman the likes of whom you no longer find nowadays!
Who got it into his head to start an investigation whereas there
was not the slightest hint of evidence. Absolutely nothing. Except
for some teenager's tittle-tattle!

When Reynalda vanished, Fiorella moved heaven and earth to

find her. One year the rumor went around that she was living in Dominica, shacked up with some English niggerman. Fiorella had immediately set off for Roseau. She took advantage of the trip to spend weeks away from her duties as spouse and Maman to the point that people began to gossip. Another year someone maintained they saw her behind a market stall in Fort de France. Off went Fiorella by boat to Martinique. But she never could find a trace of her beloved friend. At any moment she expected to see her name loom up in neon lights as an opera singer. Nothing of the sort ever happened. If Reynalda had been someone with feelings, don't you think we would have heard from her? When Fiorella gets back at the end of the summer and finds out that Reynalda is living in the center of Paris and her daughter came in person to look her up in Basse Terre, she'll have a fit. How much longer was Marie-Noëlle staying in Guadeloupe?

As he went on talking, Marie-Noëlle felt her heart gradually sink with sadness. She felt her back to the wall. The main characters in this drama were dead. Fiorella was out of reach. If she wanted to know her geography and map her identity, there was no other choice but to confront her grandmother.

This grandmother whom she could not make up her mind whether she was angel or devil, the wicked fairy casting evil spells or water-mama handing out bounteous gifts.

$$\mathscr{C}hapter\ 5$$

At the tip of the ocean's rim lies this barren rock. A land dispossessed, a land at the world's edge. A land of exile. Once a penal colony. Once a lazaretto. It is said that the king's subjects banished into exile from the port of Rochefort wept in despair on disembarking and pacing the cramped conditions of their prison. Several of them escaped the watchful eye of their guardians and threw themselves headfirst from the top of the cliffs overhanging the sea. Others went raving mad and, foaming at the mouth like rabid animals, they died after a few hours. The grave-yard by the sea at Grande-Anse houses these humble tombs, curiously engraved with names too lavish for their surroundings. As the catamaran drew closer to the coast, however, these bad memories faded. On the contrary, it seemed that the arid island became tinged with color under the sun and began to smile. It peeped out from under the water to spy on the newcomer and greet her with a reproach reserved for an ungrateful relative: "At long last! I've been expecting you for so long." Blinded by all the blue around her, Marie-Noëlle was oblivious to all that. Her heart grew heavy as she watched the inhospitable island, where her race had taken root, grow gradually clearer against the horizon. Up until the very last minute she had hesitated. Now she felt like turning back and retracing her steps as fast as she could toward Saint François, which she could still see, if she turned her head, sprawling in the distance on Grande-Terre. As if he had guessed what she was feeling Judes Anozie grabbed her by the arm and made her stand up. Once the ship had docked and was moored, amid a great commotion of pointless shouting and yelling, she resigned herself to following the other passengers. The hawkers selling shoddy trinkets on the wharf, the crowd of jobless and idlers of all sorts, inspected them out of curiosity. Though the couple was holding hands, people were not mistaken. Too absorbed in her own thoughts she was, and, what's more, showed no interest in him. People sensed those two were neither lovers nor tourists like the rest, earnest and naive, already flashing their cameras. Their trip was motivated by some special, more secret personal reason. They were not searching for what was left of an island where everything had been ransacked and auctioned off. What could they be looking for? A small procession formed and escorted them from a distance across the Square of the Begging Monk, just to see where they were going.

All Guadeloupeans are related to one another. First of all, most of them came out of the belly of the same slave ship, ejected at the same moment on the same auction block. Second, on the plantations, relationships formed between the newcomers and the others that were promiscuous and incestuous. Judes had no trouble finding a cousin, another Anozie, first name Cyrille, general practitioner and would-be politician who one day hoped to lay hands on the town hall. Cyrille scolded Judes for not visiting them more often. Things were not like they used to be. You could take the plane between La Pointe and Grande Anse. And provided you were a good sailor there was a boat service twice a day. Cyrille also discussed and debated with Marie-Noëlle the United States, which he had visited on several occasions. Nevertheless, a man of his times, he did not bother with old-fashioned preliminaries of politeness and fairly quickly got straight to the point. Like everyone on La Désirade he knew Antonine Titane, known as Nina. Who didn't? She lived up on the "Mountain." Once a month, after drawing her pension, she came down to do her shopping in the supermarket at Grande Anse. No big deal! Some saltfish, a few packets of lentils, red beans, and split peas. Sometimes, when she agreed to it, he treated her sciatica and emphysema. What had gone on in the past was past. Of course she had a reputation lingering about her like a bad smell. The children were scared of her and nicknamed her Old Hag. Some people whispered around the somber story of her daughter. Vanished, out of the blue, one fine morning. But it no longer bothered anyone, and people rather pitied her living alone in her cabin, her sole companion being a yellow-headed Creole dog. During the last hurricane she had refused to go down to the municipal shelters and had spent the night battling with the wrath of the heavens. Knowing her to be a bit peculiar, suspicious, and cantankerous, Cyrille had not informed her that someone wanted to see her. It was better to catch her off guard.

What they call the "Mountain" on La Désirade is not a real mountain, despite its name. It is merely a high plateau running down the center. On one side cliffs drop sheer to the sea buffeted by the waves. On the other, it gently rolls down to a plain running along the seashore, shaded by coconut palms. The "Mountain" has its own story. Long ago it was a place of refuge for those who were frightened of contagion from the lepers herded into their straw cabins at Baie Mahault. Our historians tell us too that a colony of maroons, slipping out under the cover of night from Grippière Grippon, set up camp there, convinced that nobody would come looking for them in their hideaway at the end of the world. Fatal mistake. The troops, hot on their trail, caught up with them and hacked them to pieces. These runaway slaves sleep in no grave-yard, and you would have a hard job finding their tombs.

Cyrille's 4 x 4 left Grande-Anse, which gave itself the airs of a capital, and bounded along the road running beside the seashore. Rows of identical little concrete houses, painted the same color, proudly replaced the hovels of yesteryear, thanks to the munici-pality. Then he changed direction, roared up a series of hillocks wooded with mango trees and pink cedars, and landed on a flat ledge that looked as if it had been balanced above the ocean. Here all was desolation. You could hear the commotion of the waves breaking below, mingled with the roar of the wind and the cries of the seagulls. Parcels of stony ground were staked out with hedges to keep out oxen. Gone were the houses with their show of wash-ing hung out to dry and children playing ball. Alone under an ashen gray *mapoo* stood a cabin. Blackened and shapeless, capped by a patched roof that sat somewhat askew. A hedge of yellow cro-tons marked out a perimeter of limestone rocks where a few cassava and dasheen plants struggled to survive. Three sheep tied to stakes were making heartrending bleats while a Creole dog barked furiously in front of the door. With a start Marie-Noëlle recognized the cabin of her dream. Yes, this was the cabin she had seen night after night. It was the same one. Nothing was missing. Only the gentle glow of the moon bathing it in unreality. As in her dream, her legs refused to carry her. She almost collapsed, and once again Judes Anozie had to hold her up by the arm. She clung to him. Following in Cyrille's footsteps they approached the cabin despite the dog's furious barking and its wide-open jaws. Cyrille repeated apologetically that Nina did not always get along with visitors and knocked on the door. After a while, a very long while, it seemed, the door opened with a creaking of hinges that rent the air like an alarm. A woman, barefoot, bareheaded, dressed in a somewhat worn, shapeless shift, appeared on the doorstep and gazed at them sullenly. Marie-Noëlle had imagined her to be very much like Reynalda. Small. All skin and bones.

But Nina was standing erect, despite her sciatica and aches and pains, and was tall, very tall. Buxom. You could make out the shape of her heavy breasts as they drooped almost down to her belly. Her arms and shoulders were plump. Despite her age and deprivation her striking face maintained its arrogant features. No doubt about it, in her time Nina must have been a handsome woman. A real force of nature. Recognizing Cyrille she forced a smile that revealed a gleaming set of strong white teeth. Then she stepped aside to let everyone in. Compared to the glare outside, the interior was pitch dark. But the stink grabbed you by the throat, like that of a pigpen. When her eyes grew used to the darkness Marie-Noëlle saw that all in all the cabin had but one room. Some old clothes had been thrown on the floor in a corner. Four uninviting chairs danced around in the four corners. The remains of a meal lingered on a table, and in what could be called the kitchenette some aluminum stewpots and billycans were hung over the sink. There was no electricity, and a hurricane lamp was placed squarely on the table next to a box of matches. Nina narrowed her big eyes, turned blue by cataracts and gazed at her visitors. The expression on her face left no doubt as to what she was thinking: What were these people after? She hadn't asked anybody for anything. What were they snooping around for on her floor? Her gaze settled first of all on the two men. Then on Marie-Noëlle. Once there, it seemed to Marie-Noëlle it stubbornly and persistently hung on, drilled into her, and would not let go. Marie-Noëlle, who had prepared her explanations beforehand in a series of well-turned sentences, completely lost her footing. All the words flew away, drifting mockingly around her in a dance, and she heard herself blurt out with a groan: "I'm the daughter of Reynalda and . . . and Gian Carlo."

She stammered. Her voice trembled like a child's. And yet she felt a wave of confidence well up inside her. It was the first time she had stated her lineage, that she had openly named the name of those who had begotten her. And it was as if at last she had taken possession of herself and made her mark on this earth.

Nina's reaction was not what she expected: embarrassment, contrition, anger. Nina began by staring at her as if she was not sure her ears had heard right. Then she threw back her head and burst into laughter. A never-ending laughter. A laughter that stretched her lips, revealed the very back of her throat and the purplish viper of her tongue. A laughter that in one blow wiped out Marie-Noëlle's convictions and hurled her back to that realm of uncertainty and anguish she thought she had left forever.

Nina's Tale

I don't know what she must have told you. All that non-sense she invented with Fiorella, I bet. That I forced her. That the first time I even held her hands. She probably said she was scared and I threatened her. And what else? She's always been like that: a liar, such a liar, wrapped up in herself and artful. Bringing such a daughter into this world has been a calamity. And for you, it's been a calamity having her as a maman. And now she's in Paris, you say? With a husband and two children living a life of ease the way she always wanted? Good luck to her! I've no need for her: I haven't got much longer to wait on this earth. At night I can hear Death sharpening her long knives. For me, I started life the way it must have been during slavery. Maman grew cotton for the "Société" that had just begun two plantation factories. Everyone on Désirade had gone into cotton because people were fed up with working themselves to the bone over corn, cassava, and beans that brought in scarcely enough to survive. You were lucky if you had a banana tree, however miserable and puny, beside your cabin, or if you could feed a goat. I'm talking about a time long ago, way before the hurricane of 1928. The "Société" no longer exists today. If you go over to Baie-Mahault you'll see the

166

remains of some walls hidden under the creepers. You'll also see what they called the tractor road. A rough track that goes from the beach at Souffleur right up to the "Mountain." The tractors threw out great dollops of fuel, and the flames caught light among the prickly pear and Turk's head cactus that overran everything everywhere. I was a baby breast-feeding when maman took me into the cotton fields. I slept beside her in a basket. She made me work as soon as I could stand on my own two feet. I learned to pick the cotton bolls, the ones that didn't have the pink weevils, even before I knew how to talk. All day long under the sun I filled the forty-pound bags that the men loaded on their backs like beasts of burden and carried to the cotton gin. In the evening we were so worn out we couldn't swallow a thing.

It's my granny I take after. Her name was Désilia Titane. People still talk about her on Désirade. It was said that if she stayed with a man she put him at death's door, so demanding she was she couldn't get enough. So the men were scared of her. They came, did their business in a rush, then left. So she never really knew who was the father of her six children. My maman, Thracie, was the youngest. Since she was red-skinned it was rumored her papa was one of the priests in Baie-Mahault for whom granny worked, because she had always refused to work in the cotton fields. She was a great dancer. They used to come and fetch her to go to the *léwoz* dances, the *léwoz* dances with caller. In fact it was at a *léwoz* dance with caller that she died. She was doing a complicated step when plop! she fell and never got up. Maman, she was quite different. Always miserable. I think it was because of papa. He was a fisherman. One October he'd gone fishing as usual on the sandbanks over by Petite-Terre, because October's the month when the migrating fish pass through. At that time of the year the dragnets are bulging, and everyone has something to get their teeth into. A bad squall caught him off guard out at sea, and his boat overturned.

The time it took for the other boats to rush over and try and help him, he was already under 150 fathoms of water. Maman was left with me starting to kick in her belly. At that time there was no Social Security. No family and unemployment allowances, no old-age pension, all those benefits you have nowadays. And then Maman wasn't married. She was entitled to nothing, and me neither. So her only refuge was cotton, cotton, and cotton. I don't think Papa would have put up with seeing Maman lose her youth the way she did. But where he was he had no say in the matter.

When I think about it those years weren't the worst, despite the work and the hunger. I had Granny. In flesh and blood beside me. Granny was not very talkative, but always had a candy for me hidden in her bodice—*topi tamboos*, pink-topped sugar cakes, and pistachio nougat. As I said, the poverty got worse after the hurricane of 1928. The hurricane destroyed everything it could destroy. It flattened everything it could flatten. Nothing remained standing. After that the "Société" decided to move to Saint François, and on Désirade the cotton plantations died a natural death.

Like Maman. She didn't last long on this earth after Granny died.

She too left me. She passed away one November evening when the great winds were roaring and battling furiously. Amid the commotion we didn't even hear her tiny voice saying farewell to the earth. One of her older sisters, Tertullie, took me in with her bevy of children, and I left the neighborhood of the Galets where I had lived with Maman. My aunt had only boys, seven in all, not one the same, each with a different papa, as was usual at the time. The eldest, her favorite because he was so tiny, had almost died from convulsions and was first-named Gabin. He was the only one who counted in her eyes. The others were nothing. And I was less than nothing. My aunt had a good job. The priests at Baie-Mahault had found her work with the Dominican nuns who took care of the lepers. She was housed inside what was known as the "camp" in one of the concrete pavilions that had replaced the old straw cabins. Despite its name of leper colony that put the fear into everyone, it was a pretty spot. The people in the camp were the only ones to have electricity and running water. All the other women on Désirade heaved buckets of water on their heads from the Cybèle gully. The pavilions had been built around a chapel with stained-glass windows painted in all the colors of the rainbow. Every morning Father Steiner from Alsace said mass. He was very kind to me, was Father Steiner. Sometimes, during the siesta hours, he had me come into his room and kissed me in a way Granny and Maman had never kissed me before. I found it strange, but I didn't say anything. I didn't like his smell, I can't say why. At the camp, everyone was nice to me. The doctors, the nurses, all from metropolitan France, like the nuns and the priest, gave me their canvas shoes to whiten, and as a reward I received brand new little coins. Apart from that we had no contact with the patients in the camp, whites or blacks, who had their own school, cinema, and soccer ground. All day long my cousins messed around, fighting, hunting birds, aiming at anoli lizards with their catapults and pilfering everything they could lay hands on. I was a girl and worked like a slave. I helped my aunt wash and iron the laundry from the camp—sheets, pillowcases, towels, doctors' and nurses' overalls, nuns' things—that we left to soak two or three days in bleach to disinfect them. I didn't have a minute to myself. That's why I never went to school, why I can't read or write, not even sign my name. Sometimes I pick up a newspaper. I look at it and tell myself how different my life would have been if I had been able to decipher it. If that had been the case I think I would have understood the world, its meaning and mystery, and my life would have been sweeter.

The problem was that the folk in Baie-Mahault next to the

leper colony were jealous of us. Because we had our bellies full and were always nice and clean. They also pretended to be afraid of us as if we were lepers as well. We who'd never had a single person sick in the family. Granny died dancing. Poor Maman passed away before her time because of all the grief she'd piled up in her heart. I must say all the snubs from the folk in Baie-Mahault had as much effect on us as water on dasheen leaves. In fact, what was there to regret in the company of folk as black as we were, who could not even speak French, who were even more wretched and deprived? They had absolutely nothing to offer us. That's what my aunt repeated, and on that point she was right.

When I was fourteen, the age when I started stuffing cotton between my legs, my aunt sat me down in front of her. She told me I was never, oh never, to let a niggerman mount me and give me a child of his misery. Better it be a white man, a mulatto, even a coolie. Niggermen, according to her, were responsible for all the misfortunes of women, all the misfortune in this world. They were hurricanes and earthquakes. I was somewhat embarrassd by her words because I couldn't tell her that her own son, Gabin, was desperate to lay hands on me. However much I threatened him he continued just the same. He spied on me everywhere I went and followed me whispering all sorts of nonsense: "Darling *doudou*, sweetie-pie, give it to me, please." I suppose he was even more desperate since no self-respecting woman would have him. At the age of seventeen Gabin did not look older than ten. Probably because of the convulsions he had when he was little, he had stopped growing and filling out. He was a real little shrimp. His face resembled a cockroach's. And he had yellow teeth and two slimy eyes like a toad. As for my aunt, she didn't see him in that light at all. She listened to him like God the Father listened to His beloved Son, Our Lord Jesus Christ. Whatever he did was above reproach. Whatever he said was gospel truth. Through constantly whining on his behalf to Father Steiner, my aunt got him accepted as apprentice to Monsieur Ernatus, a carpenter at La Pointe. He would learn a trade, and he was already boasting about it, treating his brothers like slaves.

I'll be brief about those moments that still give me goose pimples forty years later. Gabin finally had me.

One afternoon I had gone down to the river gully. I had to walk there even though it was a good distance from the camp. You wouldn't think you were on Désirade there were so many sorts of trees growing down by the cool of the water. Fruit trees, coconut and mango trees, breadfruit and orange trees. Trees from the forest too, pink cedars, *mapoos*, and silk cotton trees. Hearing the birds singing as they flew out of sight from branch to branch was like being in paradise. I lay down on the grass and dreamed I had already died and gone to Heaven with Granny and Maman, and had gone to join Papa. Gabin was hiding behind a tree and when he saw me, he just threw himself on me. He threatened me with a big stone he was holding.

I went back up to the camp crying and told my aunt what had happened. By way of consolation she gave me a mighty slap. Then she shoved me to the ground and kicked me in the ribs. Like a maniac she yelled that I was lying about her boy. Besides, who was going to believe such a story? Who was going to believe that a girl as tall and sturdy as myself, whom everyone took to be older than fourteen, had been manhandled by someone Gabin's size? How were they to know if, in fact, I hadn't asked for it, and if he hadn't given me what I was looking for?!

I don't know what he said when he returned to the camp. But nothing was ever mentioned, and he continued to thumb his nose at me. He did not have time to do it again because one week later, as proud as a peacock, Gabin left for this Monsieur Ernatus's in La Pointe. Weeping all the tears out of her body, my aunt went to see him off at Grande-Anse. Father Steiner had asked a fisherman to take him over because in those days there was no boat service, never mind a plane of course. Even so, there is some justice in this world of ours. A few months later Gabin died of an intestinal fever like the cur he was. Amid the stink of his diarrhea and vomit. When my belly began to show, my aunt showed me the door. She could not keep such a shameless hussy in the house. It was Father Steiner and the nuns who took pity on me. The nuns trotted out a little speech on the sins of the flesh. Without much conviction. Everyone in Guadeloupe committed that sin. I was not the first to have an illegitimate child, and I would not be the last. As for Father Steiner, he didn't say a word. I could see he was sorry for what he hadn't done. The nuns and Father Steiner found me a job as servant to the priests in the Parish of Grande-Anse. The priests wanted me to sleep at the presbytery to have me close to hand, I think. I refused. It was all by myself, despite my belly five months gone, that I built my cabin on the "Mountain." On the "Mountain" the land belongs to anyone. To anyone with two arms and two hands to wield a pick and a fork. It would take a clever man to come up with a deed of ownership. Even the white Creoles don't have one! I never told anybody I was pregnant by my cousin Gabin, I was too ashamed. Later when Reynalda asked me to name her father I invented any old story.

You don't carry a fetus nine months cramped in your belly without growing fond of it, without talking to it and promising it a better life, without imagining the face it will have. But when the nun placed Reynalda in my arms after the delivery she was so ugly, already the spitting image of Gabin, black-black like he was, with his protruding eyes, that all my good intentions immediately flew away. She squeaked like a rat and weighed no more. Born at term she looked like a premature baby. You cannot give orders to your heart. What's the use of lying? I have never loved that child, the only one ever to come out of my belly. I've never loved Reynalda, but I've never raised a hand to her either. Never given her a slap or the strap. I sent her to school, where, I must give her what's due, much to everyone's surprise, she worked hard. I gave her what I could to eat. She didn't have any shoes. Besides, nobody on Désirade had any. Except for the French French. But her clothes were always clean and nicely ironed to go to mass on Sundays.

I didn't love her, and, to be honest, she didn't love me either. Never a kind or considerate gesture that children make. Never an embrace. A smile. A gentle word. When she didn't have her head stuck in her books, she was busy with the birds she caught with glue and put in a cage. In the morning before she left for school I would see her talking to them, singing them songs, and sending them kisses. As for me, she looked at me like a horse that has thrown its rider and her staring, bottomless eyes, like those of a grown-up, snapped at me like a camera. I sensed the way she saw me in my old patched clothes, my bare feet, frighteningly ugly in my poverty, so ugly and so poor it was shameful.

When his grace the bishop of Guadeloupe, after his visit to Désirade, offered me that position in La Pointe, I didn't want it. It was mainly for her I accepted. I didn't expect anything ever again for me. At La Pointe she would at least have one thing I wasn't lucky enough to have, and that's an education.

I have to tell you that once Gabin had laid his hands on me he made me feel disgusted by men. Black men, I should rather say. It seemed to me that on that point too my aunt was merely telling the sad truth. Black men were creatures of hell. I can remember Gabin's smell, his grimaces and groans as he released his milk into my body and I felt like vomiting. Sometimes I was overcome with rage, and it seemed I was going mad. I felt that if a cutlass had been handy, I'd have rushed to La Pointe to hack him to pieces. So I brushed aside all those men—and there were quite a few—who hung around me. Young men, not so young, and really old geezers. Black men, red-skinned, and high-yellow. Day in and day out they waited for me as I came out of the presbytery. They waited for me on the road and walked behind me for miles. For ten years, I swear no man came into my bed or touched me.

It's probably for all those reasons I loved Gian Carlo the way I did. From the very beginning. On first sight. I became his slave like the women in the Great Houses a long time ago. People said I was his creature. They were right. If he'd ordered me to descend into hell for him I would certainly have gone. Gian Carlo was white. He was handsome with his blue eyes, his beard, and curly hair, like silk between my hands. He was the living image of a priest, a saint in a stained-glass window or the Good Lord himself. I know full well that he himself never loved me. It was for the pleasure he was deprived of. His wife had been laid up sick for years, and he didn't want to waste his money on the ladies walking the Morne à Cayes. He used to laugh that he had too much trouble earning his money to throw it out the window. And then, can you love a servant? Who, ass up, scrubs and scours the floor. Who washes the dirty laundry. Who does the shopping, the cooking, and the washing up. Gian Carlo was a miser, that was his main failing. According to him, it was because he had been deprived of everything in his young days, and every morning the Good Lord made I had to fight with him over the household expenses. What's more he was dying to be loved, dying to be admired. He never wanted to face reality, the unpleasant things, and to please everyone at the same time he put himself in terrible situations and ended up hurting everybody. At the age of twenty he married two women in the same week who were both pregnant, because he hadn't been able to say no to either one. And for that he was jailed.

Yet he would never have deliberately hurt anyone. Even less a child. All those stories Reynalda and Fiorella made up were pure invention. There is no truth to them. The only truth is this.

I slept in the attic. My cot was separated from Reynalda's by a curtain and she could hear us. Especially as Gian Carlo didn't make the slightest effort to control himself. He couldn't have cared less about Reynalda, and said that at night an innocent girl had nothing better to do than sleep. Innocent is precisely what she wasn't. I saw in her eyes as murky as pond water that she spied on us and listened to us and I was afraid of only one thing: that she'd get together with Fiorella and repeat everything to Madame Arcania, which in my opinion would have finished her off.

Deep down Fiorella was a pest, a real slut. Her papa had had to forbid her set foot inside the Lago di Como because she would shamelessly make eyes at the men under their wives' noses. Outwardly you would have given her the world, she looked so innocent. She seemed to be the loveliest and most angelic of little girls. Every year at school the nuns chose her to crown the Holy Virgin on the August 15 Saint's Day. She was the complete opposite of her close friend Reynalda. From our very first day at La Pointe, Fiorella and Reynalda became inseparable. It seemed so strange. One black, the other white. One as ugly as sin, the other like one of God's children. The truth was that they were both little hussies, both of them. Always whispering in every corner of the house. Giggling. Insolently staring at people in the whites of their eyes. They shared a diary where they wrote down all sorts of nonsense, dirty and wicked things. Sometimes Reynalda left it lying around in the room on purpose to nettle me, since I couldn't read. It was her way of thumbing her nose at me. As if she were saying: "Guess, guess what I'm saying about you." Fiorella could not bear me. It's not because she loved her maman so much as because she loved her papa, who couldn't have cared less about her. No less than the other children. If she could have killed me, she would have killed me there and then. I could see what she was thinking in her eyes because she never addressed me directly unless she was ordering me around like a dog. "Nina, my panties are dirty, do you hear? Wash them." "Nina, I've been sick. Clean it up." Gian Carlo, who never took anything seriously, repeated that even if she did tell everything to her maman it would not matter one bit. Madame Arcania worshiped her husband like the Holy Sacrament, and consequently she forgave him everything. She had always forgiven him everything. He was absolutely sure of it. Madame Arcania was not born yesterday. She knew what was going on between us and didn't care a damn. Even when they were young, even before her illness, she had never been very interested in sex. He had to force her.

Even so, I was scared. I was scared of everyone. As soon as someone was in the room with Madame Arcania, I imagined them telling her about it. I had everything to fear from the "two madams," as Gian Carlo called them, Aunt Zita and Aunt Lia. They couldn't bear me either. Naturally they were jealous, never having known a man. Imagine two old maids gone to seed who had only the name of the Good Lord on their lips, but in their heads dying to taste the succulent flavor of sin. They went to mass at dawn, at four o'clock every morning. They took Communion, and when they came back from the altar you'd think they were going to swoon they were so enraptured. By introducing them into his jeweler's shop Gian Carlo had calculated they would attract men, find husbands, and thus provide him with extra hands to help him in the business. Unfortunately no man came up to their expectations. They were offended every time a black man looked at them. Even a mulatto. As for the white Creoles, they didn't want them either because they thought themselves far whiter. Even the white Creoles, they said, had black blood in them since the days of slavery, and there was no way they were going to soil their sheets with them. Only the metropolitan French priests from the Parish of

Saint-Pierre-and-Saint-Paul found grace in their eyes. And in particular Father Mondicelli, a real miscreant, that one. He began
frequenting the house to comfort Madame Arcania in religion during the trial of her long illness. He came and went with his prayer
book under his arm. And then, I don't know how, he was all over
the place. You would find him there at any time of day. He was
confessing everybody, even Zora, even Donatella, who could hardly speak, and on Sundays he lunched with us, eating and drinking
enough for four. You should have seen those females all over him.
"Father this, Father that . . . " One of them would fill his glass,
another would fill his plate. They coddled him like a turkeycock.
Around five o'clock he regularly sat down at the piano, and the
family sang. He never failed to compliment Reynalda in particular
on her voice, and the poor wretch went into seventh heaven. It
wasn't often someone said something nice to her. He repeated over
and over again her voice was a gift from the Good Lord and she
should put it to good use in the future. As for me, he never stopped
looking at me. When I served him at table I could see full well he
was shaking. He was like Father Steiner. He was dying to get his
hands on me, but he didn't dare. Besides, I'd never have allowed
it. When Aunt Zita and Aunt Lia sat with Madame Arcania it was
to tell her all the gossip and tittle-tattle about La Pointe, all the
muckraking about people she didn't even know. Their tongues
never dried up. Madame Arcania pretended to be interested. But
you could see full well these stories bored her to death and, what's
more, tired her out. Her cheeks turned as red as shiny red apples,
and her eyes fell shut. I would hurl myself into the room like a hurricane and chase everyone out. Off with you! Out you go!

I was ashamed of what I was doing with Gian Carlo. Even so,
every night I did it again. I couldn't help it. However much I
repeated to myself Gian Carlo's words that she knew about it and
didn't care, it was no comfort to me. I was ashamed of myself, so

ashamed. For strange as it may seem, Madame Arcania loved me. I can say she was the only person in the house who loved me, simply because she loved everyone. There was room only for goodness in her heart. She loved me, me whom nobody loved, not even my own child. When I had finished washing her, perfuming her, and dressing her I'd lay her down on her bed. Then she would kiss me to thank me for looking after her so well and say: "Poor Nina, your life is like a bed of nettles. But don't think it's because of your color. Look at me. Look at Zita and Lia. We're white and suffering martyrdom. For all us women it's nothing but mourning and servitude when we don't have an education to liberate us. That's what I say to my poor children. Promise me you'll look after them when I'm gone."

She worried a lot about leaving her children behind because she knew her husband only too well. Miserly, selfish, and lecherous. She was well aware her daughters did not interest Gian Carlo. His great regret was not having a son. He didn't hide it. He never stopped repeating it, and each time it broke Madame Arcania's heart. Despite her illness Madame Arcania could have gone on for a long time like this, taking the necessary precautions. "No worrying her head," recommended the doctor who treated her. She left us so suddenly because of all those wicked ideas they put into her head when Reynalda disappeared into the blue. First of all the police who came to investigate insisted it was my fault. I was said to have mistreated her, beaten her, me who all those years had never laid a hand on her. Then Fiorella's story, the one about rape, began to be spread around. How could she have invented such muck? I still can't understand. It proves she was a hussy at heart. So the police came back to question me. Funnily enough they didn't trouble Gian Carlo in his shop. Oh, no! It was me. Little me. The fences were down. I was ready to be trampled on. For hours they asked me all sorts of stupid things, and then they typed out my answers. They called me "the witness," as if they didn't know my name, and finished off their report in a tone of voice that didn't scare me because I had absolutely nothing on my conscience.

"Since the individual cannot read or write, the above deposition was read to her. . . . " And so on and so on.

✥

It went on for weeks. When we thought it was over, it started up again. Someone came snooping around right at lunchtime and upset us all with his questions. Folks in La Pointe are always ready to swallow some spiteful rumor. They whispered around that story of rape that had made Reynalda leave the house. Like the police, they thought I was guilty. When I passed them in the street, they hurled words at me. When I went to the market, the women refused to sell to me. Madame Arcania never mentioned the subject to me. She never mentioned the subject to her husband either. But I'm convinced she knew what everyone was saying, that I was an accomplice, that I had forced the child and held her hands so that Gian Carlo could do his business. Her mind suffered agony, and her body followed suit. One morning when I came to give her her coffee, she had passed on. As simply as I'm talking to you. I lowered the shutters to keep out the sun and sat down beside her bed, not even thinking of praying. I didn't cry because in some way I didn't feel any grief. What was going on around us was too ugly, too vile for her. I had always thought she was too good and too lovely for this world. She was going to the only place made for her, the Garden of Eden. As for Gian Carlo, he wept like a baby. He realized how much he worshiped her, how much she meant to him, and despite all my efforts I couldn't manage to console him. For several months there were just the two of us. Reynalda had disappeared God knows where. I didn't care. The wretched Fiorella had

left the house and gone to live in Basse-Terre. As for Father
Mondicelli, it had been some time since he had stopped visiting.
Gone were the confessions. Gone the Sunday lunches. Gone the
singing and musical concerts. The piano remained untouched. On
the rare visits he made he had no time for Aunt Zita or Aunt Lia.
All he did was run up the stairs, two at a time, and inquire about
Madame Arcania. Once she had gone, he disappeared completely.
It was quite by chance one day that I learned he had gone to work
with the lepers. Even so, despite the badmouthing and wicked gossip, those years now seem a time of bliss and happiness. I slept in
Gian Carlo's room on the second floor. I sprawled in his vast,
locustwood bed, the mosquito net stretching like a sky above my
head. Ah! It was as if love had another feel to it in that bed. From
one day to the next it seemed I had been bewitched, and from
slave and servant I had been turned into the mistress. Free to take
my pleasure. I was no longer Nina. I had no qualms shouting and
making all sorts of noises. I was a horse without bridle or halter gal-
loping for sheer joy. Alas! Gian Carlo decided to marry again, and
I went back up to my attic. Not for very long, mind you! To tell
the truth, I was not really jealous. I pitied her rather, Ana Livia
Carloccia. I knew why Gian Carlo was after her young blood. He
was trying to have what he never had with Madame Arcania. He
was trying to have his son. It was more than an obsession in his
head. That's all he ever thought about. A boy. His boy. An heir to
inherit his money, his trade, and his name. When I think about it,
Gian Carlo was no exception. At that time, very different from
today, girls didn't count at all in the family. The men, just like the
women, only wanted boys in the family. Gian Carlo had worked it
all out. He was going to give his son his father's name: Marcello.
He already saw himself playing soccer with him and, once he was
old enough, taking him to the whorehouse on the Morne à Cayes
so he wouldn't stroke himself with his hand and come down with

all sorts of diseases. Unfortunately the Good Lord, who sees things His way, didn't want him to have that satisfaction. Ana Livia died and her son with her. It dealt him a terrible blow.

And I believe it was at that very moment, when we were once more in mourning and affliction, that the police came snooping around again. A magistrate to whom Fiorella had told her filthy stories came down from Basse-Terre, and of course it was me again who was summoned to the police station. He was very determined, this one was. I can still see him: a poker-faced brown-skinned mulatto, who obviously thought the world of himself. Once he stood all morning long on the sidewalk opposite the jeweler's shop spying on us. I can even remember when he came in to stare under his nose at the poor wretched Gian Carlo, who was lost in thought over his little Marcello laid to rot under the earth. People have no heart. Even so, the magistrate couldn't uncover anything, nothing at all, because I hadn't done any harm and Gian Carlo either. Sometimes we asked ourselves what had happened to Reynalda. I was sure she was hiding somewhere, alive and well, doing something wicked. Gian Carlo, he was more sympathetic. He said that people around here are spiteful, and someone might have done something terrible to her. Grabbed hold of her as she came out of school. Beaten her to death. Thrown her body in the bottom of a gully.

The end of our sad story is even sadder. After he almost lost an eye, Gian Carlo, who was never very fond of rum—just a shot of wood-cured rum on Sundays with Father Mondicelli—took to drinking. When he'd drunk, it was terrible, he could remember nobody and nothing. He stared at me as if he'd never seen me before. All he did was weep tears and call out Madame Arcania's name. He talked about their young days in Milan. About the time when they hid their love from Paolo Renucci, the excessively jealous papa. When they fled to the outskirts of the city. When they crossed the Atlantic on one of the Compagnie Générale Transatlantique's steamships. When they arrived in La Pointe at the end of the war. He said he never should have believed the advertisements he'd seen in the newspaper and come and settled in Guadeloupe, an island of the damned. I can't help thinking he was disgusted with life partly because of all his misfortunes, partly because of all those vile stories his own child invented about him. So he deliberately set fire to his bed. That night I was in my attic and I didn't hear a thing. He left without a thought for me. For me or anybody else. He left me with only my two eyes to weep with. He left his children nothing but debts. No country house in Vernou, up where the aristocrats live. Not a parcel of land. Not a penny in the bank. In one day they auctioned off everything he possessed, and there was nothing left. Up until the day they left, the four daughters—Eudora, Maria Adélaïde, Zora, and Donatella—had to beg for charity from Luigi Carloccia, the papa of the deceased Ana Livia. They never stopped crying at the thought of all those graves lining up behind them: their maman, their papa, their aunts, and their sisters who died in childbirth or at an early age. Sometimes I wonder what happened to them over there in Italy. I never heard from them again. When they were little, I was the one who looked after them. At the time they would kiss me and be all over me with their hugs. As they grew up Fiorella and Reynalda poisoned their minds and set them against me. I don't bear a grudge against them, and I hope they're not unhappy wherever they are. They've already suffered enough.

You see I've come full circle. I've come back here, to the place where my life began. When Gian Carlo died I was thirty-five. Had all my teeth. Had all my youth. Even so, I never wanted another man. I would never have allowed another man, black, mulatto, Indian, white Creole, French-French, or whatever, to lay hands on me. God is my witness, ever since he's been laid to rest, no man has come into my bed. I warded off all those who came running after me, excited as dogs sniffing my scent. I no longer wanted to hire out my services either. To bow down: "Yes, madame, yes, sir." And submit to other people's orders and contempt. I came back here where I was born. Despite all my years away, my cabin remained standing in the same place. I had only to turn the key in the lock for the door to open on all the solitude that awaited me. Despite wishing otherwise, I'm still alive on this earth. Because, alas, you can't order Death around. You can't tell her: "For pity's sake! Now's the time, I'm so tired. Finish me off." Yet I'd love to go and join the few people who showed some feeling toward me. Granny and Maman. Gian Carlo? Oh no! He's no longer mine. I imagine him occupying his time in paradise asking forgiveness of Madame Arcania for what he did to her on this earth. He doesn't even remember I existed. Yet I can't get him out of my head. As old as you see me here, the waters from my body still stain my sheets at night when I recall all those wonderful moments we spent together. Sometimes I wake up thinking I'm going to find him asleep beside me, heavy as a log, and I'll have to shake him: *"Boss, jou rouvrè, lévé an kaban-là, time to get up."* I'm all alone, it's true. But I don't need anyone. No so-called friends. No visitors. Nobody comes up here to spy on me and badmouth me afterward behind my back. Every day the Good Lord makes I've enough to cook in my pot and fill my billycan because times have changed. They don't let people die of hunger anymore. Public welfare takes good care of me though I never asked them. Every month they send me a money order, and you'll never believe me, but I've more money today than during all my wretched existence when Gian Carlo forgot to give me my month's wages and I didn't know how I was going to pay for Reynalda's sandals and school clothes.

You look disappointed, all upset. It wasn't this story you wanted to hear, was it? You dreamed of something else. You'd busied your head with a lot of other things and you came as far as here, crossed the ocean to find some justification to what you imagined. Unfortunately what I have to offer won't be music to your ears. I can only give you the truth. I can only tell you what happened. Gian Carlo was never your papa. Who was? Only Reynalda knows him and can tell you. Gian Carlo never laid hands on her. What would he have done with such a child who had nothing up front and nothing behind, as flat as a breadboard? He was too fond of handsome women. He was too fond of the buxom kind. Like me. Without boasting, I was quite something in my younger days. Blacks, mulattos, and whites would stop to look when I went by, even if I was barefoot, decked out in rags. But beauty's hot air, a useless thing—I understood that early on. Not only does it not go to market for you, but it makes men take advantage of you. Education is what you need, something I never had. Plus a good deal of luck. A little education, a little luck, and I'd have made Guadeloupe giddy. Alas! I was hounded by bad luck. If you want my advice, forget all of this and go back where you came from. To America. There's no place for you here. Popping up like an outsider. Here everyone knows the path he must tread from the cradle to the grave. Don't ask your maman for anything more, she's a first-rate liar. Leave her be with her fairy tales. In fact, don't ask anyone for anything more. You've got schooling. You've got education. You've got good health. Live your life.

What more do you need?

Chapter 6

⁂

"If you stayed here with me, you'd see, we'd make a great couple."

The timidly formulated offer grazed Marie-Noëlle's mind like an annoying fly on the face of a sleeper, and she was about to brush it off when she took hold of herself and attempted to find an answer. She blamed herself, for she should have realized what type of guy he was just from looking at him. A guy who cannot imagine that a woman spends a few nights in his arms quite simply out of sheer exhaustion and disillusionment. An old-fashioned, romantic sort of guy! She looked with renewed attention at the naked shape lying beside her. Nothing more than a handsome physique. Copper-colored. All muscles, since he swam every day to the isle off Le Gosier, there and back, he told her. Yet she felt nothing for him. Merely a vague sense of gratitude for the pleasure she had got, mingled with something that resembled pity. Although much older than her, of the two of them he was the more vulnerable, she reasoned. The one who had been dealt less of life's blows and was still expecting miracles. She sat up in bed, the sheet pulled up to her chin, and patiently set about explaining to him he was making a mistake. There would be no happiness with her. For the first time, she spoke to him about herself, her life in America, Stanley, and even Reynalda, who was perhaps the real reason why she couldn't point her life in the right direction. But she could sense that, instead of discouraging him, these explanations only spurred him on and confirmed his intentions to procure her this happiness which, she herself confessed, she had never known. He would, no doubt, start dreaming about her and after she had left, would develop a young man's crush.

Even so, she had to admit they had grown quite close. Once Cyrille had gone back down to Grande-Anse to be with his patients, the two of them had remained sitting on either side of the table listening to Nina's story. Darkness had settled in so thick around them that Nina had finally lit the oil lamp on the table. But the wick was badly trimmed. It gave off a sickly, yellowish flame that produced more smoke than light. Marie-Noëlle had never imagined that she would find herself liking Nina and feeling close to her as if two outcasts, needing love, had suddenly found each other again. But that is precisely what happened. All things considered, Nina had nothing fearsome about her. Behind her mask of unsociability you could sense how fragile she was, and you almost felt like taking pity on her. Slumped back against the wall, she spoke slowly, without looking at anyone, as if those who were listening were none of her business. As if it wasn't worth her while convincing her listeners or justifying herself. As if she were draining herself of this past, retched up from the very depths of her being for her own sake. When she had finished speaking Marie-Noëlle and Judes Anozie remained where they were, without stirring, for fear of breaking the spell. After a while Nina remembered she wasn't alone. She turned her head slightly and stared at Marie-Noëlle with a look that caught her by surprise. Did the gleam that sparkled in her eyes mean that she was sizing up this granddaughter who had loomed up in the night out of nowhere, and was overjoyed at their meeting? Unfortunately Marie-Noëlle could not return her attentions. For the time being she felt nothing. Merely an extreme tiredness, like a swimmer reaching her destination and realizing everything has been in vain, that everything has to be done all over again.

Until her dying day she would remember that day in November, the day before she left for Boston, when Reynalda had confided her calvary to her. After all these years she could still see every line on her face, deep in shadow. She could still hear her unmodulated voice, hoarse from what she had taken to be her suppressed sobs.

𝔇

"Down below, the house was fast asleep. Through the attic window I could hear the rum guzzlers coming out of the rum shop on the rue Barbès, quarrelling over a shot of rum as they fired off a litany of swear words.

"He always arrived at the same hour. Around eleven, eleven thirty, before spending the rest of the night with Maman, as if I were something extra or an appetizer before the main course. I could do nothing else but wait. Wait for that inevitable moment. Frozen with fear, shaking in my bed, I listened. He slowly staggered up the stairs, grousing as he stumbled, for he started drinking from the time José, the apprentice, lowered the shop's steel curtain, and at the end of the day his gait was far from steady. It was as if, helpless, I could hear a hurricane approaching that was about to plunder all my possessions, an ogre who was going to gobble me up, a *soukouyan* who was going to suck my blood. Maman, who had come upstairs long before him, after having washed down the kitchen tiles, cleared away the dining room, and laid the table with bowls and spoons for breakfast the next morning, was waiting for him on the landing. They embraced each other like animals. Then his ghostly white face under his thick mop of curly hair appeared through the cretonne curtain that divided our room in two. He smirked and then entered, asking in his strong Italian accent: "How are you, my little rabbit?" Maman came in behind him. She sat down next to me and watched. Sometimes she held my hand or my foot. When I cried she told me: "You have no idea what it would be like if a nigger did the same thing to you."

When it was over, they both left. After a while I quietly got up, without lighting the candle, without making a noise. They were so busy making their commotion they wouldn't have heard me anyway. They were too busy laughing and yelling. Maman squeaking like a rat or squealing like a hog having its throat slit. That's what I had to put up with night after night. On a night of bad weather when the rain danced on the zinc roof like a madwoman and the flashes of lightning jostled through the window, I prayed for a thunderbolt to strike the attic so that they'd die on the spot. Two pieces of wood burnt to a cinder. I went down the stairs and tiptoed along the landing on the second floor. All the bedroom doors were shut. I stopped in front of the door behind which Fiorella lay next to her little sisters. I knew she wasn't sleeping either, knowing how I suffered, but helpless to do anything. I felt alone, so alone, so forsaken, and I wondered what I had done to deserve such a punishment. On the first floor I managed with some difficulty to remove the wooden bar from one of the heavy dining room doors that creaked open in the darkness, and I crossed the yard to the washroom next to the kitchen. A faucet dripped above a small stone water tank. Oblivious to my cheeks streaming with tears, I filled the tank and slipped into the cold water that seared through my sex. I thought maybe I could cleanse myself a little and purify myself of what had just happened and what was going to happen the following night and the night after and for every night of my life until I died."

✧

Such a story could not have been invented. Such details are unimaginable. And yet one of the two women was calmly lying to her. Which one? Was it Reynalda? Was it Nina? She couldn't say, and therefore she would never know the answer to her question. Such a thought plunged her into despair. All at once she got up, still without speaking, and made her way to the door where the Creole dog lay asleep across the threshold. Just as she was about to step over it, an irrational impulse, as violent as a remorse, seized her. She turned round to face Nina, who was still sitting motionless in the same spot, still with the same expectant look, and walked back to place a kiss on her cheek. A lukewarm cheek. A cheek still firm under Marie-Noëlle's lips.

It was only once she got outside that she broke down and cried. She of all people, who had not cried for years. Not even when Terri, then Stanley, had left her. Not even standing over Ranélise's coffin.

Judes Anozie immediately took advantage of the situation to get intimate. He put his arm around her waist, and, whispering words of comfort that couldn't comfort her, he held her tight all the way back to Grande-Anse. The road down took forever. Sometimes a dirt path, sometimes a larger rough track, rutted with potholes, it wound through a landscape out of a science-fiction novel. A thorny undergrowth of cacti and agaves gave way in places to a kind of dry, spindly forest, where the patchy trees took on a menacing look. The first man on the moon could not have been more in awe of his surroundings. Up above, wedged on a cushion of ragged clouds, the moon gazed down in mockery, amused at the tangled affairs of humans. A strong wind was shifting the stars to the other edge of the sky, and to Marie-Noëlle, adrift in the middle of this desolate expanse, her feet stumbling over the rocks, it seemed as if she were living one of those childhood tales where a poor little orphan girl seeks in vain a refuge from the night, distress, and fear. At last they arrived in Grande-Anse. The town was plunged into darkness, except for the few lights shining behind the shutters and the flames from the street lamps standing on the sidewalks. All was darkness but not silence. The air was filled with all sorts of sounds. The croaking of toads sending up their prayers to unleash the heavens, the ticking of insects hidden in the tufts of grass, the barking of stray dogs, and, above all that, the rumbling of the ocean in anger, God knows why!

Quite naturally Judes entered the best room in the house, specially prepared for Marie-Noëlle and, on his own authority, set about making love to her.

⌘

"So you're leaving."

It was not a question. It was a statement of regret. While Randy and Kevin played noisily in a corner of the room, Claire-Alta was leaning over Marie-Noëlle's blouses and jeans and carefully folding them. The day before she had washed and ironed them, piece by piece, before laying them out on the bed as if she wanted everyone to see their very meagerness. She folded them; then with the same meticulous care she laid them in the case. Her expressionless face endeavored to hide what she was feeling, and yet you could guess from her stubbornly lowered eyelids, from the tight sliver of her mouth, the words of reproach that remained unspoken. At this point, knowing it would be a waste of time, Marie-Noëlle made no attempt to explain. She merely stammered in a voice that she would come back, trying to make it sound convincing. When? Soon. Very soon. During her next vacation, if possible. Perhaps she would now become one of those homesick vacationers who return year after year to the land of their childhood, seeking in vain the tree where their placenta is buried. Claire-Alta did not contradict her. Nevertheless she made a face that betrayed what she thought about these well-meaning lies and went on folding and packing the clothes methodically. Suddenly it seemed as though she had lost all her strength. She slumped onto the bed and, holding her head in both hands, began to cry. Why was she crying? Quite simply, because she was one of those normal people who cry at farewells and funerals, who laugh for joy at engagement and wedding ceremonies and clap their hands at christenings. Marie-Noëlle, a little ashamed at being somewhat unfeeling, went over to her and clasped her hand to comfort her. Claire-Alta sobbed against her for a long while, then finally said between two gulps: "I've been turning all this over and over again in my mind, and I can remember a story about your maman. I don't know whether it means anything."

Reynalda?

One evening Reynalda wrote a letter to someone. It happened after they had washed up the dinner things, swabbed down the kitchen, and scrubbed and scoured the pans they proudly hung in a neat row against the wall. Reynalda sat down on her bed, and under the glow of the Butagaz lamp, she feverishly scribbled on some sheets of paper she had torn out of Claire-Alta's school exercise books. When she had finished, after hours of writing page after page, tearing them up, and starting all over again, she read them over, sobbing noisily. Yet when Claire-Alta had gone over to try and console her, she had pushed her away, almost shoved her, as if she were afraid Claire-Alta would see what she had just written. The next morning she mailed the letter herself, going out of her way to the post office, which at that time was not far from the Saint-Jules Hospice. Then she set about waiting for the postman. As a rule Monsieur Démosthène never stopped to deliver mail at Ranélise's. Sometimes, when she saw him go by, sweating in the heat of the day—for at that time mailmen wore a pith helmet as their only protection against the sun; went on foot, shouldering a heavy bag filled with all sorts of carefully sorted letters; and did not lounge in yellow vans like Moïse the mailman does today, honking his horn to get people to come out of their houses for a registered letter—Ranélise would invite him in for a tall glass of cool water. He would empty the entire water pot, and Claire-Alta recalled the jerky motion of his Adam's apple all the way down his throat. After a few days—eight, seven, maybe less—Reynalda received an answer to her letter. It was a Wednesday. For Claire-Alta it was the best day of the week because there was no school, and Reynalda had the day off from Tribord Bâbord. After Ranélise and Gérardo Polius left, the two girls had the house all to themselves. For once they could go back and laze around in bed, drink their hot chocolate in their nightdresses, play at tic-tac-toe, and listen to the radio. And not wear themselves out cleaning the entire house from early morning and hunting down the dust, which took a perverted delight at hiding in the most unlikely nooks and crannies. Claire-Alta couldn't believe her ears when Monsieur Démosthène rapped on the door brandishing an ordinary brown paper envelope, not an airmail letter edged in red, white, and blue, and shouted:

"*An let ba sésé-aw!* A letter for your sister!"

Reynalda, who was in the other room, tiptoed over with her seven-month belly, like a quaking child afraid of being scolded by her mother. Then she grabbed the letter and whisked it off into the bedroom. She remained there such a long time that Claire-Alta became worried and, sticking her ear to the wooden door, softly called to her friend. Finally Reynalda opened the door, her eyes bright and dry, fully dressed. She hurriedly went out without saying where she was going and disappeared for the whole afternoon without further explanation.

ᗞ

Feeling weak around the knees, Marie-Noëlle sat down on the bed beside Claire-Alta. But Claire-Alta knew nothing more and, plied with questions, could not really add anything new to her story. She had only seen Reynalda write a letter once. After that she had never gone out without saying where she was going. It was true that from then on she appeared even more desperate and withdrawn. Immediately Marie-Noëlle began to torture herself, trying to guess to whom Reynalda had written this mysterious letter. It couldn't have been Fiorella, since she had moved heaven and earth in vain to try and find her. Maman Arcania? Aunt Lia? Aunt Zita? They would immediately have informed the police who would have visited the neighborhood. No, no, no! She must have written to Gian Carlo, a last-ditch attempt aimed at the father of the child she was carrying. But Gian Carlo had carefully avoided coming to her aid. At the most he had handed over a little money—not much, a few banknotes, given his legendary miserliness—to buy her silence. That idea of leaving for metropolitan France, of inquiring about a job from the BUMIDOM, was his idea. His and nobody else's. It could not have germinated all by itself in the brain of an innocent young fifteen-year-old. Had Gian Carlo confided in his accomplice, his Nina? Probably, and she must have been having a good laugh deep down when she swore to the gods she had no idea what had become of her daughter. Yet when that old face, so wrinkled, so ravaged beneath that attitude of hers, flashed in front of her eyes; when that old, languid voice, grating under the influence of Creole, echoed back to her, Marie-Noëlle found it hard to doubt her grandmother's sincerity. Her intuition whispered to her that Nina was telling the truth. Then she doubted the intuition and cast it aside, since it was motivated solely by the resentment she would always have for Reynalda.

Part Three

Chapter 1

When she closed her eyes, all she could see was white, a white glare, as if the sun were still dazzling her, as if she was unable to forget it, unable to tolerate its ferociousness as it devoured everything in its path—the flowers, the shrubs, the tar on the roads, the humpback bridges over the rivers, the hills, the mountains, and the immensity of the sea itself—leaving only this extremely monotonous, blinding blaze of light. She often got the impression she had dreamed it all: Claire-Alta's insipid, daily conversation; the futile search for a father; Aristide Démonico's complacency; Granny's rambling chatter; Nina's story, and making love to Judes Anozie on the mattress on the floor, near the open window in his tiny apartment on the seventh floor of the Glycines housing project in Les Abymes. Back in Roxbury, what she had just lived through in Guadeloupe lost all sense of reality. Running over the hardened snow to catch the bus, sinking into the gaping jaws of the subway, she would suddenly have a vision of that crossing to La Désirade at the end of her stay. The deep blue of the sea, the catamaran dancing on the crest of the waves, and behind her back, the sculptured stones of the Pointe des Châteaux, and everything seemed totally surrealistic. With the precision of a bad dream

197

she could still see the faded beauty of Nina's face in her poverty-stricken surroundings like the remains of an imposing monument fallen into neglect. Or else she would be halfheartedly chewing on a snack lunch and the spicy aroma of a curried goat out of the Arabian Nights, would fill her nostrils. And yet she refused to boil down what had essentially been a painful ghost hunt into a simple tale of an exotic journey. In one of her letters to Ludovic she had tried to explain what her return home to her native island had meant. He had replied with one of those deliberately mollifying and moralizing epistles—which he was so good at—in which he urged her to forget about all these old stories and get on with her life. Who could she go and talk to? Anthea had no interest whatsoever in the islands of the Caribbean, least of all the French-speaking Antilles, which, to her knowledge, had produced no women's slave narratives in the nineteenth century. And moreover, she was hard at work on her life's labor, editing and annotating previously unpublished material by Phillis Wheatley. There was of course Molara and the curiosity of a ten-year-old. Or the students at Roxbury College and their hardly less childish questions. For all of them Guadeloupe was like California but a thousand times better. A paradise where the word "blizzard" was not part of the vocabulary, where the flowers were like their celluloid and paper counterparts that did not shed their petals, where the trees were decked with leaves and fruit in every season, and the beaches of gold dust were fringed with waves higher than skyscrapers. Marie-Noëlle didn't have the heart to tell them they were wrong. To tell them that in fact it was a tiny volcanic bone stuck in the throat of the ocean, to which clung a handful of valiant, hardworking men and women, determined to survive at all costs. Although it's true the poor wretches were beginning to lose faith, about to give up and leave en masse to go and get lost elsewhere. Those who in the face of adversity were determined to stay put, on the island where their parents and their parents' parents had sweated before them, were fed up with working against the odds. They sensed full well that however hard they clung to their *gwoka* drums, their quadrilles with caller, *kréyol*, and quotas of bananas and white rum, they were done for. They would not survive the third millennium. Fortunately, thanks to Judes Anozie and his literary tastes, she had discovered some local authors, novelists, and poets. She included them in her French literature classes, which she renamed Francophone, and thereby handed over to them the job of constructing a mythology that suited everyone.

$$\mathcal{D}$$

After those few weeks in Guadeloupe, she was sort of pleased to get back to her usual habits, like discovering again an old, shapeless dress you are used to wearing. Unfortunately, great changes were on the way. She was going to leave the college at Roxbury, and that was not the least of her regrets. She got the impression that she was turning her back on her only friends, on those who had been behind her during the worst moments of her life in America.

Provided she finished her doctoral dissertation before the year was out, Anthea had obtained a better paid, more respectable position for her at the University of New England, where she worked. Despite her convictions, Marie-Noëlle did not have the courage to refuse such an offer. It would mean the end of a number of material deprivations, of the freezing apartment in winter, barely furnished whatever the season, of going hungry at the end of the month, and the money she constantly owed to the neighborhood Korean. Here she was just turned thirty. Her face reminded her of it, as it grew more wrinkled and hollow by the day. And yet she was hardly any happier than during those early years in Nice. So she had set about writing her dissertation. But her heart was not in her work. She was unable to muster that blaze of enthusiasm of the previous years, and the entire work of Jean Genet seemed suddenly insipid to her. She labored on even so, and remained locked up for hours in the airless, joyless cemeteries known as university libraries. When she emerged at night, the magical vision of those luminous black-and-white tombstones in the shade of the casuarinas of the other cemeteries on her island never failed to haunt her. What a stunning contrast! The latter, at least, were not lacking in style and beauty. Her dissertation gave her a good excuse to repress her vague desire to become a writer. Deep down she was no dupe. How could she write? How could she take up the pen as long as she didn't know who she was or where she came from? Illegitimate child, father unknown. A fine identity that was! As long as she had no other details to record in her family register, she would never make a success of anything. Soon she gave herself a second good excuse. Shortly before Christmas Ludovic sent her *Les jours étrangers*, the book Reynalda had just published. Despite its title it was not a novel or her autobiography, memoirs, confession, or personal diary. Reynalda was not writing about Nina, Gian Carlo, or herself. It was a well-documented essay—somewhat heavy going, it seemed—in which she dealt with migrant families from the Caribbean and sub-Saharan Africa, mainly migrant women, in fact, their social and family conditions, their traumas and—daringly enough—their sexual fantasies. Marie-Noëlle received the book like a slap in the face. Looking at the name sprawled on the cover—Reynalda Titane, five obscure syllables, apparently harmless, not very elegant or euphonius, but in fact loaded with the power to wound and inflict pain—it was as if her maman were waging a merciless battle against her. As if she were doing her utmost to block every possible escape route. She had already barred her from love and motherhood. Now she was barring her from writing. Without reading it, she put the book away on one of her bookshelves. But the sight of the white letters on the black spine made her feel so uncomfortable that she ended up putting it away where she couldn't see it. Nevertheless she couldn't get Reynalda out of her mind, and she tried to imagine her in her new role. Shaking off her reserve. Smiling. Explaining.

It was March, and everyone was fed up with winter; the last storm had piled up mounds of snow on the roads, left two thousand homes without electricity, and killed four or five homeless persons; the love story Awa was living in Mexico City fizzled out, and she quite naturally moved back in with Marie-Noëlle. Arturo, the musician she had followed to Mexico, had turned out to be a violent brute who beat her black and blue. She pulled up her skirt and showed her thighs lacerated by his ill treatment. She had had to escape in the middle of the night, otherwise he would have strangled her. Awa herself had changed. She was obsessed with returning to Guinea, for she had fabricated a surprising remorse. She blamed herself for having abandoned her aging maman in Conakry, where, she was told, the most basic commodities were lacking. No soap to wash with, no milk for baby formula, no rice, no cooking oil, or tomato sauce. She would nostalgically recall some childhood episode, now realizing that she should have thought more highly of Natasha. Maybe she was just another victim, as all women are. Marie-Noëlle listened to her. She had taken her in without hesitation. She had shared everything with her as they used to do. But they no longer got along the same way. It was not a question of being at cross-purposes. Awa had never found Stanley charming or musically gifted, and had never had any qualms about saying it or repeating it. But by placing her childhood in a different perspective, she undermined the very foundations of their close relations. Everything disintegrated. For instance, while Arturo had been playing in Paris, Awa had gone to visit Reynalda and Ludovic. Ever since, she never stopped praising Reynalda, so hardworking, so intelligent, who through sheer diligence had made a name for herself in Paris. Strange, when she was small she had thought of her as being ugly, whereas she had a charm all her own, and so on and so on. As for Ludovic, that weirdo, his only strong point were his good looks. Good looks? Marie-Noëlle was stunned by the comment. She had never thought of Ludovic as being good-looking. All she could remember was his generous heart, which had offered her refuge.

As usual Awa livened up Marie-Noëlle's existence. Spicy aromas seeped out of the apartment late at night, mingled with the sounds of wild music. Shady-looking individuals began coming up at all hours and lingering late in either of the girls' beds. And the neighbors, who up till then had paid scant attention to Mrs. Watts—who had taken her to be a respectable individual and for three years had slept soundly every night—now had every reason to complain.

⚶

"Passed with distinction."

Marie-Noëlle shook hands with the three members of the jury, who in a certain way had just issued her with a precious passport. One Frenchwoman and two white Americans. How the times had changed since the Black Panthers! Jean Genet no longer interested black America, which had abandoned him altogether to the Caucasians, and Marie-Noëlle had sought in vain an African-American professor to direct her dissertation. She had nevertheless managed to meet the deadline. In the library, among the books and journals in French, Spanish, and German, a small group of students and professors was waiting for her, all come to celebrate the occasion over one of those labored receptions the Department of Foreign Literatures was so good at: very dry crackers, tasteless cheese cubes and strawberries, and white wine so pale it looked like water. Marie-Noëlle shook more hands, embraced a few more people, and walked over to Anthea, who, with Molara by her side, was beaming with pride. Even though she was modest about it, this success was hers. She alone, and nobody else, had transformed a shy little immigrant, married to a penniless musician, into a university professor. The Race would be grateful to her, and as for those who were quick to relegate the American dream to the past, they would have proof they were talking off the top of their heads. The American dream was well and truly alive, and anyone with two eyes to see had living proof of its stamina. Anthea's and Molara's dresses did justice to the occasion. The mother was wearing baggy, Muslim-style trousers and a flared tunic, like the Ga women wear in the region of Accra, made of rich Ashanti cloth. On her head a massive headdress towered up in puffs and swirls. The child's dress was a smaller version of the mother's. Anthea hugged Marie-Noëlle to her heart with sincere emotion. Marie-Noëlle warmly returned her embrace and likewise embraced Molara. Even so, on such a day as this, she did not have the same feelings as Anthea. No satisfaction at what might pass as going up in the world. No intellectual pride. At the most she felt relieved, as if she had just gotten rid of a boring formality. Delving deeper, she felt afraid. Afraid she would become, like some of her colleagues, a "specialist" known for her publications and showered with university honors, jabbering on in a jargon that bored everyone to tears. She got the impression that, faced with two lifestyles, Awa's and Anthea's, she had, without realizing it, chosen the second. Consequently solitude and emotional deprivation would be her lot forever. What would Stanley have thought about all this, he who boasted he hadn't opened a book or a newspaper since he left school? Marie-Noëlle could be blamed for never having gone back to Eppeldorn where he was buried. It's true she never paid him those visits we imagine we owe the dead on certain dates. November 2. November 1. January 1. In the graveyard where he was spending eternity there were no fresh flowers or water on his tomb. Nothing sanctimonious to remember him by. Yet she thought about him constantly. She made known to him her intentions, her actions, and her omissions, as if she couldn't bear to leave him out of her life. Ever since she had got back from Guadeloupe, he hadn't left her in peace. The Stanley she had known so withdrawn, apparently indifferent to anything but himself and his music, was now constantly badgering her! He was blaming her. He could forgive her the way she had treated Claire-Alta so unfairly. Not a word. Not even a hastily scribbled postcard. He could forgive her the way she had behaved with Judes Anozie. Love is a battle of wits. She had had the upper hand; Judes Anozie the lower. What he couldn't forgive was her turning her back on Nina and not bothering about the solitude of her old age. When her time came, Nina would surrender to death with no one at her bedside. It would only be after several days, several weeks even, that the mailman, bringing the monthly money order from public welfare, would make the grisly discovery. He would alert the folk from Grande-Anse, who, out of duty rather than grief would climb up the "Mountain" for the wake. The wake would resemble her death, and there would be no candles, no rum, no prayers, and no thick soup. The next morning the little cortège of good souls would set off for the communal cemetery. The sun would go down over Petite-Terre. As far as the eye could see the sky would be daubed in red, and the pallid stars would be waiting for their entrance. Not a flower or a wreath would accompany the coffin as it was hauled down into the earth.

HERE LIES ANTONINE TITANE
THE WOMAN NOBODY LOVED.

Judes Anozie, who wrote often, had informed Marie-Noëlle he had gone back to La Désirade and paid Nina a visit on the off chance. But she had given him a cold reception, claiming she needed nothing nor nobody. Pure bravado! Marie-Noëlle did not believe a word. She knew in the secret of her heart that their first sight of each other had sealed a pact. Nina was expecting her to come back. She had been expecting her amid the commotion of the great winds of September, when, racing all the way from Africa, they blow up into hurricanes, uproot trees, and hurl cabins to the ground. She had been expecting her in the furnace of the dry season, when the sky is white-hot like a galvanized roof. Sometimes at night, Nina was misled by the barking of the Creole dog. She imagined a visitor approaching. She ran to open the door. But only the darkness remained standing behind the wooden shutters. Now she had come to terms with it and no longer got up in the dark. After such melodramatic visions Marie-Noëlle's heart felt a pang of anguish. How many crimes she had on her conscience! How could she purge them? How could she make amends?

D

When she got home to Roxbury a surprise was awaiting her. Wild music echoed right down to the building's entrance. On the fourth floor, all the doors were wide open, while a thousand lights shone bright. The apartment was filled with all sorts of people, some she didn't know, speaking loudly in every language on earth. Awa too had decided to celebrate the occasion and had organized a party for her. Marie-Noëlle consented to the embraces, shook outstretched hands, and kissed unknown cheeks. At one moment a glowing

Awa silenced the musicians and brought a toast to her friend, the new Ph.D. Marie-Noëlle's intelligence and determination, she said, were part of a long lineage of courageous, talented black women that dated back to time immemorial, from Africa to the Americas. A living example before her of this lineage of valiant women was Marie-Noëlle's maman, Reynalda. To support her statement, Awa brandished a copy of *Les jours étrangers*. Where on earth had she got that from? True blood never lies. Like mother, like daughter! Wherever she was, Reynalda could only be proud of the daughter she had borne. Everybody applauded and noisily approved. More kisses and embraces. Nevertheless, it was at that very moment, Marie-Noëlle felt it, that her friendship with Awa came to an end.

Chapter 2

*I*n the fall Marie-Noëlle moved to Newbury, a modest place on the outskirts of Boston. Newbury was one of those places in the United States that are considered integrated because they house an equal number of whites, blacks, Latinos, and a few Asians, whose standard of living is just above the poverty line. It was considered safe: no police sirens screaming in the middle of the night, no bodies or dubious puddles at street corners, no suspicious-looking loiterers. It was a decent neighborhood: no lines of washing flapping at the windows, no little boys playing ball behind the barbed wire of makeshift playgrounds, no bars vomiting out a noisy contingent of drunkards at all hours. And yet this respectability was enough to make her miss the pervasive ugliness of Camden Town and Roxbury. Nothing but gloomy rows of identical buildings, lined up along the sidewalks planted with trees gone spindly from so many winters. Nothing moved during the day, nothing made a sound in the evening. Looking at these lifeless façades you might have thought the houses uninhabited if occasionally a car didn't glide down the street and slip into a parking space, and a silhouette creep out, lock the car doors, and steal through the front entrance.

Newbury had one saving grace: the Charles River. Runners in colored tracksuits jogged along its winding banks, working their elbows against their bodies. When the weather permitted, mothers pushed their babies along it. Sometimes you even passed old couples tottering along amorously. The river itself changed the color of its mantle to reflect the season: a blank shimmering gray in the fall, a thick white wool in winter, a tender green velvet in the spring, bright green in summer.

The life Marie-Noëlle led reflected the neighborhood she lived in. Four times a week she went to the university, taught her classes, met with students, and lunched with colleagues to discuss curricula or student advising. When she was not at the university, she was locked up at home, attempting to transform her dissertation into an essay that wasn't too heavy going. Sometimes, anxious students rang at the door holding their papers. Apart from that she did not receive a single visit. Anthea had once again been invited to teach at her beloved University of Ghana. Every one of her letters boasted to Marie-Noëlle of her life with Molara. Both had been transformed, freed from the fear of racism, robbery, and rape. Beside Ga and Twi, her daughter now spoke Ewe, Dagbani, and Fon. She also took classes in traditional dancing and batik painting. And, wonder of wonders, Anthea, quite by chance, had come across a correspondence. In the eighteenth century, at the very height of the slave trade, Efua, the wife of the Omanhene of Ajumako, had been the victim of a plot by her co-wives, who were jealous of her great beauty, and had been sold as a slave and shipped to a *casa grande* in Brazil. There she had been forced to satisfy the sexual whims of her master, a Portuguese whoremonger. Unknown to her torturer, she had learned to read and write, and sent to her husband a series of heartrending letters that were the first texts of rebellion and liberation of an African woman as well as a unique document on Brazilian society at that time. Anthea hoped that Marie-Noëlle would come and share her happiness in Ghana by spending Christmas with her. She would take her to Kumasi, the heart of this proud Ashanti land, whose soul even Kwame Nkrumah could not conquer. Marie-Noëlle hesitated. The little she knew about Africa frightened her. She was convinced that the sight of such gaping wounds would force her to feel pity, to look for remedies when she wanted only to be absorbed in herself.

Marie-Noëlle no longer saw Awa. Living in luxury on Beacon Hill, Awa had fallen in love with the lawyer assigned to handle her immigration problems. Awa put this cooling of relations between them down to the jealousy Marie-Noëlle had always had towards her. So Marie-Noëlle racked her brains. It's true she had always been jealous of Awa. As a small child she had been jealous of her relations with her parents, the surly tenderness of her papa as well as Natasha's kisses and slaps. Later on she had been jealous of her vivacity as well as her self-assurance with men. For years she had made clumsy attempts to get Terri to talk about his love for her. Now she was jealous of her affair with a man who was neither a dropout, a bum, nor a deadbeat. A smart, thirty-five-year-old Caucasian, who had studied at George Washington University. Awa could not resist inviting her, and Marie-Noëlle had felt morose and ugly in this well-groomed setting among the sparkling, debonair guests. Ugly from being so morose. Wearing a dress that betrayed her poverty. She even wondered whether she was not deserving of the adjectives Nina and Claire-Alta had used to describe Reynalda: selfish, self-absorbed, and sly. She did not love Reynalda, but her tainted blood was flowing in her veins.

It was around this time that Ludovic's letters began to get shorter and fewer. For years his often lengthy letters regularly crossed the ocean, never failing to end with the well-intentioned lie: "Your maman, brother, and little sister share with me in sending our affection." As their closing indicated, they were somewhat conventional, even grandiloquent. They gave the impression that Ludovic was intent on giving his family and its members a semblance of normality. That he was hiding behind the role of papa he had given himself and that he wanted to avoid any deviation from the norm. Marie-Noëlle, however, was cruelly blunt in her answers. It was the ideal opportunity for her to get everything off her chest. What she didn't dare confront in the open she dared write down, and Ludovic was hard put to find the appropriate objective, understanding, and well-meaning answers. So he was not offended by her description of her stay in Guadeloupe. In answer to her suspicions, accusations even, that Reynalda was, as Nina said, a "first-rate liar" he had merely been content to sum up the facts as if he were trying to solve a mystery story. Reynalda's belly had not borne the fruit of the Holy Spirit. It was, as the Creole saying went, a mountain of truth you inevitably came up against. Even if Gian Carlo was not the guilty party, then this belly was not something Fiorella and Reynalda had made up. Could she think of another man who had been in the house on the rue de Nozières and might provide a clue? He had ended his letter urging Marie-Noëlle to care for her grandmother in her old age as best she could. For every sin can be forgiven. The time for forgiving and forgetting was long overdue. This superfluous advice, as effective as a Band Aid on a wooden leg, amused Marie-Noëlle. Did he lavish it also on Reynalda?

When Ludovic's letters got fewer, Garvey's began to arrive, written in the same scratchy handwriting that tore through the sheets of paper as if the son had used the father's hand. Just as conventional, his first letter came enclosed with a picture of himself, one arm on the shoulder of Angéla, his little sister, who was giving a toothless smile beside her big brother. Marie-Noëlle saw that he was tall, as tall as her basketball-player students, skinny, his handsome egg-shaped skull closely shaved without a bump, his eyes narrow and shifty-looking. One generation apart, he could have been one of the MNA's musicians—he had that look about him. In his first letter Garvey apologized, still very conventional, for not having written for so many years. Even so, his older sister had always been in his thoughts and his heart. The proof! He owned all the recordings of the late Stanley Watts, who hadn't got the recognition he deserved and whom he revered as one of the greatest! Patience: His time would come as it always comes to those who deserve it. Garvey confessed that his own life was not a success story. Nothing he could boast about. He had been expelled from public as well as private schools. He had done more wrong than been wronged. He had pilfered everything that could be pilfered from supermarkets and department stores. He had stolen a good many cars, spent the night in a good many police stations, narrowly avoiding jail, but he had always kept off crack—that was fatal. He had recently turned over a new leaf and, like Ludovic, was working for a trucking company. He shared lodgings on the boulevard du Temple with four friends, two North Africans, a Turk, and a guy from Benin, who had done up the apartment all by themselves. Once he had enough savings, he would leave Paris with his backpack and set off to see if the earth was really round. He would visit the United States, some countries in South America, and, above all, the Caribbean, a silo where so many races had been fertilized before setting off to sow the world. She shouldn't get him wrong! In no way was he on the age-old quest for identity. He was a European. A West Indian from an immigrant family. He did not long for a mythical past nor was his heart set on winning back a beautiful native land. His placenta was buried under one of the plane trees in Savigny-sur-Orge. During the day his turf was walking to the beat of the urban jungle amid the noise and the squalor. At night it was the neon lights that glared back at the light of day, and the mean and dangerous streets. He recalled the time when he used to go out stealing with his gang, relishing the taste of forbidden fruit and the voluptuousness of fear. It was only in his fifth or sixth letter that Garvey began talking about Reynalda—a subject he could talk about forever.

⫷

For the boy whose maman doesn't love him, the earth provides no shade. The sun burns him. It scorches his brain and shrivels him down to his heart. His mouth is parched. His eyes are blinded. He has no friends. He doesn't look at girls. He doesn't play with himself. His obsession never leaves him alone.

Admittedly Ludovic couldn't do more for the boy. He was a model, doting father. He did the cooking, he signed his report cards, attended the PTA meetings, took him to see *Pinocchio*, demonstrated the butterfly stroke, and had him listen to *Peter and the Wolf* on the record player. Yet all this devotion missed its mark, for it underscored the cruel absence of the other. The few times Reynalda took him to school she abandoned him in the yard as if she were getting rid of him. In the evening, once Ludovic had bathed him and tucked him in under the sheets, she would come and sit on the edge of his bed to read to him so halfheartedly, with such an expression of being trapped, that the story of Little Red Riding Hood in distress set him to crying as much as his own misery. She couldn't be bothered with him. She couldn't be bothered with anything that had to do with him—that he understood very quickly.

Until he was fifteen, until he refused to go any longer, week after week, Ludovic dragged him to the Muntu meetings. Some people wouldn't hesitate to give Muntu the murky name of sect, because during the Sunday services members reinterpreted the

Gospels and then ladled out the holy stew made of vegetables and baked beans without salt. In actual fact little consideration was given to religious matters. Muntu, which drew its inspiration from a number of sources, had been founded by a West Indian working in Abidjan, Ivory Coast, as a tax inspector and who ended up as a prophet in Brussels. One morning as he was strolling along the Ébrié lagoon, a black God was revealed to him in a vision among the debris of weeds and wood floating on the surface. He had the revelation of how the black race should purge itself of its ungodliness. In next to no time he abandoned his name Paulius Polydor, slipped on a white robe, and let his hair and beard grow. Thinking he had gone mad, his superiors at the ministry where he worked had him dismissed. He therefore returned to Europe, where he calmly began denouncing the ravages of the white man's values, for he was not a violent person, rather a gentle crank. At Muntu they worshiped hard work, especially manual work. They learned self-respect, forgiveness, the sense of the word "solidarity" as well as love for one's brother—that is, anyone who was black. Ludovic was one of Muntu's cornerstones. He had been attracted by the Mallam, as Paulius Polydor was now called, while he was a musician in Brussels, and he had helped plant his doctrine in the fertile soil of the Paris suburbs. Armed with these simple, some would say simplistic, precepts, he worked wonders in his role as educator, effectively placing a check on juvenile delinquency. On the other hand, he only had to look at Reynalda's attitude during the services to realize that she couldn't care less about what was going on around her. She only came to life before communion when the singing started. For someone who never even hummed a lullaby to her son, she would stand up for all to see in the very midst of the worshipers and belt out the hymns. She was gifted with a magnificent mezzo-soprano voice, an organ of amazing power and range that rose up from a breast of such small proportions. The pleasure she took in singing transformed her. It broke the mask of boredom and apathy she constantly wore and clothed her almost in beauty. Despite his resentment, which had hardened like a crust, Garvey could not help bursting into tears as he hung on every word he heard her sing. He thought he had died and gone to heaven. One day when she had surpassed herself, when the congregation, which was not exactly fond of Reynalda and always ready to criticize her, had cheered her again and again, she had returned home to Savigny-sur-Orge and confessed that her great regret was not having been able to pursue a musical career. With technique, lessons, and a teacher she would have become one of the greatest singers of the twentieth century like Marian Anderson, so lauded by Arturo Toscanini; Leontyne Price; or Jessye Norman. In the past there was someone who had appreciated her exceptional gift and given her to believe she would be able to study at a conservatory in metropolitan France. Worried about her color she had asked anxiously whether a black soprano was not even more out of character than a bald soprano. The person had shrugged his shoulders and assured her that all God's children were alike. She had believed him. But it was merely idle talk, a lot of hot air, hollow words designed to take advantage of her. Recalling this still-painful memory, her face had puckered up. Then tears had filled her eyes and flowed down her cheeks, leaving shiny streaks. It was the only time Garvey had seen her show any emotion, a time when she had conceitedly dreamed of grandeur, when she had selfishly pitied herself.

Hoping to track down a clue, Marie-Noëlle, in her reply, had bombarded her brother with questions. Had Reynalda let slip the name of the person who had encouraged her to sing only to disappoint her in the end? Was it the bishop who had already played a role in her life? Was it Gian Carlo Coppini? Or someone else whom nobody suspected? Alas! Everyone is wrapped up in his or her own problems, and Garvey could no longer remember.

As a child he had never been able to confide his hurt to Ludovic, who could see full well the growing silence and distance that was building between mother and son. Days would go by without their speaking to each other or even their eyes meeting. But Ludovic preferred not to see and barricaded himself behind ready-made considerations: "Your maman has suffered a great deal. Her childhood was taken from her. You must try and understand her." Such words were especially enigmatic since Garvey had no interest in his mother's past. Nothing prior to her life at Savigny-sur-Orge interested him. He had never asked questions about the father of his older sister, whom he knew to be different from his own. There was nothing unusual about that. Madame Asdrubal, the neighbor, had six children by three different papas. The most he knew was that he was from Guadeloupe, like his mother. Guadeloupe, an island that corresponded to no pictures on the wall, no exact mental image. Some of his friends went there on vacation and came back complaining of the foul things they had to eat. Garvey never wondered whether there was a family, a grandmother, aunts, and uncles, whose tenderness might have brought a comforting warmth to his existence.

In his last letters Garvey implied that serious disagreements were emerging between Ludovic and Reynalda. She no longer found Ludovic good enough for her. It was as if she were ashamed of him. His weird looks. His dreadlocks. His demeaning jobs. She herself was a changed person, not a hair out of place, manicured, almost elegant, and no longer seemed troubled by her former problems. The only time she stayed at home was to give interviews to journalists. The rest of the time she was absorbed by a whirl of cocktail parties, receptions, seminars, conferences, meetings, and discussions devoted to immigration on local radio stations, independent or otherwise. In short the couple was going to the dogs. Marie-

Noëlle was careful not to ask too many questions, but was overjoyed at the news. At the same time she was ashamed to admit that she was jealous of her mother and envied everything she possessed.

Shortly before Christmas, Marie-Noëlle made a decision that upset Anthea. She decided not to join her in Ghana, where plans had been made to visit the forts at Takoradi, Dixcove, Elmina, and Cape Coast, witnesses of the memorable encounter between Europeans and Africans, and still filled with the memories of slavery. Instead she chose to go to Paris.

Chapter 3

etting off the plane, Marie-Noëlle found nothing beautiful or salutary about the overcast sky shrouding Paris or the fog that misted her vision. She had been used to more violent, more contrasted colors. The misleading yellow of the sun above the crackling white crust of winter, the great gaps of metallic blue sky, and the harmonies of an Indian summer. This enveloping grayness made her heavy-hearted. Garvey was waiting for her, accompanied by a boy he briefly introduced as Soglo, his buddy from Benin. The disappointment she felt embracing the two of them made her realize how much she had hoped someone else would be waiting for her.

This trip no longer had its *raison d'etre*. Why exactly had she come to Paris where, finally, she did not know anyone and hadn't set foot for years? Of course, there was that old trail, now gone cold, she intended following. But above all she was convinced she had come to look for something she had always desired, something that had always eluded her and she was now bold enough to want to possess it. Perhaps she had never seen this airport before. Ultramodern, a complex of moving escalators, all glass tubing and bubbles. Yet, it seemed familiar. It took her back years, twenty years or more, and in her imaginary memories she saw the little girl she had once been, clutching a rag doll to her heart and searching in vain for a smile in the crowd. She saw her everywhere, this little girl. In this child half asleep beside a baggage cart. In this one daydreaming, sucking her thumb. In this little Indian, this little Chinese girl, this little blond, long-haired American. What mattered most was the look of distress. These flashbacks added to her sadness and took away most of the pleasure of the reunion with her brother. And yet he had done his best. He had borrowed a car driven by friend Soglo, that rattled along the dismal highways surrounding Paris. They left the airport and drove past warehouses as desolate as those in the suburbs of Boston, past hotels, hangars, and more warehouses. Suddenly, the damp sky burst onto the roadway and the gray of the sky mingled with the gray of the air and the gray of the rain.

Was the whole world turning ugly?

Fortunately the heart of Paris doesn't change. However much they stick a fast-food restaurant here, a home electronics shop there, a pyramid of Plexiglas, sex shops, and pizzerias just about everywhere, they can't manage to disfigure it. Under the Mirabeau Bridge the Seine still flows. The familiar architecture remains. It's like the face of a beautiful woman which the ravages of age or sickness leave unscathed. Marie-Noëlle rediscovered the stone lacework and the elegant facades of centuries-old monuments. Yet she realized she was feeling no emotion. Paris was a sumptuous, empty stage, a decor where none of her dramas had been played out. She had loved nobody there, buried nobody, wept for nobody. However, all this beauty did not last. They quickly left the well-to-do neighborhoods. Garvey lived near the Place de la République. Once they managed to park the car in the dirty, congested street, the puddles of rain grew larger, as dubious as pools of blood. In the stores the crowds of shoppers looked sullen and needy. A lot of the women's faces were black or pallid, tattooed in blue, women from North Africa, each with a cluster of children clinging to her. The imposing appearance of the building where Garvey lived was deceiving. Once you pushed open the large carriage door, the full extent of its dilapidation struck you. The automatic light on the stairs was broken. There was no elevator, and the steps of the monumental stone stairway, patched here and there with colorless carpeting, were cracked. Garvey laughingly recounted the war being waged among the building's various social categories. On one hand there was the clan of proprietors, very French, old couples retired from the Civil Service who had miraculously survived the Second World War and remained barricaded behind their locks and safety bolts. On the other, the clan of dusky foreigners, tenants or more commonly squatters, casual laborers, the jobless or petty truants, an extraordinary assortment of cross-cultures. In their fear and distrust the proprietors saw no difference between a tenant and a squatter and refused to give them the time of day. They tolerated no noise after 10 P.M. and if the peace was disturbed their favorite pastime was to call the police in a fury. The police no longer bothered to call around, and they were now plotting to write to their representative in the National Assembly. Garvey and his friends lived on the second floor. The windows of their apartment looked out onto a kind of dark, narrow passageway, which meant the rooms never got any light. Even at noon the lights were on all the time. Except for a giant TV screen, where Walt Disney characters rollicked about in silence, the living room was virtually empty. A carpet, some poufs, and a few cushions were all there was in the way of furnishings. Marie-Noëlle did not mind because it brought

Garvey closer to her. She would have had trouble confiding in him if he had succeeded in life.

When she thought about it, it was perhaps for this reason she had felt so remote from Claire-Alta and the folk in Guadeloupe. Success was still their religion. Life must have the appearance—at least the appearance—of marching on victoriously, from the belly of the slave ship lying anchored, waiting in the mangroves, to the blaze of sunlight at the top of the hill. Perhaps Judes Anozie was an exception with his rumpled clothes, his Japanese jalopy, and his speeches about the environment. All in vain, she tenderly reminisced, since the trees were withering, the housing projects mushrooming amid a desolation worse than the old cabins on four stones, while in the backcountry the gullies were drying up. From a distance, Marie-Noëlle began to see Judes Anozie as a friend, mistreated and misunderstood. How could she make amends? He deserved better than what he had got from her. Without waiting for her to answer, he wrote her letter after letter. He sent her news of the island, of politicians and priests, and a host of people she had never heard of. Above all he sent her news of Nina. He had finally broken her reserve, and from time to time he took the boat over to La Désirade, just for a chat. The Creole dog no longer barked. Nina opened the door to him, neither pleased nor displeased to see him, in her sullen indifference. He helped her around the house. Fearing the devastating effects of hurricane Ferguson—thankfully it vanished somewhere in the Atlantic—he had climbed up on the roof to nail down the sheets of corrugated iron. On each visit he set about weaving the bonds left unwoven and talked to her about Marie-Noëlle. When would she come back in person? It was her duty to come back and make up for what another had failed to do. She couldn't let her grandmother set out on the voyage of no return without a last kiss. Marie-Noëlle did not know how to respond to this reproach that turned up over and over again in every letter. She had nothing more to do over there, in Guadeloupe. Lucky Garvey who knew where his placenta lay! Property developers had dug up hers. They had thrown it away. Then built a city of concrete in its place.

Around one o'clock a few friends arrived, and Soglo served up a dish he had cooked in honor of the new arrival. All kinds of cigarettes passed from hand to hand. Numerous bottles of cheap wine and beer were emptied. Soon the only thing missing was the live music and the voices with foreign accents for Marie-Noëlle to be transported back to Camden Town. That journey back in time was no pleasure trip either. Her memory had left those years intact. Like today she had been alone. Nobody paid her any attention. Garvey, a little drunk, had finished talking to her, as if he had already told her everything during the eight months of correspondence and there was nothing left to say. Even so, both of them had been able to see for themselves that their childhoods had not spoiled everything for them. Childhood had not shrivelled their hearts, and there was still room for affection. At the end of the afternoon, Marie-Noëlle retired to the room they had made up for her: cold and empty like the apartment, though two roses in a cheap vase pathetically conveyed a welcome. She closed her eyes and eventually dozed off, facing the dirty gray rectangle cut out by the window.

✑

She must have slept for a long time. When she returned to the living room, night had fallen and all the guests had gone. Garvey and Soglo, somewhat drunk, were sprawled over the cushions. This time she had the strength to ask Garvey the question she had been turning over and over in her mind.

Where was Ludovic?

Garvey lowered his voice as if the sound of his own words frightened him. Ludovic had just left for Belgium, taking Angéla with him. They had spent the night at Garvey's before catching the train for Brussels. What was behind this departure, Garvey did not know. Naturally he had been dying to ask questions, but had refrained. He had not even mentioned Reynalda's name. After dinner father and son had left Angéla with Soglo in front of the television and walked as far as the Place de la République. It was raining that evening as well. The wheels of the cars, as shadowy as hearses, splashed buckets of water over the sidewalks. Amid the darkness and the damp a single sign flashed out: the green crosses of the pharmacies glittering like gems. Despite the weather and the late hour, a carousel was making its rounds. Children were throwing tantrums at their parents, and the streets were crowded. That's what Garvey liked about big cities—the constant hustle and bustle like the agitation of ants. Day and night the world never stopped revolving. In a certain respect you were never lost because there was always a lost soul like yourself you could tell your misfortunes to. Ludovic and Garvey had pushed open the door to a café unimaginatively named A la République. Inside there was a party's-over atmosphere in which the lonely, the sleepless, and those who drift aimlessly in the night made a last stop. Garvey felt sorry for his father, who never took his eyes off his glass and suddenly looked gaunt and haggard and fifty years old. They had sat a long time silently drinking beer after beer in the muggy atmosphere. Finally a man came and sat at their table and told them the story of his life. Some pre-posterous story that he must have made up, in part about the savagery of women. The next morning when Garvey woke up

Ludovic and Angéla had gone, conspicuously leaving a letter for Marie-Noëlle on the television.

✑

The next morning when she woke, the weather was just as mournful. It was still raining. The same dreary gray. All night long Marie-Noëlle had rediscovered the forgotten, morbid pleasure of crying. Like when she was a child, knowing that nobody would come and comfort her. That she would have to wait for the dawn, get up as if nothing were wrong, get ready for school, face the other children, the teacher, life, in other words! The apartment was deserted. On the kitchen table someone had clumsily laid out the breakfast things. Marie-Noëlle preferred to go out. In the damp street, passersby hurried along and she hurried on likewise. Yet she had all the time in the world. The decision she had come to scared her like the thought of an operation she had to undergo for her own good. She had tried every avenue possible, and only this last remaining one stretched out in front of her. Yet for some time now she had asked herself why not go on living as she was. Without an identity, like someone whose papers have been stolen and who drifts aimlessly through the world? Wasn't she freer like that? It's a terrible thing wanting to know at any cost where we come from and tracking down that drop of sperm that gave us life.

The street she chanced to wander along was lined with shops selling all manner of gaudy and cheap goods. Enormous earrings, heavy pendants, and gilt metal brooches, specked with sequins and multicolored pieces of glass. She stopped to look at her dour reflection in a shop window, then went on her way. After a while she came out onto a square, elegant and austere with its pink and gray façades that looked as familiar as a postcard. To kill time, she entered a café as deserted as a tomb.

Madame Duparc had answered her letter immediately and agreed to see her. But she had warned her she had nothing dramatic to reveal. All things considered, she had kept good memories of her little domestic from the 1960s. Marie-Noëlle promised herself that after this visit she would renounce this search that led her to places that suited her the least. Last year Guadeloupe. Now Paris. Besides, it was all becoming useless. Useless? She was no longer so sure since she hadn't seen Ludovic again. She never stopped wondering why he had left for Belgium without waiting for her. It looked too much like an escape. She now had the courage to confess she had only come to Paris to see him. Why had she ignored the truth for so long? In fact all the men she had met in her life had been a way of looking for Ludovic, and each time she had been cheated.

At two o'clock precisely she got up, crossed the square, and took a taxi. The driver was from Guadeloupe like herself. Well, his family came from Guadeloupe. He had gone there for the first time three years ago after having dreamed about it all through his teens. To say he had been disappointed wouldn't be telling the truth. It was something else. The extraordinary beauty of the island had intimidated him, as if he were walking on foreign ground. His own universe was the dismal suburbs, the stadiums, and the soccer fields. He had never felt comfortable there. He was always the odd man out. He knew that behind his back they were making fun of him. He spoke with a French accent. He didn't wear his hair short enough. He wore African clothes to prove God knows what identity. He had only felt his usual self once he had got back to Paris. And yet he didn't consider himself French.

In actual fact Marie-Noëlle was hardly listening to his story, as tedious as a scratched record. How many were there across the planet Earth who shared the same tormented life? Enough to form another race, enough to people another world.

Spellbound in spite of herself she gazed at the scene that was the heart of Paris. The rain paused, and the Seine, swollen with water, flowed violet. Clouds of the same color chased one another over the bridges. Already the light was fading, and day was getting ready to take up its night quarters.

The taxi drew up in front of 305 boulevard Malesherbes, and Marie-Noëlle inspected the tall stony façade. It had sheltered a fifteen-year-old Reynalda. Perhaps it knew her secrets but was not telling.

Chapter **4**

IMAGINATION! Imagination!

This was not how Marie-Noëlle had visualized the apartment where her maman had hired her services. She had imagined it to be more luxurious, richly furnished in soft tones, in beige, gray, and fawn, like those dream apartments you see in glossy magazines like *House & Garden*. In actual fact, with its heavy rep drapes and its walls tapestried with portraits of ancestors and reproductions of old masters, it was nondescript, somewhat stifling, and rather gloomy. Matisse's goldfish swam glumly round and round in their bowl in the print hanging over the piano. She had imagined Mme. Duparc to be quite different too. Elegant, even a little scatterbrained. Whereas the woman standing in front of her was well-dressed, though nothing unconventional, with a God-fearing expression, wearing her gray hair carefully brushed back into a chignon. A widow, since Jean-René had prematurely abandoned her on this earth. But surrounded by her devoted children. A little maid decked out as a perfect soubrette, a replica of what Reynalda must have been thirty years earlier, silently busied herself around the room, pouring tea, serving millefeuilles and coffee eclairs. Marie-Noëlle was first subjected to an interrogation which she answered as best she could, feeling, nevertheless, that everything she said was being held against her. To be honest, she hadn't chosen to live in America. Life had dragged her over there. That's all. No, she had lost her husband and had no children. No, she had no plans to return to France or to Guadeloupe. Well, yes, she liked living over there. Mme. Duparc switched on her smile for the occasion and leaned over the photo albums, laid out on a low table in anticipation of her visit. But these amateur snapshots, already yellowed, were nothing new to Marie-Noëlle. She had already seen this ill-dressed, sulky, skinny girl, who made no effort to smile as she held three boisterous children by the hand, or received her slice of birthday cake in total indifference, or stood, stiff as a poker, behind a baby carriage. What was she thinking in the refuge of her head? Just by looking at her you could guess that life at the Duparcs' didn't interest her, that she didn't even pretend to love the three children in her care, Nathalie, Phillipe, and the youngest, so adorable, Charles-Emmanuel, whom everyone called Chamanou. Her ambitions were set elsewhere.

Mme. Duparc began to speak in a neutral tone of voice as if she were gathering together the facts for a letter of recommendation. Reynalda was clean, conscientious, hardworking, and discreet. She kept so much to her place, you forgot she was in the apartment. Gradually, however, her voice grew agitated and betrayed her. After all this time her heart had never forgiven Reynalda for having treated her like an employer instead of a benefactor. Once she left the boulevard Malesherbes they had heard nothing more from Reynalda. Not a letter, not a card. She had left behind a good many personal things in her room—photos of Guadeloupe, a radio, some paperbacks by Zola—but she never came back to fetch them. Just think of everything the Duparcs had done to reap so much ingratitude. Mme. Duparc was not someone whose conscience was easily satisfied: by giving her, for instance, her old clothes, her leftovers. Oh, no! The day after Reynalda arrived, she took her to the nearby department stores and dressed her from head to foot. Every day, she scrupulously left her enough time to prepare her lessons and do her homework, giving the children their evening bath herself. In fact she had never treated her like an inferior, more like a relative in trouble. Never a word of blame, never a reproach. Jean-René and she practiced the word of Christ: Him who is without sin among you . . . That sad story in Guadeloupe, of which in fact they knew very little, was not their business. What mattered was the little innocent child who had not asked to be born, who had remained behind in Guadeloupe in the care of a stranger! Just think of the child! (And here Mme. Duparc became vicious). Reynalda did not seem to care one bit. Not a single photo among her things. You never saw her buy a trinket or souvenir for her. Christmas, New Year's, and birthdays came and went. Everytime they tactfully tried to broach the subject, not out of curiosity, but out of sympathy, for they were parents themselves and Christian parents, Jean-René and she came up against a wall. Naturally they made an effort to be sympathetic. It was understandable. An unwanted child has trouble finding a place in a heart that never wanted her, and obviously Reynalda had never wanted her daughter. So in the best interests of her future, they had consented to pay her far more than the average wage. They had opened a savings account for her and made her make monthly deposits. And that's not all! They had never asked to be reimbursed for her fare from La Pointe, a fair sum at the time.

Thereupon Marie-Noëlle ventured to interrupt this torrent of bittersweet words. How come? Wasn't it the BUMIDOM who was in charge of dispatching Reynalda to Paris? The BUMIDOM? Mme. Duparc appeared taken aback. Yes, she had heard of this government agency that used to place domestics from the

Caribbean. But the BUMIDOM had nothing to do with it. She would never have agreed to introduce someone into her home on the recommendation of some anonymous civil servant. Marie-Noëlle insisted. She recalled the unequivocal words of her mother, sensing at last a crack in the edifice of solid rock Reynalda had constructed and that, thanks to Mme. Dupare, the truth, the truth, might come to light. She insisted with a trembling voice. If it wasn't the BUMIDOM, who was it, then? Mme. Duparc joined both hands together as if she were about to pray and calmly described her version of the facts.

The Duparc family was no ordinary family. It included a good many exceptional individuals—eccentrics, adventurers, and especially saints and martyrs. Nobody knows exactly how many Duparcs set off with rosary and sandals to evangelize Africa and distant lands. One of them ended up at the hospital in Lambaréné helping Albert Schweitzer. Closer to home, another Duparc, after having spent his time hunting down the outlawed priests in the back country of Haiti, became bishop of Guadeloupe. His name was hallowed in the remotest parishes on the island. He gave the appearance of being a jovial fellow with a ruddy face, a little too fond of rum punches and cacao bean liqueur. In actual fact under his paunch and his ruddy complexion beat the heart of a true mystic constantly concerned with acts of kindness. He paid regular visits to France to attend councils and synods, make pilgrimages to Lourdes, and never missed an occasion to stop by the boulevard Malesherbes to bless the children. One day in 1960 they received a somewhat mysterious letter from him. He was asking them, his young relatives, to come to his aid and at the same time put their Christian faith to the test. It was about finding a job as a children's nurse for Reynalda Titane, a fifteen-year-old mother, rather the unfortunate victim than the hardened sinner, as lonesome as loneliness itself and afflicted with affliction. A few years earlier he had wanted to help her by finding her a job in La Pointe, but in fact he had exposed her to the worst of temptations. He felt responsible for her misfortune. Counseling from the Duparcs and the example of a close-knit family might put her back on the right track. The bishop's answers to the couple's legitimate questions had not made matters any clearer. He merely explained that the young Reynalda could not bear her maman, a woman of somewhat loose reputation, and she had neither family nor friends. As for the father of her child, (he refused to simply call him the guilty party) he could say nothing more for he was bound by the oath of secrecy following a hasty confession stammered out in the shadow of a confessional. All they need know was that the unfortunate wretch was consumed by his guilt, and the rest of his life would not be long enough to expiate it. Moreover, he himself would see to it, bishop's honor. Mme. Duparc admitted she was, deep down, quite against the idea of hiring a sinner to look after her little Nathalie, her nine-year-old angel. But Jean-René, who was rather taken by the priesthood, was not of the same opinion and quickly sent his great-uncle the money for her passage. One month later Reynalda arrived and the uneasy cohabitation that was to last four years began.

Surprised at the distress into which her story had plunged Marie-Noëlle, Mme. Duparc racked her memory. But however hard she tried, she could remember nothing more. She knew nothing, absolutely nothing else. They had not seen the bishop again, and shortly afterward he was struck down by a heart attack. Too many rum punches. Too many cacao bean liqueurs. A crowd lamenting a saint carried him, even so, to his last resting place in the cemetery at Basse-Terre, for he had requested to be buried on his beloved Guadeloupe at the foot of his beloved volcano. And his secret with him. It seemed practically certain that Reynalda no longer kept in touch with the father of her child, presumably somewhere in Guadeloupe, because she never wrote or received any letters.

𝔇

What does one do in such cases? wondered Marie-Noëlle. Perhaps I ought to drink myself into oblivion. Not that I feel like it. Then do something dramatic? I haven't got the strength. From now on I shall quite simply have to live with the unknown, this area of darkness behind me. I came out of the dark. I came straight out of the brilliant head of my mother, totally unprepared and ill-equipped for life. There's no point in confronting her. She'll stick to her story. Besides, I'm sure she's ended up believing it. Perhaps she's mistaken herself for one of those wretched girls whose stories she had to listen to. Or else she dreamed it all up. For it's one of those stories that is too good to be true, that are the making of novels. She's basically a writer, my mother, and she has constructed her fiction. I'm living it and must search for the truth elsewhere. Where? It needs a new reading, starting all over again from the beginning—from that morning when Nina and Reynalda got off the boat, *J'espère en Dieu*, which in those days made the round trip between La Désirade and Saint-François twice a week.

𝔇

Nina was walking in front, striding along, balancing her light load on her head, without a thought for the child trying to keep up as best she could behind her with her pigeon toes peeping through her torn sneakers. Nina's heart was a bag of mixed feelings. She thought she had done the right thing for Reynalda's sake. But she was unhappy at leaving La Désirade. Okay, her life was tough over there. She had eaten her fill of wretchedness. She had stuffed her belly and her child's more often than not with stews of root vegetables and rancid oil. Yet that's where she was born, where her maman was born as well as her maman's maman, and where both of them were taking a well-deserved rest facing the sea. That's where her cabin was pitched. What she'd heard about La Pointe was far from her liking. Nothing but thieves, swindlers, and loose women. A country bus was waiting near an Esso station and she slowed her gait to allow Reynalda to catch up with her. The girl was sweating. The sweat soaked her picky hair, and, in spite of herself, her heart took pity on her child's ugliness. She held out a piece of bread she had been keeping between her breasts, but the child shook her head. She wanted nothing from her. It had been like that from the very beginning, when three days after her birth she had refused her breast. Nina and Reynalda sat on the back bench in the bus, and Nina immediately fell asleep. Reynalda, however, sat examining everything around her with her inquiring, inscrutable eyes. The road from Saint-François to La Pointe seemed endless. There was little else to be seen under the burning sun but sugarcane field after sugarcane field. Scrawny-looking oxen dragged their chains along the tarred road or lowed as they craned their muzzles in the direction of the ponds. Here and there was a mango tree, its arms outstretched. The driver sounded the horn as they drove through the villages, all alike in filth and poverty, and hordes of dogs and bare-bottomed kids charged after the bus in wild excitement. Late afternoon, just before dark, they arrived in La Pointe. The bus went and parked itself opposite the Bergevin market amid the day's-end smell of spoiled fish and rotting papayas. The last market women were packing up what could be sold the following morning, turning a deaf ear to the pleas of the poor women begging.

Everyone knew the way to Il Lago di Como. Folks took pity on

Nina and her child, with her airs of a country bumpkin, and they showered her with so many intricate directions they muddled her more than anything else. "Make a left. Then walk straight on. Go as far as the upstairs-downstairs house. That's the home of a doctor. . . . " At the corner of the Vatable Canal, a town crier was beating his drum, and people were rushing over to hear him out of curiosity as fast as their legs would carry them. Neither Nina nor Reynalda had ever seen such a sight with their own two eyes and were convinced it must have been one of the wonders of La Pointe. The man pushed his kepi back, put away his drumsticks, and drew himself up to his full height. Then he began to read in an incomprehensible voice a lengthy notice to the population indicating, in short, that the schools would soon be open and parents needed to enroll their children at City Hall. He then swaggered off toward the rue Frébault. When he had disappeared Nina and Reynalda resumed their way. They arrived one behind the other in front of Il Lago di Como at the moment when José was about to lower the steel curtain halfway, a signal to the customers they should take their leave, for tomorrow is another day. On the sidewalk opposite, in front of the hosier's shop, the owner's son, Aziz, was shrieking at his nursemaid.

What must their first evening have been like?

The bats fluttered ungainly out of the attic windows and wheeled around the house. Arcania lay exhausted in her room on the second floor. While Nina familiarized herself with the kitchen range, the pots and pans, Aunt Zita and Aunt Lia took pity on poor Reynalda, and without asking Gian Carlo, who, with an exasperated look, was holding court at the head of the table, they made room for her at the place she was to sit at every meal until the day she disappeared, between Donatella and Fiorella. It was that very evening the friendship burgeoned between Fiorella and Reynalda, two girls who were complete opposites. Reynalda looked around at her new surroundings, at the heavy oak Henry II furniture, the gilt-edged scalloped plates that decorated the walls, the reproductions of miniatures by Viator Gentini, the naive paintings of a Sicilian whom Gian Carlo had been fond of in his youth, and she tried not to cry. Why, in fact? What was there to miss on La Désirade?

Suddenly, Fiorella nudged her with her knee under the table and whispered:

"Do you know the story of Aïda-Gros-Tété?"

Reynalda opened her eyes wide in ignorance and Fiorella launched into some farfetched story that made her split her sides laughing. Gian Carlo rapped his spoon on the edge of his plate to request silence and Aunt Zita, who was going round the table serving the meager dish of codfish potluck, made an attempt at scolding her: "That's enough of that, Fiorella!"

Shortly afterward Nina entered, statuesque in her faded madras dress. She was carrying the tray of lemon grass, the teapot, and the chipped porcelain cups. As if he were the Holy Sacrament itself, she turned her head in wonder to gaze at Gian Carlo who too was looking at her. Little realizing that the crazed angel of love and desire had just hurled his javelin, Fiorella giggled even louder: "Your maman, your maman, she's just like . . . Aïda-Gros-Tété in person!"

Once the dinner things had been washed and put away, Nina and Reynalda climbed up to their attic. In their ignorance they had left the shutters open, and bats had flown into the room. Frightened, Reynalda crouched on one of the beds while her mother lunged after them armed with a broomstick. At the end of the struggle, six tiny black, hairy corpses lay bleeding on the wooden floor.

Was that how the first evening went? And the day after? And the following days? Where had the nameless, faceless man come from who had given the girl her belly? Had he raped her, waiting behind a sandbox tree on the Place de la Victoire to pounce on her one fateful day and drag her to his home despite her kicking and pleading? Or had she been duped by his seduction and consented to surrender? Meeting him in his tenements' yard on the Morne La Loge and staying with him as late as the afternoon hour permitted? Together they would watch the first black threads of night tangle with the white threads of day. Then she would run back as fast as she could to the rue de Nozières. One might wonder how they had been able to meet so often out of the house, how they had managed to elude so many children, so many pious women, three in all, and a confessor who never stopped coming and going, prayerbook in hand, always prepared to confess anyone at any hour.

Unless . . . Unless . . .

An icy cold numbed Marie-Noëlle's legs, crept into her heart, and she almost collapsed then and there in that rather dirty bar selling cigarettes near the Gare Saint-Lazare, where she was drinking a coffee. At the counter a woman was wolfing down hard-boiled eggs. Huddled on a bench, two lovers were kissing.

Why hadn't she realized it earlier? Everything fitted. All the scattered pieces of the puzzle were locking into place. The confession. The music. Cherubino. *Voi che sapete che cosa è amor.* My child, what a beautiful voice you have. I will help you to study in France. You'll be *paggio* at the Opéra. You've got a beautiful voice and beautiful eyes, you know. Come here. Come closer. . . . Oh! What have I done? Perish the day I was born! Why did I not give up the ghost when I came out of the belly? Or why didn't I die at my mother's breast? Father, you will never, ever be able to forgive me. From now on my place is among those I resemble. The pustules of their bodies cover my soul.

If only I had someone to talk to, someone in whom I could confide my agony. If only I had a man on my arm, as Judes Anozie would say. It helps. Alas! They've all abandoned me. My grandmother Nina believed education was the key to happiness. She thought her life would have been different had she known how to read and write. Me, I've got an education. I earned it with the sweat of my brow. And yet I'm no happier for it. Why? I asked myself. Because I had no idea of the legacy I was paying for.

Chapter 5

As soon as they left Paris it began to snow. Big snowflakes, in a hurry to reach the ground, huddled together as if in fright. In a question of minutes there was no other color blanketing the houses, the trees, and the cars but a blinding white. Pressing her cheek against the cold of the window, Marie-Noëlle gazed out at this dead landscape, so similar to the one she carried in her heart. It was a Wednesday. Off peak. This was no express train. The few passengers, a man wearing a pair of worn-out shoes, two ill-dressed women, in odd getups, to tell the truth, were shivering in the second-class compartment. The man handed round his packet of cigarettes and soon, amid the smell of Gauloises, all three began to talk dispiritedly. About what? About the government making life difficult for the workers. About how the previous government had done the same thing. Republics and presidents come and go and nothing changes. Just by looking at them you could see these travelers were run-of-the-mill types. Normal people. From normal families. Nothing worth mentioning. Copulations of the ordinary kind. Affairs and one-night stands with little consequence. A little fellatio here and there. Not even a bit of sodomy. Marie-Noëlle's heavy conscience made her feel

237

out of place. She hid her face behind a newspaper she had bought mechanically. But these chain-saw massacred corpses in Burundi, thrown into the silos of Rwanda with their genitals exposed, these decomposed bodies drowned in the mud of Pakistan left her ice cold. Since living seems impossible, why doesn't the world just give up? And get it over with! Return to the delights of nothingness. She let the newspaper fall into her lap and turned back to the window. Behind the glass, the countryside had replaced the town. The hearselike train was unrolling its metal coils across a white plain, as flat as the palm of your hand, here and there bristling with unrecognizable shapes. Warehouses? Trees? Copses? Piles of bones? Animal corpses? She did not dare ask herself what she would find at the end of this three-hour train ride. In any case, it couldn't be worse than what she had left behind.

In the compartment the conversation dragged along. The two women laughed at one of the man's jokes. But it was obvious they had to force themselves. Above their stretched lips revealing the yellowed enamel of their teeth, their eyes remained tired and hollow. Finally one of them put an end to the masquerade. She wrapped herself in her coat, threw her head back, and settled down to sleep. Marie-Noëlle thought she ought perhaps to do the same. She hadn't gotten any sleep for hours. She had started off the night drinking cheap red wine, the sort that stains, with Garvey and Soglo. The thought of Christmas approaching in the solitude of Paris brought tears to their eyes like the kids they still were. Leaning against the cushions in the living room they kept trotting out the same stories over and over again until they had lost all sense of reality. Soglo had come to France as a child after a coup d'état had thrown out the African dictator who had sworn himself in for life a few years earlier. Soglo's father, an ardent disciple, had had to follow his master and hide his family away in a villa in Fontainebleau, sumptuously furnished with the people's money. Soglo had never seen Africa again, and at the age of twenty, night after night, his desire for her soaked his sheets. One day soon he would leave in search of Africa. He would rediscover her in the furnace of the midday sun and on the scorched shell of her land he would rip her open with his rod. Garvey scoffed at him and shrugged his shoulders. Africa was not something to dream about or mate with. She was there to be molested, plundered, and raped. If there was a world to be coveted it was the one they lived in. They must fashion it to suit their ways. It was Soglo's turn to laugh and shrug his shoulders as the same old debate grew more bitter, day in and day out. Around midnight they had stopped their empty palavering and set off for the Soho Club they visited nightly. A nightclub behind a dismal façade in the Réaumur-Sebastopol district, where a quintet was playing Caribbean jazz. Its dark, narrow confines were filled with all types of Martinicans, Guadeloupeans, as well as Africans, for once in close contact, elbowing each other in a brotherly fashion. The air was heavy with nostalgia and identical dreams. For a moment, the music had poured its balm into Marie-Noëlle's heart. This clash of harmonies, these discords sounded familiar to her, and it was as if old friends had got together to play for her sorrow. Unfortunately the lull did not last. Someone struck a chord that brought the pain surging back. At the break the trombonist, with the languid eyes of a bolero singer and a Gabriel García Márquez moustache, stepped off the stage and came and sat at their table. Garvey was so proud of her, of his big sister, professor at a university in the United States, that he had announced her visit to everyone. What an honor for the Soho Club! He himself had known her late husband, Stanley Watts, and had the good fortune to play with him at a concert in London. Oh, yes, Stanley Watts was one of the greatest. He was way above all the rest, even Jimi Hendrix and Bob Marley, who were mere cherubim compared to him. But there you are, the world was not ready yet for his music, and espe-cially not for his message. Nobody wants to hear that immigrants are not the wretched of this earth. They are the salt of the earth as well as the light of the world. Karl Marx was an immigrant. And Einstein. And Pablo Picasso. At one time Ho Chi Minh was one. And Nicolas Guillen. The list went on and on. Hearing these platitudes, Marie-Noëlle's eyes filled with tears, proof that she was far from being her usual self. She could see Stanley again, as inaccessible as a strongbox for which she never had the key. And Terri, who had left her without a word. They had probably both sensed the truth about the girl they had let into their bed. A cripple. A monster. During the Renaissance it was believed that monsters were born from unnatural copulations, so horrifying that just the thought of them froze the blood. Virgins ripped open by dogs, leopards, bulls, and hairy apes with massive erections, chased by bloodsuckers, incubi, and fire hags. The monster, even though she does not openly bear the signs of her deformity such as no arms, no legs, a fishtail, a ram's horn in the middle of her forehead, or an epsilon on her breast, can but cause a void around her. Her proximity terrorizes. Apparently the trombonist was not terrorized since he stared at her engagingly and asked her about the United States. In fact he wasn't asking her. He was speaking from experience. Racism. He knew that. He had spent a few days in New York and those yellow panthers, the cabs, had flexed their muscles and bounded out of his reach. Violence. He knew that. Coming out of Sylvia's restaurant he had seen two bodies lying bleeding on the sidewalk in Harlem. Homosexuality. He knew that. Two leather-clad colossuses had chased him all over Chelsea. Fortunately at this point, the break was over and he had to join the other musicians. Nothing to report. They were a good quin-tet. Able musicians. She thought, however, their improvisations lacked versatility and the unexpected. Stanley, who was so demanding, would have thought twice about hiring them for the MNA.

$\maltese$

As they left the Soho Club the night paled, and the eyes of the stars were already closing. Garvey and Soglo joined a group. She followed the trombonist. She drank a lot more cheap red wine in his apartment squeezed under the rooftops. He no longer talked to her about America. Nor anything else, come to that. His hands wandered over her breasts, and his male member dug deep into her thighs. But she pushed him away with all her strength, for she was in no mood for that sort of thing. Then she found herself under the gloomy glass roof of the Gare du Nord railway station. In the company of the already exhausted early morning commuters who had had barely time to wash. She had taken the first train leaving for Belgium.

The compartment door slid open, and two passengers entered, obviously a mother with her small son. They kept their eyes down. Not a word to anyone. They sat down, unwrapped their provisions, and immediately began to eat. With a disgust mixed with envy everyone watched as the blackish-brown slices of farmhouse bread colored purple with salami and *jambon de Parme* were greedily bolted down.

All of a sudden, Marie-Noëlle collapsed into sleep. When she opened her eyes again they were entering the station at Brussels.

$\maltese$

Cramped into his old cardigan, as reassuring as a palm tree on the edge of an oasis, Ludovic was waiting at the end of the platform. Beside him stood Angéla. And Marie-Noëlle imagined he had brought the child as a rampart, as an obstacle placed between them. Garvey had exaggerated. Of course, Ludovic's dreadlocks were graying around the temples, for age was creeping up on him as it creeps up on us all. Of course, his forehead and the corners of his mouth were furrowed with more than one wrinkle. But he didn't look at all like someone who had been disappointed in love. On the contrary he looked fit and full of energy. He pushed the two sisters up against each other, and Marie-Noëlle, hugging this child she had never met, was surprised at the gentle affection she radiated. Angéla was small for her age and looked more like her father than her mother. She had Ludovic's light brown *kako* eyes. Garvey's too. A hesitant smile fluttered on her lips as if she did not know whether she ought to give it. Ludovic took Marie-Noëlle affectionately by the arm and led her toward the exit. As usual, he talked about everything except the essential. He asked her whether it was snowing in Paris as well. It looked as though it would be a hard winter in Europe. In Belgium, Germany, and the Netherlands it hadn't stopped snowing for days. Yes, he had had to leave suddenly for Belgium because they needed him in a center for young delinquents where he had once worked. Cilas, the director and friend of twenty years, had gotten tired of living in exile and had decided to return home to Cameroon with his family. Eight children all born in Europe. Ludovic was not unhappy to be back in Brussels among the immigrant community, feisty and welcoming like a family. He had invited Garvey and the inevitable Soglo to leave Paris where nothing much happened and come and join him. Marie-Noëlle listened and said nothing. Since Brussels did not interest her she did not look out at the gray façades as they drove from the station to the suburbs, or the congested streets, the sidewalks dirtied by winter's mud or the glimpse of parks, on the contrary, coated in white. Her heart was anxious about how to switch from this tone of affection and confidence to another? She remembered when she had had her first periods she would stuff her soiled panties into a corner and then later in shame lock herself in the bathroom to wash them. Ludovic had unearthed this stinking treasure. Without raising his voice he had simply taught her how to use the washing machine. He had treated a boil she had tried to hide on her left buttock. When she had the flu he would lift up her nightdress and roughly rub her chest and back. How can a father possibly rape his child? How can he manage to forget all these memories and transform such a familiar, such a commonplace body into a place of concupiscence?

At the Georges Simenon housing development, Cilas and his family had one or two days left before they vacated the apartment they were leaving to Ludovic. So they were living in a chaos of children of both sexes, of trunks closed, cases open, cardboard boxes half filled and items half wrapped. While Cilas hammered down the boxes, Céleste, his wife, majestic amid all this commotion, her newborn clinging to her back, scolded her boys and kept an eye on the girls as they cooked the midday meal. She kissed Marie-Noëlle as if she were her older sister, reunited with her after a cruel separation, while her lovely eyes shrewdly looked her over and wondered about her real reasons for coming. Céleste did not hide her feelings. She was dutifully obeying but she was not at all happy about returning to Africa. She had said as much to Cilas, who had not listened and done exactly as he wanted, since men make the mistake of never listening to women. He had no misgivings because someone had promised him a job in Douala. But everyone knows that promising and keeping a promise are two different things. Especially in Africa. After a few months they'd be lucky if Cilas wasn't locked up between the four walls of a jail, accused of having plotted against the president; Cilas had never been able to hold his tongue and was probably on some blacklist. She would then find herself all alone, out of money and out of work. How would she manage to feed these famished mouths?

There would be no use relying on the family. Neither hers. Nor Cilas's. Nowadays, the word family no longer had any meaning. Neither did the word "tribe." Or "village." Or "community." Or "Africa," come to that. For Africa was no longer Africa. It had become the realm of darkness and vultures.

Around one o'clock everyone sat down in a circle on the floor to do honor to an excellent meal, for despite all their giggling and secret whisperings, the girls had done a good job in the kitchen. Then Ludovic and Cilas disappeared together as men mysteriously do. The children, boys and girls alike, scattered in all directions. Céleste laid her baby to sleep and took Marie-Noëlle by the hand. This was one of Ludovic's ideas. He was very eager for her to speak about her life in the United States to members of the association La Main Ouverte, meeting for a special session just to listen to her. In a neighboring building about forty immigrant women of varying hues and ages, and almost as many very young children, were noisily waiting. Some of the women came from Africa and had their heads shaved or hair braided and woven. The women from North Africa were veiled up to their eyes in chadors or else wore a flowered scarf over their long braids dyed red with henna. A few were bold enough to wear their hair short and curly. But all of them stared in single delighted disbelief at the sister who was not much to look at, no lovelier or more majestic than another, and yet had climbed to the top: professor at a university in the United States of America! Confronted with these stares Marie-Noëlle realized her imposture. If she described her real life, her solitude, her failures, her depressions, and her sleepless, loveless nights, no doubt the room would empty, and she would be faced with nothing but row upon row of empty chairs. Instead, she began to fabricate a story worthy of a Republican congressman, full of clichés picked up here and there that she herself did not believe in. Democracy. Liberty. Multiculturalism. Yes, America was the blessed land of opportunity. Yes, if you knew how to use your two arms and your two hands you could build your own log cabin and lead the life you wanted. Yes, your wildest dreams could come true. It was a fact that over there, more than in any other country on earth, the immigrants and their children composed a national treasure. Charlie Chaplin. Nabokov, Auden. Joseph Brodsky. The most revolutionary ideas came out of their heads. Marcus Garvey. George Padmore. Stokely Carmichael. With each name her conviction grew stronger, and it was with the fervor of an electoral address that she ended her homily. There was silence. The applause was lukewarm. Then one woman soon followed by another, then another stood up and there followed a barrage of questions very different from what she was expecting. Had she had dinner with the president? In New York, did she have her own house? Did she drive a car? Did she earn a lot of money? Did she have someone to clean her house? Do the cooking? Do the washing? To all these questions Marie-Noëlle was obliged to answer in the negative. The women became restless. One of them asked whether her husband was American. How come she didn't have a husband? No children either? All alone then? At that moment, if Céleste hadn't mercifully indicated they could continue to the second half of the program, Marie-Noëlle would have been totally unmasked.

In the early evening she was back with Ludovic. They sat down next to each other on the sofa that looked the worse for wear from the feet of so many children. Cilas, Céleste, their children and Angéla had gone to visit old friends. Peace at last. Just the two of them. In many respects the apartment reminded her of the one at Savigny-sur-Orge, and it was as if the past had caught up with her. It was easy to see herself sucking on a pencil, having trouble with her English homework as she sat at a whitewood table. Garvey was squealing in his playpen. Ludovic was moving back and forth between the kitchen and the living room, casting a glance at her exercise book every time he passed by. You could hear the rattle of Reynalda's typewriter as she locked herself away in her world. She pictured the scene without melancholy or bitterness because for the first time she realized that Reynalda's silences and lies had spared her. What would have become of this poor little girl if very early on she had been aware of her deformity? How would she have gone through life that was already so heavy on her shoulders?

Timidly she turned to Ludovic, for the moment had finally come to get down to essentials.

Ludovic's Story

’m not heartbroken, you understand. I’m not bitter or disappointed, heart and soul darkened by a thirst for
revenge. I always knew one day she would let go of my hand. I
always knew one day she would leave me like she left everyone else
who was a hindrance or no longer any use to her. Like the crab
loses her pincers; the anoli lizard, its ragged green coat by the way-
side. Her mother. Fiorella. Ranélise. Claire-Alta. The Duparcs and
so many others we don’t know. If she turned her back on me after
so many, many years, after so many emotions and so many memories together, it’s because now she has nothing to be afraid of.
Neither the darkness of the night. Nor the commotion of the great
winds. Nor the screams of the madwoman that is life. Of nothing.
She knows how to unravel the tangle of life’s threads. And that’s
okay by me.

As for her story, don’t ask me for explanations. Don’t count on
me to fit the last piece in the puzzle and tell you the name of your
papa. Like the end of a detective novel and being told: “It was him
or it was her! How come you never guessed?” I never asked her
about anything. Mainly because I knew she would tell me only
what she wanted to tell me. And then I’m of the opinion that

everyone has a right to their share of secrecy, of privacy. It's like a woman washing her menstrual-stained rags in the river for everyone to see in the glare of the noonday sun. Wouldn't we turn the other way, embarrassed by the open display of her bloodline? And then what about me, whom you believe to be irreproachable, who knows how many pairs of eyes brimming with tears, how many pregnant bellies and fatherless children I left behind wherever I went? In Africa, America, or France I've always adored a woman's body and had my fill of sexual pleasure with them. Reynalda never held it against me. On the contrary, she asked me all sorts of questions. She would breathe in the smell of the other women in my hair and my fingers. She wanted to know what it meant to be a man and maintained that we should all be entitled to two lives. One as a male. The other as a female. I used to laugh at all the day-dreamings that filled her head. It's true she could remain for days on end without saying a word. She was tortured by a memory that haunted her day and night. Something terrible, something monstrous had occurred in her childhood that she was unable to share with anyone else. She was highly susceptible because of her arrogance and took everything the wrong way. She would cry every day for the slightest reason. A dream. A bad memory. A look. A harsh word. Even so, despite her melancholy, we had our moments of bliss. When I had dried her cheeks with my kisses I would clutch her against my chest like a precious doll, and then we would make love. Afterward I would whisper in her ear: "Tell me! Get it out of your system. You'll feel better for it." But she shook her head, and I couldn't make her. Occasionally she would reveal snatches to me. She couldn't forget one humiliation. When she was working at the Duparcs', one day little Chamanou had grabbed her hand and kissed it, saying: "I love you." His maman, furious, had shouted in front of everyone: "Please, Charles-Emmanuel, not the maid!" The students at the school on the boulevard Brune made fun of her and called her "Bamboula" and "Snow White." One day in the Métro some boys had chased her, calling her "monkey." The person she mentioned time and time again was her maman, Nina. She loathed her. I never managed to understand why. Her descriptions of her were ragged and patchy. Her smell. Her vulgarity. Her disgusting dirtiness. Her vices. I think merely she blamed her for being what she was: an uncouth niggerwoman from the country who hired her services to a family of white folk and was only too pleased that the master slept with her. She had nothing good to say about that Gian Carlo, a good match for her mother, according to her, miserly and lecherous. Sometimes she talked about Arcania, whom she would have preferred for a maman, as angelic as Nina was diabolical, and about Fiorella, her only friend. The two of them had worked on writing a novel, *Gondal*, and some poems. Such childhood foolishness had surely prevented her from going mad or taking her own life. She talked to me about the people she had detested and the people she had loved in the same way you talk about people long dead whom you will never meet again on this earth. Guadeloupe, thank goodness, was finished with. She would never set foot there again. When I reminded her of Nina, her maman, and the solitude of her old age, she did not even answer. All in all she didn't tell me very much. And, as I said, I didn't wear her out with questions. It's not wise to venture down into the gullies of other people's pasts.

You'd like me to begin my story at the beginning. But where is the beginning? Perhaps it started the moment I was born in a cabin with a straw roof, not far from the edge of the cane fields, at Ciego de Avila; perhaps it was written I would travel around the world three times only to be brought to heel at the age of thirty by a frail little soul who would bear me two children and keep me twenty years by her side. Whereas up until then I had cut loose from the moorings of my responsibilities, kicked up my heels, and sowed my wild oats in every bed. Already as a young boy, my mother would tie me to a table leg. It was the only way to stop me from running all over the place.

It was one Saturday, at a dance at the neighborhood town hall, Place du Panthéon, that I met Reynalda. At that time—I'm talking about the end of the sixties—immigration was not a dirty word. No graffiti on the walls, no police blunders, no suburbs torched and up in arms. Every month the West Indian Associations organized a dance for their fellow countrymen. The bands that played the tangos, the boleros, and cha-cha-chas went by the Spanish names of Esperanza, Los Matecocos, and El Calderón. The musicians wore flowery ruffled shirts and pretended to be Cuban. Their god was Aragon. When Celia Cruz and the Señora Mantecera came to play in Paris, there was almost a riot. Those dances were quiet, good-natured places. No crack was passed around. Here and there a cigarette of *marie-jeanne* that didn't yet go by the name of *ganja*. These town hall dances were a cure for homesickness where you could speak Creole, drink rum and brag in your suit and tie in front of your fellow countrymen. Me, who never had a homeland, unless it was Haiti or else Cuba or Canada or the United States, I had been invited by Violetta, a Guadeloupean girl I used to go out with, among others. Violetta had come with a friend whom she secretly begged me to dance with. I don't see why she begged me. I would have done it without asking for her permission. Her friend had neither her pearly white teeth nor her wasp waist nor her dimples. But even so, though you wouldn't think it, there was something tantalizing about her somber looks, her drooping eyelids, and her guava-bud breasts squeezed into her faded blouse. You would have taken her for a schoolgirl. You wondered why she wasn't doing her homework. She first of all refused, saying she didn't know how to dance. But when I grabbed her for *La Cumparsita* she clung to me like a collar stud. I'll spare you the rest of the evening: Violetta's increasingly downhearted expression, her tears, her girlfriends' reproaches, and the insults from her brothers who were fighting mad. It all finished the way it was destined to finish: walking across Paris at two in the morning and making love on the bed in my room. When I woke up, the classic situation: She had vanished. But she wasn't a thief. She hadn't touched a cent in my wallet.

Weeks went by. I thought I'd forgotten her.

As usual I had a good many problems. I had come back empty-handed from two years in Senegal. I'd been an Overseas Volunteer. But they accused me of meddling in politics and terminated my contract. At the urging of friends I came to Paris, and then I lost my job. I was looking for another one, with no luck. To my prospective employers I was guilty of having the wrong look, as they say nowadays. They wanted me to comb my hair and shave my beard. At that time I didn't have my dreadlocks, mind you; those came later. They also thought my English sounded American and wasn't "Queen's" English. As for my Spanish, it sounded Cuban and not Castilian enough. From time to time I strummed a guitar or else blew on a saxophone in a band. Sylvio, one of Muntu's members, stuck by me, and he was the one who took me in and saved me from dying of hunger. But it was far from satisfactory. Sometimes I got it into my head to return to Belgium, where I had lived before going to Senegal. Pride kept me in Paris. One evening, I found myself climbing up the six flights to Violetta's to enquire about Reynalda. Violetta lived in a maid's room at Denfert-Rochereau. She had been cooking red snapper on her two-burner gas plate, and the entire landing reeked of fish stew. Her room was filled with Guadeloupeans sucking their fish heads and listening to songs by Manuela Pioche. They looked at me in a strange way. As for Violetta, she forgave me immediately. She filled my plate, then whispered to me all the bad things she could

invent about Reynalda. Titane? That was a name from La
Désirade, that's for sure. It might very well be a leper's name, for all
we know. Anyway, she had bad blood, you could see that. Blotches
on her face. She'd been a domestic somewhere in Paris. A maid. A
mabo. Ever since she'd started at the school for social workers,
nobody knows why, she'd grown too big for her boots. The school
for social workers? That's all I needed to know.

I stood watching on the sidewalk of the boulevard Brune until I
saw her come out. As she walked toward me I almost turned away,
wondering what I saw in her, she looked so ordinary. And then her
eyes met mine. And I stood rooted to the spot.

A few months later she completed her studies, framed her diploma, and got her first job at Savigny-sur-Orge. We set up home
together, which suited me fine. Because although she needed me,
I needed her even more. My friend Sylvio had got married to a
gawk of a girl, and I had to get out of his apartment. Still no per-
manent work. Miserable jobs. One month here, another month
there. Reynalda gave me a roof over my head and shared everything with me. Her money, her bank account, they were mine. It
was she who got me that job in a center for juvenile delinquents
because, at City Hall, everyone bent over backward to do what she
wanted. We never got married, which shocked people. All the
Caribbean girls love to have a ring on their finger and their picture
in a Pronuptia wedding dress in an album. So, in the secret of their
hearts, people in the housing development despised us. That was
okay by us. What did we need the mayor for, never mind a priest?
Reynalda felt a loathing for the priesthood, even more than I did.
There was, however, a ceremonial blessing at Muntu. My old
friend, Paulius Polydor, the Mallam, came down from Brussels for
the occasion. I had met him during one of his tours that had
brought him to the village in Senegal where, up to my ankles in
sand, I was drilling wells with the peasants. He was already getting

on in years, but he still had the gift of gab. He told us how he chatted every night with Jesus, a niggerman Jesus with a python coiled around his neck. I didn't believe in all his nonsense. Even so, I admired the work Muntu did for our community. Reynalda took part in the ceremony with unusually good grace. She sang better than anyone, louder than anyone when the time came to sing. She went down on both knees when everyone bent theirs. At the moment of communion she put her hand in the dish and ate the holy breadfruit stew without salt. But when it was time to leave, the Mallam drew me into a corner and advised me to be wary. He who loved me like a son, he did not appreciate the likes of Reynalda. He believed she was capable of anything. He communicated his distrust to the entire congregation. It was especially unjust since she had never given cause for blame. She was in charge of choir practice. I don't know whether you have ever heard her sing. You can't imagine the voice she has. As if a nightingale were hidden inside her throat and suddenly poked its head out. People would cry listening to her. However strange it may seem to someone like me who has no ambition, she dreamed of becoming a great singer and earning respect. Of making a name for herself. I guess she had a need for such a revenge.

Very quickly Reynalda gave me what I had always longed for. A child. I watched her belly grow round, and I trembled. Me who had never been any good at anything, I had worked a miracle. I had become the master of the dew. I had found water. I had brought it to the plain. Garvey was born one January twenty-fourth at nine in the evening. Reynalda had been admitted to the maternity ward the day before and lost a lot of blood. At one point the doctor had envisaged a cesarean: The baby was big. It was badly positioned. I must confess I wasn't too busy thinking about her, drawn and pale. All I could see in front of me was my son, wrinkled and covered in hair like a baby chimp in his white undershirt. I adore Angéla. I was the one who

wanted her. Yet it's not the same. I can never describe how I worshiped my son. That winter, the winter he was born, I did not feel
the cold. I went out in short-sleeved cotton shirts. It was as if there
was a great fire burning deep down, and its sparks were flying inside
me. My nondescript life, my messed-up life took on a meaning. With
my head in the clouds I built dreams. I wanted my son to achieve
everything I had never been able to achieve. He would be educated.
He would become an engineer and hang the Golden Gate over San
Francisco Bay. He would write books that would be translated into
every language on earth, like the Bible. He would be Johann-
Sebastian Bach or Mozart, the musical prodigy. Yes! His name would
be a household word. Every day I was in a hurry to finish my classes
and get home to make sure his heart was beating under my touch
and cradle him, warm and sleepy, in my arms.

One evening while I was tickling and showering him with kisses, Reynalda, sitting next to me on the sofa, began to cry. This was
nothing new. She refused to give any explanation, but I guessed
she was blaming me for worshiping Garvey and neglecting her, as
she would put it. I was getting ready for one of my usual appeals
and a session of caresses. But that evening there was something
else. Without looking at me, she revealed to me what she called
her shame. She had another child—a little girl. The child had
remained behind on the island under the care of one of the many
devoted souls back home, a certain Ranélise, and that's all she
knew. Amazed, I asked her the child's age. Almost ten by now.
Ten! I imagined you with two braids greased with palma christi oil
bobbing on your shoulders, as lively as a wildcat and gracious as a
sprig of lily of the valley accompanying your "maman" to church,
singing with her "I believe in Thee, my God," and immediately, I
began to love you. I didn't say a word of reproach to Reynalda.
Besides, I was speechless. If I told you that at that very moment I
wasn't thinking of leaving her, I would be lying. And then I man-

aged to control my anger. I considered it a punishment for all the harm I'd done to other women. To Violetta, for instance, whom I had betrayed so despicably with her own friend. From that moment on I could not rest until she had made amends, or rather I'd made amends, by getting in touch with this Ranélise. Day after day, morning, noon, and night, I kept up the same old song. You had to come and live with us. Your place was with us in Savigny-sur-Orge. For the first time since we had known each other, she stood her ground and wouldn't budge. She gave me all sorts of excuses. I didn't listen to her. I was convinced that once Reynalda had set eyes on you she would love you. The opposite happened.

Our myths are hard to dispel. We believe the ties of parenthood to be the strongest. Blood is thicker than water, repeat over and over again the voices out of Africa. All those tortured, dismembered, and abused children, all those fetuses thrown out as garbage, left to rot in the depths of the forest, have not silenced these fables, and here we are still repeating things that reality contradicts. Remorse overtook me when I saw you become a ghost of your former self, as I watched your smile vanish, your cheeks hollow, your eyes cloud over, and even your hair lose its lovely color of cornhusks. Weren't you better off where you were? Weren't you happier with this Ranélise? You now lived under the same roof as someone whose heart was as barren as a desolate savanna. You constantly reminded her of memories she would rather lose track of. I would have liked to give you more than I did, but I couldn't. I often got the impression I was sacrificing one for the other. In the end you can't reinvent childhood. You have to live with it.

Your life is only just beginning, and you imagine it's already over. There is a place ahead of you made for happiness that you'll slip into once you've stopped peeking over your shoulder. Once you look at your future. You've got it into your head that you want me. But in fact you only want to take revenge on your mother. I will not make love to you. That would be too easy, too despicable for both of us. You will only ever be my daughter, my firstborn. The one I didn't know I had, who loomed up at the age of ten to claim her backlog of tenderness. I'm telling you, if there's one piece of advice I have for you, it's go ahead with your life. Reynalda has shown you the way. She has proved to you that the past, however painful it has been, in the end fades away, and that passion achieves aspirations that seem out of reach to others. After writing *Les jours étrangers* she told me she was going to publish a novel, the autobiography she's been working on since I've known her, since Savigny-sur-Orge, since the boulevard Brune and even before that. In that way she'll liberate herself once and for all from the truth. But knowing her as I know her, her truth will, of course, be fiction. Besides, what else do we construct when we talk about ourselves? I must confess that although I encouraged her to write her thesis, which was to improve her career and get us out of Savigny-sur-Orge, I never took her ambition to become a writer seriously. It was as if she told me: "I too want to set foot on the moon." A fantasy. A daydream. When she was in her good moods, she'd let me read excerpts. I didn't think much about it. For me it was time stolen from her serious work.

Don't you worry about me. I'm not lacking in resources, and after all I've got Angéla beside me, my walking stick for my old age. For the time being her hand is holding mine until it too lets go. Leave me where I am. You still have your America to discover, the America you haven't yet discovered.

Chapter 6

Through the windows of my office perched on the fourth floor of the university I can see the Charles River, a pale ribbon between its banks undecided whether to thaw. By the calendar, spring is not far away. Yet there are no signs of it approaching. The entire city is still shivering, wrapped in frills of soiled white. I feel like someone recovering from a serious illness. Weak. Exhausted, even. Yet reassured that the worst is over. For weeks I didn't see the snow fall or the sun try unsuccessfully to elbow its way into the sky. I didn't hear the cavalcade and the laughter of the wind as it galloped like crazy around the trees. I was deaf, dumb, and blind. Then one morning my senses returned. I could make out shapes and colors. The yellows, reds, and blacks of tulips peeped out from the flower beds and the air tasted of fresh milk. I have office hours with my students until noon. It's the rule. I have to listen to them, discuss with them, and communicate with them, and irony of ironies, I have the job of helping them solve their problems, I who have trouble managing my own life. We have been working together for weeks and, white or black, I can hardly distinguish one from the other. Muffled up the same, wearing the same shoes and the same smiles in front of me. In class they listen to me in a religious silence and respectfully ask questions. I'm a long way from the fiery debates in Roxbury.

There is no shame in offering oneself to a man. Sociologists even maintain that in most cases it's the woman who makes the first move. Especially when such a man openly admits he has a craving for women. It's strange! All through my childhood I thought Ludovic was perfection itself. It wasn't really his body I desired. But his heart, his affection. In actual fact he was nothing but a womanizer like all the rest. I was hurt when I learned it and at once racked my brains to find out what was wrong with me. What Reynalda and all those unknown women possessed. Through constantly asking myself this question and never coming up with an answer, I ended up acquiring a kind of fatalism. I now admit he didn't want me, that's all. He told me over and over again that by continuing to look behind me, over my shoulder, I had turned into a zombie. Yes! That's precisely what I am at present, a zombie, and I don't know who will ever place a pinch of salt on my tongue. He claimed that all my troubles were caused by the fact that I had no goal in life. I don't know what he was talking about. I always thought that happiness was the only goal in life. All the fuss some people make about literature, politics, religion, and charity work is merely a mask for hiding this truth.

What's this student telling me? Black hair. Black eyes. Black clothes. He's not an American of old stock. Another immigration story! He's the son of Iranians loyal to the shah who came to safeguard their millions under the California sun. His French nannies taught him to speak perfect French. He was even a French teacher at Tefila, a small town in Algeria, and, priding himself on his knowledge of the field, he wants to write his thesis on Rachid

Boudjedra. *The Repudiation*. Why not? I give him my encouragement. Next.

Ludovic got annoyed when I talked about my monstrosity theory. He who knew her better than anyone had decided to take Reynalda's word for granted. It was obvious: The guilty party was Gian Carlo Coppini. He refused to discuss any other theory and claimed I could conclude nothing from the contradictory and uncertain relation of events that dated back thirty years. In the end he didn't realize that I had ended up liking this identity, real or imaginary. In some way or other my monstrosity makes me unique. Thanks to it I have no nationality, no country, and no language. I can shrug off all those tiresome bedevilments that bedevil human beings. It also provides an explanation to everything surrounding my life. I can understand and accept that there never was any room in my life for a certain kind of happiness. My path is traced elsewhere.

This student, an African American, has decided to work on Amadou Hampaté Ba, though he hasn't been to Africa yet. His father, however, told him about a magical world without writing, without manuscripts, without books, and without libraries, and he intends to capture the secret of the *griot* poets, those word tamers. I approve as well. What magical force is there in Africa that can resist so many pictures of desolation and torture that fill the screens all over the world? Soon Anthea will return from Ghana, her head full of her imaginings. I can already hear her. She'll tell me every detail of the story of Efua. She'll repeat the stories dreamed a hundred times of the lost paradise. Of the Middle Passage, that terrible journey we all took before we were even born. Of our scattering to the four corners of the earth and of our suffering. In exchange I shall have only my own little tales of misfortune to tell her, the real reason for my journey to Europe, and the circumstances of yet another failure. My nervous breakdown.

The beginning of my recovery. Ashamed, I shall keep silent until I too learn to invent a life.

Without warning, everything has now gone dark outside the windows. It has started snowing again. A light snow that scatters in the wind and crumbles under the feet of the passersby.

It is, we hope, one of the last snows of the season.